Healing Time

Healing Time

Anthony Owen Colby

Seaview Books

NEW YORK

Trade distribution by Simon and Schuster
A Division of Gulf + Western Corporation
New York, New York 10020

Designed by Tere LoPrete

Library of Congress Cataloging in Publication Data

Colby, Anthony Owen.
    Healing time.

    I. Title.
PZ4.C683He   [PS3553.0439]   813'.5'4   78–653
ISBN 0–87223–482–7

In memory of my mother and father, Enid and John, who courted each other with poetry and, if an afterlife exists, continue that courtship with the words of Tennyson and Keats and Wordsworth.

Healing Time

SUMMER 1976
SPRING FALLS, IOWA
Friday, June 18

"Hold on and don't jump," Ned said, "I'm going to inject all around the cut to make it numb. I have to go pretty deep, Willie. You got a tendon."

Willie Stecker lay on trauma cart two in the Emergency Room of Spring Falls Community Hospital. He was proud of his wound. "Figured it went deep. Knew I'd do something. Can you fix it, Ned?"

"Hope so." Ned put on sterile gloves and draped the wound with sterile towels. After injecting the Xylocaine, he prodded and sponged. A tendon was severed. Willie had been cut above the wrist by a small circular saw. Ned moved the man's hand, looking for other damage. After prodding for several minutes, Ned found the part of the tendon going into the hand; the white strip popped in and out of the fatty tissue. He grabbed it with a pickups. "Now move your wrist up—backwards." Ned was able to touch the ends of the tendon. Blood pooled in the wound. Ned daubed it with his free hand and checked the wound again.

"You do good work, Willie. You'd rather fish than work,

wouldn't you? You cut a tendon all the way through. I'll
fit the ends together, then I'll put your arm in a splint for
at least six weeks. Maybe longer."

"I figured as much," Willie said. "It had to happen.
They put Jackson on the lathe next to me. The son of a
bitch talks like a maniac. Cars and pussy."

"How old are you, Willie?" Ned asked.

"Fifty-five."

"You're not too old for cars."

Willie studied a hidden code written on the ceiling.
"Seventeen years and never a scratch. Then Jackson comes
along."

"I need a nurse!" Ned yelled. "Nurse!"

Ms. Sherman appeared with a cup of coffee in hand.
"Need help?"

"Need you to hold and cut suture."

He was dressed in sterile gloves when the phone rang.

The nurse answered the phone. "It's your kids, Dr.
Owen. Ellie."

"Again?"

"Come over to the wall. I can hold the phone to your
ear," she said. As the nurse held the phone to his ear, Ned
floated his gloved hands awkwardly in the air.

"Your mom will be home. You know that!"

"We're starved."

"Dummy! There's a pizza in the freezer. There's two
cans of cheese Spaghettios because I only ate one last
night. You can make popcorn in the microwave."

"Mom says we can't. It might explode."

"It hasn't yet."

"Dad? Where's Arizona?"

"Near Mexico."

"That's where Mom said she was going."

"Ellie. I'm in the middle of an operation. It's yukky. You
understand? Your mother isn't in Arizona. The farthest
she could have gone is to the club pool and you can get
mad at her for not taking you."

"She told us you'd make us supper tonight."

"She didn't tell me."

"Are you coming home?"

"I'm not going to Arizona. Now Ellie, you're being a big brat. You called me twice. What's the matter?"

"I'm bored."

"Maybe you should put popcorn in the microwave."

"Why?"

"It might blow up; then you wouldn't be bored."

"Now you're being dumb."

"OK. If your mom doesn't get home before I do, we'll go out on the highway and find some place with fish sticks."

"Can we ride behind the seats in the Mercedes?"

"Yup."

"Top down?"

"All the way."

Ned spent several minutes touching the ends of the tendon. The cut was slightly jagged and at an angle. A small portion of the tendon had been torn away. He could approximate the ends fairly easily. After staring motionless at the wound, he decided that a primary closure would work. He instructed the nurse to pour hydrogen peroxide in the wound. The liquid foamed, turning blood to pink and wound edges to white.

To fit the tendon ends together Ned used a figure-of-eight suture. He pushed the suture needle through one end, then brought it back up on the other portion of the tendon. He then looped it back through the same portion and across again to his original location. While he was pulling on the ends of the thread, the tendon came together easily. He tied the synthetic suture with four knots and told the nurse to cut the suture as closely as she could. Once it was repaired, he asked Willie to move his wrist. The green suture moved back and forth with the tendon. The skin was closed quickly, and Ned fashioned a plaster splint over cotton batting.

"How can I fish with this thing?" Willie asked.

"You'll figure it out."

As Ned was writing his report on the Emergency Room chart, his younger daughter, Lizzy, called.

"What if it gets dark and no one is home?" she asked.

"Ellie's home."

"I mean someone big."

"You're big enough, the both of you."

"Do I get to ride in the car, too?"

"If your mother doesn't get home before I do."

"I hope she doesn't."

Ned couldn't think of a word while describing his tendon repair on the chart. He gave up and finished the report.

The nurse handed him another chart as he was leaving. "One more."

"Who?"

"Borodini."

"What the hell's the matter with him now?"

"Belly pain. For three weeks."

Ned threw the chart against the desk. "Give me some coffee first. Does he look sick?"

"Does he ever?"

"Has he had a bath?"

"Doesn't smell like it."

Ned sipped half a cup of coffee before seeing the patient. Borodini spoke of no previous life and no one knew of any. A gift from the world to Spring Falls, he looked like a cross between a Magyar tribesman and a Sumi wrestler—five feet seven, over three hundred pounds, always smiling. He also would show up at any time to fix a flat or deliver gas or consult Ned.

"Got this bellyache, Doc," he said. Borodini's smile was molded like a death mask.

"How much does it hurt?"

"A lot."

"How come you're smiling, then?"

"I'm not smiling," he said with a smile.

"Where does it hurt?"

"All over."

"How long?"

"Three weeks."

"Jesus Christ, Borodini. You have had belly pain that long and wait until eight o'clock tonight to let me know. Why didn't you call me at my office?"

" 'Cause I just thought of it."

"Lay down," Ned ordered. The man lay down and Ned unbuttoned his filthy shirt. His belly was huge and muscular, offering stiff resistance when Ned prodded. Ned checked for signs of localized pain. With reluctance, he slid the man's trousers down and felt through an unwashed scrotum for a hernia. The man's penis was tucked away between folds of foreskin and fat, more of a biologic afterthought than an organ of aggression.

Ned leaned back and stared at Borodini's face. The smile never changed! Ned could tell him his days were numbered and nothing would alter it. The world's gift to Borodini!

"What's the matter, Doc?"

"I think you're OK."

"So'd I."

"Then why did you bother me?"

"Just to make sure." Borodini pulled a filthy undershirt over his belly.

"Next time, come during office hours," Ned said.

The patient grunted in an effort to tie his shoestring. "That's hard to remember sometimes."

Ned hastily composed a note at the nursing station.

"Do you want me to give him something?" the nurse asked.

"A trip to Shelly Lynn's." Ned gave her a chart on which he had scribbled "no diagnosis."

"Any meds?"

"Why not? Give him five milligrams of Compazine. Make sure he's not allergic to it."

Ned sat at the desk and called home. The phone rang at length. Lizzy answered.

"What took you so long to answer?"

"Watchin' TV."

"Your mom home?" he asked as he heard Borodini protest against his shot.

"She's outside."

"Get her. I want to talk to her." He waited several minutes, playing with the phone cord and reading procedural memos for nurses tacked to a bulletin board.

When his wife answered, Borodini and the nurse were laughing in the hallway. Ned turned from them.

"What took you so long?"

"Those birds that fly this time of day."

"The swallows?"

"I was watching them. Some of them fly with only one wing."

"Where were you?"

"Nowhere."

"You told the kids you went to Arizona."

"It's too hot in Arizona."

"I know that but they don't. Why did you give them a hard time? They've been calling me since six. You even told them I'd cook supper."

"Likelier I'd go to Arizona than that."

"What the hell!" he insisted. "Why did you scare those kids?"

"They're not frightened."

"They were. Something you said scared 'em. They don't usually call me every five minutes."

"This book says you have to have an occasional secret."

"What does that have to do with all this?"

"To have a secret you have to lie."

"God damn it, Win."

"Don't swear, Ned. Don't swear."

"Do you want to go to Arizona?"

"No."

"Would you like a trip? Up north to Canada? Where it's cool?"

"It's cool in our house with all the air conditioners."

"OK. I give in. How was it in Arizona? Did you have a good time?"

"Arizona is a great place to be, thank you," she said. Ned relaxed. *Arizona is a great place to be, thank you.* Her proper name was Bronwyn. Her father had been a miner in Wales and gave her the native tongue. The family was poor though she never acted like it. Ned's parents were third-generation Welsh, hence common in his mind. He had placed Win a cut above himself because of her direct heritage and accent. *Arizona is a great place to be, thank you.* When she said the word *great*, all was absolved. *Great:* said with a soft *g* and an *r* that was more slurred than rolled. The *e* was a long *e*, but muted because she was born in the States and her accent wasn't pure. Her voice expanded implications of speech past simple definition.

"Win. Why don't we go on a trip? It would do us good."

"Your practice would up and wither," she said, playfully.

He put one foot on a chair and bent over, speaking quietly. "Don't you want to go anymore?"

"We're too old for that."

"For a trip? That's crazy."

"It's all crazy. The whole of life."

"No, it isn't. Why don't we plan on going somewhere next week?" He moved out of the way as the nurse reached above him for a chart.

"There'll be an epidemic of swamp fever and we'll never leave town."

"You're mad because I wasn't home at six. I didn't know you wouldn't be home and I can't help emergencies." Orderlies slowly pushed a cart holding an old man whose eyes were fixed. The man's wife followed, carrying a brown paper sack filled with the man's clothes.

"That's why I went to Arizona."

"What do you mean by that?"

"You can't help emergencies—I can't help Arizona."

"Where were you?"

"It's a secret."

"I don't care where you went, just let the kids know you'll be late or let me know. That's all. I could have driven home and put some food on, you know."

"Maybe you should come home sometime to find out for yourself."

"That doesn't make sense! I'm either at the office, the hospital or home. Sometimes you act like a spoiled kid. If I do one thing, you want something else."

"If you were here, you could tell me how those birds fly with one wing."

The hospital operator spoke over a loudspeaker, ordering all visitors to leave. The sick needed their rest.

"It's an illusion. The sun is going down."

"I can only see one wing."

"I'll be home in a minute."

"Doesn't matter now, they've all gone."

It was about half an hour until sundown. Ned dropped the phone and walked toward the side exit of the Emergency Room. He reached around and took his pocket page radio from his belt.

"Sherman—Julie." He yelled for the nurse.

He asked her to follow him outside. Parked near the door was his 1969 280SL Mercedes convertible. Its top was down.

"This is my magic trick for the night." He turned the radio to "off" and put it in his glove compartment. "The radio's staying in there for at least half an hour. I'm going to cool off and take a ride in the country."

"If I didn't have to stay here, I'd come along," she said.

"You just take care of me, huh? If anything serious comes in, call Byron. Otherwise, fake it."

"Call when you're back."

He jumped into the car and headed for the highway.

Traffic was light. The left lane was clear for miles. The median lines clipped by like emanations from a strobe light. Everything was being sucked up: the green fields, the evening air, road signs, Volkswagens, an indignant finger. The only sound he heard was the purr of the motor.

Ned was soon going over a hundred and ten.

He drove through the cultivated prairie. Each square mile contained houses and barns and cattle and people; he didn't see any details.

Ten miles out of town he was spotted by the highway patrol. He saw them in his rear-view mirror. At that speed, their sirens sounded like a single sustained note on Curly Ray Cline's fiddle.

Ned called them sons of bitches, piss-ants and pricks. There were two cars. He must have passed them as they shared a cup of coffee by the roadside.

He sat up. The patrolmen were driving Fords. Panicked, he almost expected to see six-guns blazing. No, he reasoned, they wouldn't shoot a doctor.

His choice was to stop and try to explain, or—

Run.

The Interstate moved on. But for him and the highway patrol the scene could have tucked and folded itself into a Grant Wood farmscape.

He blew his horn for courage.

He slowed very carefully to narrow the gap between the patrol cars and his Mercedes. The Epworth exit was two miles ahead. Ned concentrated. The patrol cars were gaining. He hoped religiously there weren't any trucks in the way—not for his sake but for the men stuck with the Fords. He had to figure it perfectly. There were too many variables to assess. He couldn't follow a logical checklist. He accepted the challenge: His tachometer showed 5350, he was hurtling past something blue and white, he had good tires, he didn't know if the patrolmen were good drivers. A piece of paper dislodged itself from beneath a seat and popped into the air.

Ned heard the sirens clearly. They moved into a block-ing position, side by side. Gaining. He cut into the right lane and held at a hundred.

Eighty yards from the Epworth exit Ned pushed his brake pedal to the floor. Flesh stood on his face. The Mercedes didn't swerve.

He managed the off-ramp doing seventy-five.

The patrol cars braked in panic. The car on the left detected a collision and accelerated as the other car began twirling round and round like a stunt driver at a county fair. When the patrol cars came to a stop, they made a sharp turn and drove against oncoming traffic to regain the chase.

Ned drove three miles, then turned onto a gravel road, flinching as small pebbles smacked the finish of his car. He could hear the patrol cars in pursuit.

Turning blindly into a farmer's driveway, Ned skidded to a stop near the house. A chicken flew from a wire fence, terrified.

It was an old farmhouse, unpainted. Amish people. He heard the rutting of hogs and the clanking of a water pump. Reaching beneath his seat, he grabbed his bag and ran into the house. Sirens were approaching.

Standing at a primitive sink was a woman of fifty who was wearing a black satin dress and a white bonnet. She was Ned's height, about five feet eight, twice his weight.

"Pretend you're dead—please."

The simple woman didn't show an emotion or move.

Ned held his bag high. "Please."

The patrol's siren growled like a predator as the cars spun into the driveway.

"Twenty dollars," Ned yelled.

Car doors flew open and there was the scuffling of boots against gravel and chicken sounds and the inevitable slamming of the old metal gate.

The patrolmen arrived in time to find the doctor breathing into the mouth of a perfectly healthy Amish woman who loved garlic and hadn't seen a dentist in twelve years. Mrs. Hilda Miller was sprawled on the floor of the darkened room, lifeless. Ned reached for his bag only to find one of the officers handing it to him. A minute later he rose, and in the silence of that homely kitchen announced that she would live.

"Chicken bone got stuck," he said.

Sunday, June 20

At two-thirty in the morning Ned was sitting in a mild rain on his deck, waiting for a storm. Spring Falls was caught between two major fronts. The first struck at full force about ten. It extended across the Midwest from Kansas to Lake Michigan. Ned had waited on his deck as a solid wall walked toward him. Lizzy and Ellie waited at the French doors opening onto the deck. When lightning was popping all around, they yelled at their dad, telling him to give up and come in. Ned laughed at them. He was drenched with rain and pummeled with hail.

"Daddy, Daddy!" they screamed.

A bolt of lightning struck close by. "Jesus Christ!" he screamed, tipping over his chair as he ran into the house.

The kids clapped.

"Made it," he said.

"Close the doors," Ellie said.

"You're stupid, Daddy," Lizzy said. She was eight.

"You just say that because Mom said it," Ellie said. "He was having fun." Ellie was ten.

"He almost got lightninged," Lizzy protested.

Ned stood with his nose against the glass. Water dripped from him into a puddle. The storm was exciting: Windows rattled with the wind, lightning spit and crashed, leaving afterimages of the storm's anatomy, rain blew against the door in sweeping waves. Ned and the kids watched in fascination until the storm eased into a persistent rainfall.

"Go to bed now, kids. We're going to see Grandma and Grandpa tomorrow."

"Can we go in the Mercedes?" Ellie asked.

"Can we!" Lizzy insisted.

"Don't think so. You're getting too big to sit behind the seats. We have to go on the highway, you know."

Ned went to his study to read the *AMA Journal* and watch a late movie. The broadcast was interrupted for details of the storm and an announcement of another front that had snuck down from the Dakotas. The radar showed the situation: The first front was massive, a band of white across the screen. The new front intersected at the Nebraska border, creating a Y formation. Each sweep of the radar revealed separate storm cells, like balls of cotton, extending to the north and east. Ned decided to stay up for the new storm.

His wife, Win, passed by his room, peeked in a moment without speaking and went to bed. She adjusted the air conditioner before accommodating herself to the bed. She lay on her side, her right arm and leg touching the edge of the bed. As a matter of habit, her right hand grabbed the edge of the bed; holding it firmly, she went to sleep.

By one o'clock the wind was shifting and came from the northwest. There was lightning far off. Ned wandered downstairs, found a beer and walked through the bedroom to his deck.

Their house was as large and as old as any in Spring Falls. It sat on the very southwest corner of town, the most fashionable part of town until the banker and other men of commerce moved to Golfview Estates, a rural subdivision created so that the most expensive lots bordered the golf course. Ned's deck was built for the precise reason he was using it, to watch storms, a compulsion inherited from his father, who, as a carpenter, was once burned by lightning as he worked on a roof. Ned was drawn to the storms of the Midwest as those on a seacoast make ritual of watching sunsets or as New Englanders find solace walking forest paths beneath stands of maple.

The hospital called at one-thirty. A woman with asthma was wheezing. He ordered an injection of epinephrine.

Rain fell slowly. The wind picked up a bit, but the lightning stayed to the north. Ned looked around to see if there were other signs of the new storm. The few clouds he could see were moving due east. He sipped his beer slowly, hoping the weather would move toward him. At two-thirty nothing had changed. He opened another beer. For a few minutes thunder sounded, but it quit and Ned could hear raindrops falling on the empty beer can next to him.

Past three the clouds separated and he saw a star. He closed the French doors on his way to bed. Tucking a pillow, he lay on his back across from Win, carefully, so not to touch his wife.

When he woke, Win and the kids were dressed and leaving for the Baptist church.

"What time are you done with church?" he asked.

"We have a potluck after services. Maybe one-thirty," she said.

"Why don't you hurry because we should be at my folks' house by three."

"Why three?" she asked.

"You know. If we get there later, Mom will get on her high horse and cook up a big meal."

"She'll do that anyway."

"Not if we get there early."

"I have to help clean up after the potluck."

"Get someone else to do it. You do so damn much already, you'd think you had stock in that church."

"I can't just walk away."

"OK. One-thirty. At the latest. I'll eat at the hospital." The phone rang and he responded slowly, picking up his two empty beer cans on the way.

"This is the Emergency Room, Dr. Owen. We have a pretty sick little girl. Sally Fromm. Eighteen months old. High temp. Her mom says she's really listless. I agree. She won't respond much at all."

"I'll be over. Get out a spinal-tap kit just in case. She move her head all right?"

"She just lays there. Her eyes are glassy."

Ned shaved and took a quick shower. He dressed in tan slacks, a light-colored shirt without tie, and dress boots the color of honey. He rarely wore anything else.

After putting the top down on the Mercedes he hurried to the Emergency Room. The sick child lay on a trauma cart, crying weakly, her eyes wandering aimlessly about the room. Her forehead was hot and dry. Ned quickly examined her ears and throat and chest. The child's neck was supple, but at her age it didn't exclude the possibility of meningitis.

He ordered the nurse to open the spinal tray.

He took Mrs. Fromm aside. It was possible the child had meningitis. The high fever and listlessness were very suspicious. To prove it he would have to do a spinal tap and look at the fluid. If she had meningitis, the spinal fluid would have infection cells in it.

"Will it hurt her?"

"A little. But if we don't do it, we'll really be in trouble. It'll only take a few minutes. It'd be best if you waited outside. It looks worse than it really is." He put his hand on her shoulder and smiled at her.

"Let's hurry," he yelled at the nurse. She found a

nurse's aide and the women positioned the child for the procedure. They lay her on her side, holding her neck and feet, curling her into a ball so that her back formed a curve. Spinal processes were visible as bumps in a row along her lower back. Once she was in position, the aide opened the spinal tray while Ned put on sterile gloves.

The aide poured tincture of Zephiran the color of cherry soda into a small cup. Ned took a cotton swab and applied the solution to the child's back, beginning at the spot where he would insert the needle before making ever wider circles with the red antiseptic. He did this three times. A drape with a hole in it was placed over the child's back. Ned felt her hipbone and used it as a guide to locate the level for the tap.

"Are you going to use Xylocaine?" the nurse asked.

"No. She's so out of it she won't feel much."

He carefully felt the hollow between two bumps of the spinal processes. After he visualized the plane of her back, he judged the direction the needle should go. He checked the spinal needle. It was hollow, with a center stylus which would be removed when he reached the spinal fluid.

The needle was aligned perpendicular to a plane between her hips. After he had inserted it slightly, the child screamed, extended her body and almost rolled off the cart.

The nurse grabbed the child and wrestled her back into the proper position.

"Don't break her neck," Ned said.

"She's strong."

"I think that's a diagnosis," he said.

"What do you mean?"

"I don't think she's got it. Too active."

He again pushed on the needle. The child squirmed and yelled, but the nurse held tightly. He pushed the needle inward, slowly, concentrating on the feel with his fingers. After it had gone in a ways, he felt a very slight pop.

"I'm in. Give me the tubes. Quick."

He removed the stylus, and spinal fluid came out a drop at a time. He took a tube from the aide and filled the bottom. Holding the tube to a light, he saw that the fluid was clear.

"Looks good." He put fluid in the other tubes, slid the stylus in the needle and removed the needle.

"Give her a band-aid." With the tubes in his gloved hands, he ran to the laboratory. A technician helped as he drew up a violet-colored solution into a pipette, then added the spinal fluid. He put a drop of the mixture onto a special microscope slide. After adjusting the focus, he searched for cells.

"Clear," he said to the technician.

He walked to the waiting room and talked to the child's mother.

"We're all right," he said. "She doesn't have meningitis. She really looks out of it. Sometimes plain old viruses do that. I have an idea she'll run a temp today and be better tomorrow. Just to be sure, I'll put her in the hospital and we'll watch her."

"She'll be all right?"

"She gave us a good scare, but she doesn't have anything bad."

"Thank you," she said. "Poor kid. I was so worried. You don't know. Her eyes looked so bad." She thanked him again.

Ned drank coffee with the Emergency Room staff before he made his rounds. He didn't have many patients in the hospital, mostly elderly ones with congestive heart failure or strokes. He took his time, reading bits of the Sunday paper at each nursing stand, talking to the nurses, joking. He ate stale baked chicken and sweet potatoes in the cafeteria. Three nurses joined him and they talked about the rain and gardens.

"Damn," Ned said. "You know what? If I don't get out and weed my garden, I'll have a jungle next week."

"Get your wife to do it."

"If I planted it behind the Baptist church, she'd have it as clean as Byron Markham's sport coat."

"We could arrange it," one of them said.

"Don't you dare. I'm allergic to churches. Especially hers."

"I'm sure they'd love to have you as a member."

"I'm as welcome as a horse. I swore at the preacher once."

"He's your patient, isn't he? Didn't you and Dr. Markham do a hernia on him?"

"He wouldn't dare go to anyone else. Not with what Win gives to his church. If it was General Motors stock, I'd retire."

He checked his young patient before leaving the hospital. Her temperature was down a bit, but she was still groggy.

Win was late. She said she wanted to change clothes, but Ned insisted they leave. Win ran into the house to get a book. They drove away in the station wagon.

His parents lived in Colfax, about forty miles away, directly on Interstate 80. Win read from her paperback, *Tales of Winterhaven*, a book with the picture of a nun staring through the gate of an ancient convent.

"How was church?" he asked.

"The same."

"Anybody bring any good food?"

"Daddy, Johnny made ice cream in an ice cream maker," Ellie said.

"Was it good?" Ned asked.

"We only got a taste," Lizzy said.

"That a good book?" he asked Win.

"I haven't read much."

Ned followed a semi and was able to go seventy-five. When they turned from the Interstate toward Colfax, Win reminded Ned that they had agreed to visit her parents' graves. They didn't make it on Memorial Day.

"Then don't let Mom start cooking. We'll say hi and visit, then leave. OK?"

Ernest and Ruth Owen were well into their seventies. He was a large-boned man with thick hands who moved and spoke slowly. Ruth was squat and spry, with alert eyes. They hugged the kids and kissed Win.

"Hi, Dad. Hi, Mom," Ned said warmly. "Sorry we didn't make it last time. I got caught up in the Emergency Room. A couple of teen-agers messed themselves by rolling a pickup."

"You'll stay for supper, won't you?" Ruth asked.

"Sorry, Mom. Have to get back. We'll just visit. We have to go out to the cemetery."

"We can eat early," Ruth insisted.

"Mom. No cooking today. Save your energy. We'll just visit. Are you watching baseball, Dad?"

"The Cubs are playing. Doing good," Ernest said.

Ruth scurried to the kitchen, where she cut a pie and served it to everyone with ice cream. "Have to eat something," she said.

The kids ran around outside. Ruth and Win followed them. They talked about the new carpeting in Win's church. Win donated most of the money for it.

Ned and Ernest watched a baseball game on the big Zenith that Ned had given him. Ernest sat forward, intent. In the Cubs' half of the fourth inning, Manny Trillo hit a stand-up double.

"That's the Cubs," Ernest said. "Like that Mexican they got. See how they play. They're doing good."

"Dad. He's not Mexican."

"All them guys are good. They're skinny and can run fast."

Ned laughed at him. Ernest didn't take his eyes off the set.

"You ever play ball, Dad?"

"Nope. Had to work."

"You probably could have hit a lot of home runs."

"I wasn't good at running. Never liked to."

"If you hit home runs, you could walk around the bases."

"Look. See there? That pitcher almost threw the ball away. Too bad, 'cause he could have got to third."

Ellie and Lizzy found flowers in the neighbor's back yard and gave them to Ernest. He boxed their ears like a gentle bear.

"You kids are gonna be as big as your dad. Maybe bigger."

"You're silly, Grandpa," Lizzy said.

"Do you like the flowers?" Ellie asked.

"Did you steal 'em?"

"Sort of."

"The neighbor, he don't care. He's never home anyway."

Ned told Ruth they had to leave when she made threatening gestures in the kitchen. "Win and the kids ate a lot right before we came and I ate too much. Next time we'll come and take you out to eat."

She protested but Ned got his way.

Ernest stayed with his game as Ruth walked the family to the car.

"When are you coming back?" she asked.

"Month or so. About the same," he said.

"Thanks. It means a lot that you come so often." Ruth hugged Ned.

The cemetery lay on a hillside outside of town. There were a few large monuments, but most were less expensive. The Skunk River Valley and its marshes were plainly visible from the hillside. Ned and his family walked through the front gate toward the rear of the cemetery, past names of rooted familiarity; Welsh names: Morgan and Thomas and Jones and Llewellyn and Jenkins and Thomas and Lewis and Owen. The Welsh came to run the mines near Colfax at the turn of the century.

By the thirties the mines had gone bad, so the men became farmers or worked at the Maytag factory in Newton. Win's father, Albert Jenkins, came to Colfax when there was no work and he spent his life drinking beer and telling stories. "A workin' man is entitled by law to his pint," he often said. Albert never worked at anything. He was buried next to his wife, Esther, near the back of the cemetery. Lizzy and Ellie were toddlers when they died.

Each grave was marked with a small flat stone inscribed with their names and dates of their lives.

Ned followed Win to the graves. Beyond the fence was an open field with a few oak trees. Stopping at her father's grave, Win began to sniffle. Staring ahead at the trees, she kept her eyes open and head erect as the tears flowed across her face. The children quieted and dropped their heads. The tears stopped when she looked down at the modest grave markers.

"Did we know Grandpa and Grandma?" Lizzy asked.

"You were little when they died."

"Why did they die?" Ellie asked.

"They were getting old," Win said without emotion.

"Like Grandpa and Grandma Owen?"

"Sort of."

"It's sad they're dead," Ellie said.

"It is for us because we can't see them," Win said. "It's not sad for them." She kneeled at her father's grave. Her voice brightened. "Do you know what your grandpa told me? He was old and knew he wouldn't live much longer. He said that when Welsh people die, they go into the ground and come back to the earth as beautiful things, like animals and flowers and trees. He told me to look for him after he died." Win's Welsh accent became richer. "'Look for me in the forests and in the gardens.

Look at the beautiful animals that live in the wild,' he said."

"Really?" Lizzy asked.

"He said Welsh people are magic," Win told her.

"Win." Ned pointed. "Heaven is up there."

"Heaven is anywhere," she said.

"Is that what the Baptists say?"

"They might. Heaven is where God's spirit lives."

"Wait a second. You just told the kids that when people die, they come back as animals. You mean your old man is down there by the Skunk River turned into a raccoon or an old hoot owl?"

Her reply was thinly audible. "Blasphemy. That's blasphemy."

Ned pranced in delight about Albert Jenkins' gravestone. "Blasphemy, blasphemy," Ned mocked.

"Let's run over there." Ellie pulled Lizzy toward a statue near the front of the cemetery.

"Win, you're crazy. According to religion, God makes you whole after you die. If you're missing an arm, you get it back. For God's sake you don't turn into an animal!"

"How do you know?"

"I went to Sunday School when I was a kid."

"The Welsh have other ideas."

"They're not Christian ideas."

"You wouldn't know. You haven't seen the inside of a church since we were married."

"I only asked a question. How would you like to die and wake up a pigeon or a groundhog?"

"The Welsh stories my dad told were for fun."

"It seems to me you use any story that suits you."

He left her and joined the kids. They left Win alone with the graves.

On the Interstate going home, Ned drove peculiarly slow. He had switched on the air conditioning and turned the radio to station WHO for a Bluegrass concert. Win read her book and the kids argued in the back seat. Ned told them to quiet down and they did, in their own manner.

"Were all the grandpas and grandmas there when you got married?" Ellie asked.

"We had grandpas and grandmas and aunts and uncles and a billy goat," Ned said.

"You're lying," Lizzy said. "I don't believe it."

"The minister was a billy goat," Ned said.

"Dad—" Ellie said reproachfully.

"Was Mommy pretty?" Lizzy asked.

"Sure she was," Ned answered.

"Did you have fun?" Ellie asked.

Win had placed her book against the door as the sun was bothering her. "Your dad's hands shook all day," she said without moving her eyes from the pages.

"That's because your mother had a gun," Ned said.

"There were no guns to be found anywhere," she muttered as she lost her place.

"Where did you go on your honeymoon?" Ellie asked.

"To a hospital," Ned said. He looked over his seat and winked at them.

"A hospital! That's silly!"

"We were married two days before I was an intern. We went to Toledo, Ohio."

"Is it nice there?"

"It's a city. Not like where we live," Ned said.

Win turned a page and adjusted the air conditioner vent on her side of the dash.

"Gee. We weren't even born then, were we?" Ellie wondered.

The kids sat back and were quiet. Win peeked at a road sign from behind her book and Ned proceeded slowly, in silence.

He took an access road into Spring Falls, past a small gravel pit and stored dump trucks. They passed modest houses, some impoverished, some painted brightly, with

American flags stuck from doorways. He showed the kids Mr. Bayer's grotto. The eccentric had collected geodes of questionable worth, split them in half so they looked like sand-blasted grapefruit and cemented them together to form a small chapel and a liberty bell.

"Why are we driving around here?" Win asked.

"Thought we'd take a drive," he said.

She didn't protest further.

They passed the Williams furniture factory, which had expanded from a long brick building into three rows of stainless steel and a barren parking lot. As they neared the college, houses were larger, many of them Victorian. Several were freshly painted, trimmed with rich brown or green or lemon. Ned turned onto another street with newer homes, simple in design. Win's church was surrounded by these houses. The church itself was old; siding facing the street was sagging, and new cement steps had shifted, leaving a gap between the stairs and the church.

Ned drove to the college. "Cathlin College, Its Heart Is Our Home," announced a sign over an archway.

They passed older brick dormitories, the Colonial-style library, newer buildings of vagrant architectural style. The college lawns were massive, with great open spaces between buildings. Ned wove around the driveways and headed for Denby Manor, the president's home. It stood on the very highest point of the college. Parking the car, Ned told everyone to get out for a walk.

Suddenly three cars roared around a curve. They were filled with teen-agers. Ned heard the loud mufflers and saw the huge racing tires on the cars. The lead car turned sharply from the roadway and spun onto the lawn near the library. Girls in the cars screamed as if they were on a roller coaster. The other cars gave chase and the trio drove across the campus, around trees, digging tire tracks in the sod.

"Son of a bitches." Ned ran at them with an outraged

finger, but they disappeared behind the power plant and left.

The kids climbed out of the car, but Win waited inside with her book. She told him to leave the motor running so she could read with air conditioning.

Denby Manor was an old Victorian house; long, thin windows graced the living and dining rooms. The house was a whim of Sir Charles Denby, founder of Cathlin College, named for his wife. It was a hodgepodge of turrets and towers and walkways and stained glass that had survived one tornado, innumerable hailstorms, doubtless personal feuds within, the Scopes trial, bombardier school in World War II, beatniks and antiwar rallies. Above the second-story front was a square and steeply angled roof that ended in a small flat top. A walkway circled the base of the roof, trimmed with filigree ironwork. "See that, kids? That's a witch's hat. We could see everything from up there. Wouldn't storms be fun if we could stand up there?"

"Where would you run when it got bad?" Ellie asked.

"Through the window."

"Then it would be OK," she said.

"Could we live there?" Lizzy asked.

"If I was president of the college."

"Can you do that? Since you're a doctor?" Lizzy asked.

"I'll find out. President of the college can't do more than I do. I think I'll apply for the job."

"Really?" the kids asked.

He drove home through the original town site. The streets were named Lucas and Chambers and Grimes and Briggs and Kirkwood for early governors of the state. The section had special secret places, overgrown back yards, newly sandblasted century-old settlers' houses, lawns populated with plaster images of geese and donkeys and human minorities. Untrimmed hedges and lilac bushes and weedy alleys isolated houses into secretive hideaways. Ned drove past College Row, where professors lived, then to a street with four Civil War homes, which led to his house.

At home, Ned spoke to Win. "We have to work on the garden today."

"I have church tonight."

"If we don't do something today, the darn thing will go to weeds. I'll do some but you should help, too."

"It's hot outside."

"We'll do it fast. I can hoe if you pull the big weeds."

"We never use the garden," she said.

"We still can get some green beans and tomatoes."

She agreed to help only after persistent nagging. In shorts and sandals, Ned led the charge to the garden and began hacking away at weeds that had taken a position of superiority. Win slowly caught up with him and daintily pulled long weeds from the edge of the garden. They worked that way for fifteen minutes, Ned swinging the hoe with gritted teeth and Win sauntering around the garden, never leaving the grass to venture onto the dirt.

"Why didn't you tell the kids about when we got married?" he asked.

"You seemed to be doing very well with the talking today," she said.

"That was dumb. You told them about what happens to people after they die."

"It's only a story."

"Tell them the truth."

"There's plenty of truth I could tell them," she said, stopping her work. "They asked about our marriage day. Did you want me to tell them you had to get me pills because I was sick and you were nervous because I might vomit in the church?"

"That's our business."

"That was the devil's work. What we did."

"We were like anyone else."

"So everyone's pregnant when they get married?"

"So does it matter?"

"It matters a lot," she said.

"I was twenty-four and you were twenty-one. You didn't mind back then. You wanted to get married. You said so."

"The preacher says it was the work of the devil."

Ned threw the hoe halfway to the house. "Win. I really get pissed off at that crap. Religion is fine. I don't mind your going to church. All you talk about anymore is the devil and how bad we were and a bunch of crap that doesn't make sense. That preacher is a nut. I wanted to tell the kids something nice today. They asked about us getting married. I wanted to tell them you were the nicest person I ever knew. You used to be nice to everyone we knew. I loved to hear you talk. People like the way you talk to them. They like your Welsh accent. We used to have people over to the house, but you don't do anything but go to that damn church anymore. I don't like it."

"I don't expect you to understand, Ned Owen."

"The hell you don't! I'll tell you what I understand. You've turned from being the nicest person in the world into a cuckoo. You mix up stories of the devil with your old man's bullshit. You said the devil made you pregnant. The hell he did! I did! If the devil was responsible, then half the world belongs to him. We were old-fashioned. Every seventeen-year-old girl in this town is on the pill. They're not getting pregnant but they're screwing their butts off. You ever thought of that? Does the preacher tell you that?"

"I won't hear anymore." Win turned from him and ran in a shuffle to the house.

"Bear fuck and bullshit!" he yelled as he kicked a row of leaf lettuce gone to seed.

They ate bananas and bowls of Kraft's macaroni for supper.

"I have church at eight," Win said.

"I'll go to the hospital now and be back early so someone will be around the kids."

Sally Fromm was running around her hospital room as if she'd never been ill. Ned reexamined her, looking at her ears and throat, feeling for lymph nodes in her neck and listening to her chest and heart. The child was normal as could be.

"Her fever broke about three and she's been fine since," Mrs. Fromm said.

"Funny business, isn't it?" Ned mused. "I see this about twice a year, a virus that really makes kids groggy. We'll watch her tonight and you can take her home first thing in the morning."

"I was scared to death this morning. Thank you."

"She scared me, too. Kids can be funny with infections. They can scare the pants off you."

"I hope you got some time off today," Mrs. Fromm said. "I hated to bother you on Sunday, but I didn't think it could wait until tomorrow."

"Oh, no, I'd be mad if you didn't call. She was sick. I had a nice day. I even got to my garden."

Ned made brief social rounds, saying hello to visiting families. He checked out of the hospital and drove through Main Street. The only signs of life were four cars parked in front of Mike and Al's bar, an old brick building, erected in 1882, on the corner of Denby and Cherokee. Windows were painted black but light seeped through where the paint had cracked. Ned parked the Mercedes in front and walked in.

The floors were sagging pieces of dirty hardwood covered with debris. Ned nodded to Mike, standing in front of rows of cheap liquor and a picture of Al, who had died years back of cirrhosis. The bar could stay open on Sunday because they served sandwiches prepared in a microwave, qualifying as a restaurant.

Four men were playing pool in the rear. Ned knew all of them. They were patients who spent about as much time shooting pool as he spent in his office. The expert was Barney Poepsel, a retired farmer. Barney was well-to-do, heavy in the chest, and suffered from a condition, rhinophyma; his nose was twice the normal size. The others were Delmer Wade, who sold insurance to farmers; Ralph Flint, a farmhand; and Barney's grandson, Jeff.

"You guys looking for trouble?" Ned asked.

"I think you're lost, Doc," Jeff said. "Haven't seen you here all year."

"Just checking you out," Ned said.

"Your old lady give you permission?" Delmer asked. "That preacher don't like pool."

"She sent me over here to make a little money." Ned walked around a pool table that was lighted with a plastic Tiffany lamp. Posters covered the walls: Summer Hills Rider's Saddle Club Show, Denby Country Beef Days, Coon Dog field trials, Republican Picnic featuring State Secretary of Agriculture Robert H. Loundsberry—tickets 25¢.

The men watched him as Ned checked the rack of cues.

"Table open?" Ned asked.

"It is for you," Barney said.

Ned took ten dollars and slapped it on the table. "I'll take you on, Barney."

The others laughed in amazement.

"You'll get yourself in trouble, Doc," Barney said quietly.

"Ten bucks says you can't beat me playing left-handed."

Barney scratched his huge nose. Taking a cue in hand, he stroked it into the air, left-handed. He looked at Ned seriously, then reached into the rear pocket of his overalls.

"Money breaks," Barney said.

Win left shortly before eight. She drove down Denby Street and saw Ned's car. Two blocks further she turned onto a side street; driving slowly, she turned again, into an alley. She drove halfway up the alley and parked in a narrow lot between two cars. She walked up an old wooden stairway. The railing was unsafe, so she guided herself with her left hand against the brick of the building. The very top step was rotten and about to fall away, so she jumped over it. She walked across the landing and opened a door to a dim hallway.

"Thought I heard you. You're on time." Johnny Inglebretson stuck his head from his door.

Win walked into his apartment. One end was a kitchenette with old appliances. The living room had two stuffed chairs and a broken sofa. Win kissed him and walked to the window, pulling the shade.

"How can you stand it up here without an air conditioner?"

"I don't mind it. Sit over there by the fan."

"Johnny. Can you carry me over your shoulders?"

"Why should I do that?"

She showed him her book with the picture of the nun. "See her. She was forced to live in the convent by her mean parents. They gave her to the nuns. One day a young man came to prune the trees. She talked to him a long time and he decided to help her. So he lifted her on his shoulders and she climbed over the wall. He saved her. I wanted to know if you could lift me on your shoulders."

Johnny was bewildered.

"Here." She stood facing him. "Put your hands on my waist and lift me up to your shoulder. Come on, Johnny. Let me see if you can do it."

He obliged. With a grunt he lifted her and she climbed over his shoulder. He carried her around the room like a fireman.

"You can do it! If I was that nun, you'd save me."

He put her down and they sat by the fan. It was getting dark outside. Light from a vapor lamp in the street seeped through his window shade. Win's hair was snarled from their playing. The effect of the peculiar light was to mummify her face and create shadows between her teeth, making her look like a hag.

"I hate him," she said.

"I know you like me but you shouldn't hate him."

"He mocked my father. Right over his grave."

"He shouldn't do that."

"There's no fun in him. Everything has to be real. He thinks I'm silly. He always has. Today he called me a cuckoo. That makes it easy for him. If I'm a cuckoo, he doesn't have to worry about me."

"It seems he always wants to hurt you," Johnny said.

"He'll find out about hurting," she said. The effects of the vapor lamp were stronger. Her face darkened to lavender. "He'll find out. When I leave him and he's all alone in that big house, he'll know who's cuckoo."

Monday, June 28

High on the inner aspect of Gail Tamlin's left thigh was an angry infection which had grown worse overnight. It had darkened to an ominous crimson. Skin over the center was very thin. Gail rested her foot on her bathtub, complaining. "Ouch, ouch, damn, damn." She poked a finger about the periphery of the infection, trying to think of a name for it. She was posed like a ballerina and might have passed for one, but for five or six extra pounds. She felt her forehead for a fever, then looked in the mirror, examining her face from several angles, wiggling her mouth. There were no signs of general illness.

As she walked to the bedroom, the infected area rubbed against the other thigh, touching some nerve deep in her stomach. After the nausea passed, she allowed herself ten minutes for self-pity.

She dressed, gingerly, in summery slacks, old tennis shoes and a gingham blouse. Breakfast was a peanut butter sandwich. She scoured the kitchen for the letter from the owners which lay in a ceramic bowl on top of the refrigerator. Midway through it said: *"If you get sick, call Ned Owen. A good man and his politics are right. He's busy, so use our name as reference."*

Ned walked to the scrub sink, casually tying the strings on his scrub pants. He whistled.

"Where you been?" Byron Markham yelled through the operating room door.

"Out driving, Byron." Ned pushed the water button and began his scrub.

"You're late," Byron said.

"Did you start without me?"

"I've started and stopped. She's fat, Ned. Fat. I'm through the subcutaneous fat and she's got so many bleeders I thought I was doing an aneurysm." The surgeon covered the incision as a mother would tuck a baby in a bassinet. His forehead was a mass of wrinkles which twitched as Ned scrubbed. "I'm glad you decided to come, Ned. I was afraid I'd fall in the incision and there'd be no one to pull me out."

"It's my birthday. I was out driving. It's nice out."

"That's a peculiar way to celebrate."

"Gets my blood going."

Byron lifted the towel covering the incision. "Yuk," he said as he dropped the blood-clot towel into a waste-basket. "Come on, Ned, let's get going."

"Use the mechanical hand."

"If such existed, I'd have it salute you with one finger."

"You told me a long time ago you didn't need an assistant, only a mechanical hand."

Ned finished scrubbing. Byron yelled, "Let's move, Ned," and gave him six clamps. Two small vessels bled from the wall of the incision. They were clamped and tied. Byron took a knife and separated a thick band of muscle. They caught the bleeders and then opened the perito-neum, the protecting layer of the abdominal cavity. Byron pushed his hand inside as Ned hummed and tapped his feet. The surgeon felt the contents: stomach, liver, spleen, kidneys, intestines, and uterus with ovaries and Fallopian tubes. "All clean."

There were three or four large stones within the gall-bladder. Byron motioned for Ned to feel. "Did you drive fast?"

"A little."

"I heard about your encounter with the smokies. That's what truck drivers call the highway patrol, you know."

"Who told you?"

"The ambulance crew. The patrolmen questioned them. The crew lied for you."

"How in the hell would they know what I was doing?"

"A hundred and ten. Clocked. That's the word."

"Somebody's been telling stories."

"Town gossip has it that way."

"Gossip is wrong."

"Ned, you can't get by with anything in this town. Like the time you punched that drug addict in the ER."

"Baloney." Ned's hand reached the gallbladder. It felt like bloated kelp.

Byron rolled a cloth inside. Ned lay his hand on the cloth to separate blood vessels and ducts which ran from the liver to the gallbladder and small intestine. Byron dissected fat so that the area was well defined, each vessel and duct separate and distinct.

"Get X-ray, get suction up, have some more lap pads ready, give me a big clamp. Ned. I never said anything about a mechanical hand. Now give me some good exposure. That's right. Hold."

Ned held his fingers over the cloth so that the parts of anatomy were properly spread out. He would hold this position until his fingers would cramp and ache.

The surgeon slipped silk suture over the artery and tied it. Another suture was placed over the duct loosely as Byron cut a hole in the duct and inserted a small plastic tube. He tightened the knot. X-ray was positioned over the duct and Byron injected dye into the tube. While the X-ray was being developed, Byron tied off the duct and removed the gallbladder by carefully snipping it away from the liver bed. He held the gallbladder in the air. It looked like a plump dead rat.

"How old are you, Dr. Owen?" the scrub nurse asked.

Ned raised the tips of four fingers of his left hand to his forehead. The tips of the fingers automatically aligned themselves.

"Don't contaminate yourself, Doctor," Ellen said.

"He's too old to learn any new tricks," Byron muttered.

"You're still mad that I'm late."

"Why shouldn't I be? You refer me this fat farmer's wife and let me grub around in her fat while you're out having a birthday party. And the reason you're having your party is because you don't have the common sense to do it properly later. Ten o'clock tonight you'll be in the Emergency Room."

"I'm not a gentleman doctor, like you," Ned said. "What time do you get home, Byron?"

"Three-thirty. Four, maybe."

"Gentleman doctor!" Ned said to Ellen. "A New York fancypants who comes out here to live like a country squire. Where do you get your clothes, Byron?"

"Brooks Brothers."

"He looks like a stockbroker on his farm."

"I wear riding clothes at home."

The X-rays were back and showed the common bile duct to be open, free of stones. "Let's close," Byron said. He attached Kocher clamps to the inner edges of the wound. Ellen gave him a long catgut suture and he began to close the peritoneum. Ned held one end of the suture as Byron worked.

"Ned. You haven't learned about proper living. If I was in New York, I'd be teaching at Columbia, working until ten every night. You should move to New York. You'd love it. Work your hind end off just to keep up. You're a ready-made New Yorker."

"What am I supposed to do if someone calls at night?"

"Tell them to wait until morning."

"I need the money." Ned winked at Ellen.

"You need money like I need one of your Vietnam hippie stories."

"You want me to tell you about the time I kicked a Vietnamese out of a helicopter?"

"The helicopter was on the ground." Byron tugged at the suture, his voice sharper. "You're illogical, to say the least," Byron lectured. "You tell far-fetched stories to justify your consorting with hippies and you justify obsessive behavior with equally absurd stories. The truth is, medicine is a big joy ride for you. You're addicted to it, Ned. We all know you're from a small town, your old man was a carpenter and you never cared about money and you don't give a damn now. If you did, you'd take your wad, invest it and leave tomorrow. Medicine's a game."

Byron's forehead signaled no further discussion. They closed her incision.

The farmer's wife was rolled onto a cart and they talked to her husband. After the man was assured of his wife's recovery, Byron took Ned aside. His voice was abrupt. "I want to talk to you."

Ned looked at him.

"Let's not talk here." Byron led Ned past the dressing room. He walked two paces in front of Ned until they were near the nurses' coffee room. Byron's forehead was flat as the wall. He stared at Ned intently.

"What—?" Ned stammered.

"Bring him in."

Half of the hospital staff, the entire operating room, people from the Emergency Room, and some of the floor staff filled the room. Pink and blue streamers flowed from a decorative urinal. They sang, "Happy Birthday, Ned," as Ellen unveiled a cake sitting on a Mayo stand. On it was a drawing of a diapered baby and the name NED.

"How does it feel to be Spring Falls' youngest doctor?"
Ellen asked.

"Damn you, Byron," Ned said.

Gail put a volume into the canvas bag of her bicycle. The
book contained transcripts of the Senate Committee on
Banking and Currency, 1932–34. She rode up a long hill
from her rented house in College Row to the library. It
was impossible for her to pedal without bumping the
infection. The bike had been her husband's, a blue Gitane
with straps on the pedals. As their divorce settled into
pettiness and acrimony, Gail made a selfless offer: Willy
P-3, her husband, could have the M-l6 sail boat if she
could have the bike. "Now I know why I married you,"
he said.

"Ouch, damn it." She swore as she dismounted.

The reference librarian stood beneath a heraldic tapes-
try. Gail limped to her.

"Have they come? *Sons of the Wild Jackass* by Ray
Tucker and Frederick Barkley and *Rogues and Heroes of
Iowa,* an Iowa State Press publication."

"No."

"Damn," Gail said. "Is there any way we can trace the
books? I was told they would be here by now. It's important. My time is limited. I have to be finished by the
end of the summer session. I can't get the books out east.
They're about former Iowa Senator Wildman Brookhart.
He's one of the sons—of the Wild Jackass. Can you help
me?"

The librarian's face was marmoreal, as though she'd had
a face lift at the age of thirty-two.

Gail pleaded. "Can't you help me?"

"I can say I can but I can't. There's a computer for the
libraries. It's in Des Moines. It's not very friendly and it
doesn't cooperate, so it doesn't do any good to bother it."

"Like the Wizard of Oz?"

"I wouldn't know." She gave Gail a card. "Fill it out."

"Again?"

"If you want the books."

"Crap," Gail said.

"You're the one!" The woman's face livened.

"Which one?"

"You're staying in the Raffensberger house. The place in College Row by the lily pond."

Gail nodded.

"What's it like inside? I bet it's beautiful."

"It's a very lovely house and the woodwork has been preserved."

"Do you ever go outside and sit under the willows by the pond?"

"God, no. The mosquitoes are murder. In fact, I think that's why I have this damn infection."

"Isn't there a lily pad?"

"The neighbor kids smashed them chasing bull snakes." The woman's eyelids twitched.

"What time do you finish work?" Gail asked.

"Four-thirty."

"Stop by on your way home. Without those books I don't have anything to do. I have to visit the doctor and my seminar gets over at three-thirty. I'll be glad to show you the house. I haven't had a soul over since I came. Sure, stop by. If I look like I'm going crazy, don't worry. This place is driving me nuts. Summer here is as exciting as Dachau."

"You sure you won't mind?"

"Not at all. Oh, could you tell me how to get to Dr. Owen's office?"

"Sure."

"Is he OK?"

"He's nice. And he's an honorary member of the AFL-CIO."

"Christ, that's all I need." Gail made a face and looked

at the floor where countless students had shuffled their feet as they ordered books from an indifferent computer.

Ned arrived late at his office.

"Good morning, Doctor." His secretary, Ann, cleared her throat. "Number one. Happy birthday. Second. Can Mrs. Princeton have her Valium refilled?" Ned grunted yes. "Third, then, do you want to take out Timmy Parks' stitches Tuesday or Thursday?"

"Thursday."

"Then"—she shuffled charts—"yes, you'll love this, the pharmacy ordered too much Novahistine DH and would appreciate it if you prescribed it for a couple of weeks. They'll sell it ten percent off."

Ned's face was blank.

"I told them you would be excited." She plopped the charts on a shelf. "Doctor, Sheryl and I feel sorry." She hung her head. "It's your birthday and you told us not to spare you. Well, we didn't. The schedule is impossible." She thought a moment. "I mean, we're not even sparing ourselves."

"I like being busy."

His nurse, Sheryl, gave him a single chart. "Ready? Happy birthday. Elmer is in the second room."

Elmer Groote was a grain hauler with a nose like the beak of a Baffin Bay puffin. He was leaning over the examining table. When he saw Ned, he unlatched the shoulder straps of his overalls, slipping them to the floor. His body was white, flowered with gray hairs which were matted like tundra. He smelled of baby powder.

Ned found an examining glove and KY jelly.

As he was about to insert his finger into the man's rectum, Ned asked, "How's things goin', Elmer?"

"Fine, Doctor, just fine."

Ned pushed his finger easily through the anal sphincter. The man's prostate gland felt like two mounds of rubber.

Ned applied force with the end of his finger, stroking the gland along parallel lines to express fluid. Elmer waited with Kleenex. Only the tip of Ned's finger could move, which pulled the small muscles of his hand and a muscle in his forearm. His finger began to hurt. The pain wouldn't stop until the procedure was over.

"Dr. Markham told me about a mechanical hand."

"Oh," Elmer said.

"Maybe it could do this."

"Maybe so."

Ned felt discomfort to his elbow.

"That's good," Elmer said.

Ned exhaled.

Elmer waited for the last drop of seminal fluid to appear before he hitched up his pants.

After Elmer left, the office was quiet. The waiting room and the examining rooms were empty.

"That was your birthday present," Ann said.

"Elmer," Sheryl drawled.

Ned sat by the microscope and the incubator.

"Nervous?" Ann asked.

"No."

"Because—there's no patients out there."

"Don't worry. We set this up," Sheryl said. "It's your birthday! We don't have another patient for fifteen minutes."

Ann put a cake next to the incubator. The cake was decorated with an open car surrounded by something that looked like the pillars of Stonehenge.

"Now your real presents."

Ann gave him a magazine advertisement of a resort in the Bahamas. Forty cabanas, a blue ocean, two sea gulls, a black man serving a green daiquiri. Clipped to it was an application blank for a Traveler's Express Card. His name was typed on it.

"You haven't taken more than three days off since I began," Sheryl said. "We daydream about being here by ourselves—with you gone—no patients."

"I wouldn't have told it quite like that," Ann said.

"Really, Doctor. Don't you ever think of taking a vacation? You told us about that place in the Philippines. Isn't this picture like it?"

"If I left for two weeks, all the patients would leave."

"That's not a bad idea, either," Sheryl said.

"It's not that I don't want to," Ned explained. "I forget."

They gave him an expensive tennis shirt and a can of tennis balls.

Their first patient arrived.

Susie Minks had a croupy cough and a fever. The cough frightened her mother. Ned asked, but there were no other symptoms. The eight-year-old sat on the examining table. Her face was red. She smelled of child's vomit.

"She barks," Mrs. Minks said.

Ned lay the girl on her back and put his left hand beneath her head, lifting it to her chin three times. She didn't have meningitis. He looked at her ears and eyes, then slid a tongue depressor over her tongue, looking for her epiglottis, a small piece of tissue. He had to push firmly at the base of the tongue. She gagged and turned from him.

"I'll vomit," the child said.

"She will, Doctor," her mother insisted.

The child moved away from him, but he repositioned her and forced the depressor backward, arching his neck to see. Susie made noises and struggled, but he persisted until he saw a small arch of tissue, flesh pink.

She vomited on his arm.

"She'll be fine." He walked to the sink and washed his sleeve.

Tears came to the child's eyes.

Ned laughed. "Got you, didn't I?" He prescribed codeine elixir.

The surgery room looked like a dry goods sale at the Goodwill Industries. Pam and Jerry and Ron and Steve and Rhonda Thomas waited in their underwear. Pam had a small spot on her shoulder. Jerry had two in the middle of his chest. His didn't itch. Ron had a spot on his cheek, arm and belly. Steve had something on his back, and Rhonda, the others informed, had it on her butt. Ned looked at the patches carefully. "Ringworm." He gave them salve and pills.

Delmer Wade came for insurance physical. He also sold cattle, farm land, antiques, and drank Schlitz for exercise. His wife collected Danish Christmas plates. After the exam, Ned shook Delmer's hand. "For a man with a gut like that you're in damn good shape."

Gail waited cross legged on an examining table. The infection had reached a point of crisis. If she pushed the palm of her hand between the infection and her groin, the pain lessened. She experimented this way until she discovered a mixed sensation of pleasure, itching and pain.

Through the window she saw the heads of two dying hollyhocks, dust covered, peeking at her like curious century-old dolls taken from an attic chest. Pushing her palm almost to her underpants, she shuddered with the odd sensation.

She heard a voice over and over again. It laughed a lot. Other voices laughed as well. She created pictures of Ned. It was her pastime and occupation to master images of people unseen and unmet.

Mrs. Carley's son Tom-Tom had returned after living a year with his dad in a commune in Arizona. She couldn't get his hair unmatted. He was eleven, barefoot, tanned and dirty; the boy had the most generous face Ned had ever seen. His hair was peculiar. As Ned was about to touch it, something caught his eye. He moved closer. Lice covered the boy's head like a plague. Ned felt itchy all over.

"I tried Clorox and acetone," she said.

Sheryl knocked at the door, asking Ned to step into the hallway.

"Can you come with me?" She led him outside. The temperature was over ninety. "Bear with me," she said. "I know you might think this is different."

They walked to the rear of the building. It had been a grain warehouse before it was converted into a doctor's office. The storage room opened onto the alley, its entrance an old loading dock. Two figures were sidelighted against the dark of the room.

"This is Rodney Miller." Son of Dr. Miller, the chiropractor.

Ned pulled the chain of a hanging light bulb. Rodney sat on a box of disposable pads amidst other supplies. His eyes were sick, he was shivering.

"Do you mind seeing him, Dr. Owen?" Mrs. Miller asked. "And you won't tell his dad?"

"No."

Sheryl handed him a light and a tongue depressor.

"My God!" Ned exclaimed. The boy's tonsils were swollen and touched each other in the middle of his throat. The back of his throat was crimson. Cream-colored pus oozed from the crypts of his tonsils. Ned poked around looking for an abscess.

"Can he take penicillin?" he asked.

"Yes."

He sent Sheryl for two prepackaged syringes.

Rodney slipped his pants to his knees and bent over a box of Ace bandages. Ned injected penicillin as thick as the stuff on the boy's tonsils. Mrs. Miller's forehead was dripping wet.

"Let me see him in a week," Ned said.

"Here?" the woman asked.

Ned looked at the dusty walls. "I think it's safe," he whispered on his way to his next patient.

"Gail Tamlin, I'm Doctor Owen."

Gail looked at his lips, the softest part of his face. He wasn't like her image.

"I bet it hurts!"

"Like hell," she said.

He asked her the necessary medical questions. Her infection looked like an infrared picture of a volcano. Ned touched the skin around it. If he touched it gently, it didn't hurt.

He bent over her, observing. His eyes turned from the lesion to her underpants. They were a rich blue, slightly faded from several washings. There was an old stain, teardrop in shape, deep between her thighs.

With his fingers flattened, as when he felt his hairline, he crept his fingers under her pants to feel for lymph nodes. He found two at the top of her thigh.

He looked at the blue of her underwear, then at her face.

"Are you a housewife?"

"I've got my boil down there. Not in my head."

"No kids?"

"Or dogs."

"What do you do?"

"When I'm not showing off my legs?" Gail's hair was walnut, streaked with lighter-colored strands. She unconsciously played with loose hairs over her ear. Her voice was bright but slightly husky; precise. "If it's important to you, I talk to dead people."

Ned played with the bell of his stethoscope, hesitating. "Do they talk back?"

She laughed. "Only on the first day of my period." She grimaced after looking at her infection. "I have a lot of pain with my IUD, so I take anything I can get to stop it. After a few pills they might talk back."

"And you get paid for this?"

"I get paid for talking to live people. I teach American Studies. My area of concern is the depression and the people involved. Like Herbert Hoover. I don't think he's talked to me, but then I blocked him out for a long time. But Andy Mellon talked to me. He was Secretary of the Treasury under Hoover. He owned lots of railroads and steel mills. Andy told me he was going to give me all his money."

"You must get blitzed out of your mind."

"A medical necessity."

Ned selected instruments from the cabinet, putting them on a stand. Then he pulled a chair next to her, jotting notes on her chart. "Do you only talk to rich people?"

"Are you writing this down?"

"Just curious."

"I occasionally condescend and associate with union people."

He didn't respond.

"I said that because a lady told me you were a member of the AFL-CIO."

He stood, reached beneath his white coat and found his billfold. "See that?" It was a worn union card from Local 327.

"It says you work in a furniture factory."

"Mostly on weekends."

"You can't get by with that."

"Why not?"

"Your hands betray you."

"I'm an honorary member. For giving a speech for labor at a county Democratic convention." After she had given him his card, he looked at her. "I don't know any schoolteachers with union cards."

"I'm not a schoolteacher. I like to think of myself as a professor."

"And I'm a union man." He put a tall stack of gauze sponges on the tray. After placing drapes around the infection, he filled a syringe with Xylocaine.

"Can I talk when you do this? I'm nervous," she said.

"Really?"

"I'm leery of shop stewards attacking me with knives. Can you tell me what you're going to do?"

"Put some stuff in there to make it numb, then make a cut to let the pus out." He asked her to lie back. The wound was carefully examined again. He checked her arms and stomach and chest for other infections. There was a smattering of freckles on her stomach, larger than those on her face.

"You haven't told me what it is," she said.

"It doesn't make any difference as long as I let the pus out."

"Is it a boil?"

"A carbuncle. I only told you because you're a school-teacher."

Gail arched her head back, looking at the ceiling. Resigned. "A name is the difference between a Chevy and a Cadillac."

"If you have to look at the nameplate, you're in trouble. That's what they don't tell you in school."

"You obviously have a thing about teachers."

"I never liked them."

"Did you give them a hard time?"

"Usually."

"For any reason?"

"I got bored. Then I'd do things." He forced a needle under her skin. He told her it might hurt and it did. He continued to inject until his needle entered the cavity of the infection. Without telling her, he took a knife and plunged it through the skin. Gray-yellow pus rolled out; he daubed it with sponges. The smell was rank. Four sponges were completely soaked with pus.

"A lot of stuff in there," he said.

"Smells terrible."

"All done." He temporarily covered the incision with two sponges.

"That quick? It didn't hurt after the shot. Very good."

"Maybe it was a boil."

"I think I'll tell you what I was thinking when I was waiting. I created a picture of you. You were like a pirate, tall and dark with a long scar across your cheek."

He noticed a spot of blood on his boot, leaned over to remove it. "Bad guess."

"Maybe not. You said you were a rascal in school. Are you a rascal now?"

"I don't know."

"I know what the problem is."

"What problem?"

"It's this mortuary of a town. No one can be a rascal here. Ever since I came I've felt a sense of terror that I'm slowly turning into Ice Nine."

"You don't like it here?"

"God, no. Do you?"

"It's great."

"Can you expand on that?"

"You haven't been here long enough."

"What would I discover? Does it come alive at three in the morning?"

Ned cleaned the skin around the wound, throwing dirty sponges into a wastebasket and placing the used instruments on a corner of the tray. His back was turned to her as he removed the knife blade from its handle. "What are you looking for?"

"A good restaurant. People to talk to. Live music. A decent bar. Movies. Civilization."

"We had a wife-swapping group until this guy brought back the disease from St. Louis."

"I'm not a wife."

"We have great storms. It's fun to watch them."

"You're putting me on." A line of thinned blood streaked down the side of her thigh. He quickly caught it with a clean sponge.

"If you think this place is bad, you ought to see Des Moines."

"I have nightmares about being stuck here. Makes me think of Charles Ives. He spent his whole life without recognition, in a vacuum. It must have been like living here. Do you know his music?"

"Was he a fiddler?"

"A composer. Now that he's dead they say he was great. Doesn't do him any good now."

Ned put a tidy dressing over her wound. "Change the dressing at home. Keep it covered until there's no drainage. You'll have to be on antibiotics for a week. Check back with me then. Maybe I'll think of something that'll make you excited."

"I think the secret wonders of Spring Falls are very secret."

"Schoolteachers should be able to figure a few things out."

"Professors have more of a problem."

Ned laughed at her. "You're welcome to come here. I could show you some sights."

"I don't like working that much."

"It's the closest thing to Disneyland this side of the Rockies."

He looked at her again, at her legs, her blue underpants. He smiled in resignation. "See you in a week."

At precisely noon Lizzy and Ellie called.

"You have to come home now," they insisted. "Mom's gone but we want you to come anyway."

"Is there a party?"

"No. Something special. Please come."

Ned saw another patient, then ducked through the laboratory door to avoid three remaining patients. He drove as fast as he dared. His house, on the edge of town, marked the end of Spring Falls and the beginning of a cornfield.

Ellie, the ten-year-old, took him by his hand and made him wait at the bottom of the open stairway of their old house.

"Close your eyes until you can't stand it any longer," she said as she ran up the stairs. "Keep 'em closed."

Suddenly there was a loud flapping and bumping and the hysterical giggling of his two daughters. Ned looked up as they rode a rubber canoe down the stairway. He caught them at the bottom.

"Happy birthday," they yelled.

"For me?"

"For us, too. For the pond."

They made him sit in it.

"We got it from Bean's," Lizzy said.

"It's for the pond," Ellie said, "but most of all it can go anywhere. It can take white water, Dad. Really."

"If it can take white water, it can take anything." He hugged them both.

Wednesday, June 30

Bronwyn Owen changed into her faded orange nightgown, a morning habit. It was the color of an old pumpkin gone unpicked. She wore the gown mornings and some days into the afternoon. It was sheer nylon and she wore little underneath, but she was thin and only when she assumed odd poses, which was seldom, were the contours of her body revealed. Her hair, coal black for a miner's daughter, lay against the gown, bunched and loose like freshly combed angora waiting to be spun. Her face had high cheekbones, a proper chin and flesh like royalty—her mother had been compared to the Queen herself. The hollows of Win's face were more apparent than the highlights. She was a person of shadows, shunning too much light and sun. Some ounce of flesh was missing; in meager light she looked fragile as a hungry child, the effect vanishing when she looked up from eyes the color of a cold sea.

The phone rang. Although it was only across the bed, it rang four times before she said hello.

"Yes, it's all right," she said. "If it wasn't, do you think I'd be standing here talking?"

Her voice was softer than Irish or Scotch, with a different cadence.

"I might read a book," she said, answering a question. She held the phone to her ear and closed the doors to Ned's deck.

"It's a furnace out there." She turned on the window air conditioner and pulled the drapes.

"It was cold in the book I'm reading," she said. "Raining and snowflakes on this mountain." She listened for a while and laughed.

"That will be good." She hung up.

She crawled into bed, slowly, like the fabled Southern rich girl, mythical in her ease. She read from a 1970 *Reader's Digest* book, then napped until Lizzy bowled her way into the room.

"Mother," Lizzy yelled. "Ellie says I can't go swimming."

"You both are going. Don't let her kid you."

"Are you coming, Mom?"

"It's too hot."

"To go swimming? That's silly."

"I've got to clean the house."

"Today? No you don't," Lizzy argued.

"Mrs. Watson bragged on herself that she could take all you kids by herself."

"You can come, too."

"I go with you tomorrow. That will be enough for us all," she said. "You be ready and waiting out front when she comes and be sure and take money for ice cream."

Lizzy exited, yelling for her sister, pounding her heels into the stairs, running through the living room and out the door with a slam.

Win was alone and surrounded by the house.

She rose from the bed, in no hurry, uncanny, as if she'd perfected a new form of locomotion combining levitation

with somnambulism. Five bedrooms opened onto the upstairs hallway. She walked on a runner which made the
upstairs feel stately and weary, like an old hotel. She
entered Lizzy's room. Small pictures of animals from
Ranger Rick's were taped to the wall. The hermit crab
was torn. A pillow lay on the floor on one side of the bed
and her sheets had fallen to the other side. Win picked
up the pillow, lay it on the bed and tugged at the sheets
until half of them were on the bed.

Continuing her rounds, she walked past the door to
Ned's study. Beneath four years of medical journals was
an oak desk. She didn't bother the room. The smallest
bedroom had the best TV, but no one used it so she
stored broken things there. Ellie's room had bright red
walls and a thick white shag carpet. Win walked to
the window and leaned against the sill. Lizzy and Ellie
were dragging a plastic wading pool across the lawn.
Water splashed from it. Lizzy fell on the grass. Win could
see that the child was crying, but Ellie continued without
her. Ellie's bedding was rolled into a ball at the foot of
the bed and several stuffed animals were under the bed.
Win inspected the room and left. Barefoot, she made no
noise as she walked the length of the hall. No noise
penetrated from outside. In the bathroom she picked up
three towels and checked a title on another *Reader's
Digest* book.

Guiding herself down the open stairway, she descended,
towels in arm, to the living room. She walked through the
kitchen, took three steps down the basement stairs and
threw the towels into the void. They landed, *huuuufff,
huuupppp,* on the cement floor.

Her toaster could make thirty pieces of toast in ten
minutes. She dropped a slice of bread into it and carefully stepped over a soup spoon and three kernels of popcorn to reach the refrigerator and the strawberry preserves.
There was a golf ball and a frying pan with half a cold
egg on the stove. Win carried the pan to the sink, flipped

the egg into the disposal and ran water in the pan. Two plates, one with dried ketchup and a pickle, lay on the table. Win buttered her toast and spread preserves on it. After eating, she dropped the pickle where the egg had gone and put the plate with ketchup into the frying pan. A hand towel had fallen between the stove and refrigerator. After turning on the kitchen air conditioner, she picked up the towel and lay it near the stove, wiping the very tips of her fingers.

She walked gracefully and unhurried into the dining room, like a great yacht enjoying light airs. She turned on the room air conditioner. Someone had pushed the throw rug under the dining room table. She tugged at it with her toe, but the rug was caught. She arranged two of the high-back chairs next to the table. A Smokey-the-Bear doll sat in a silver service on the table. She put it on the shelf of the china closet next to cracked geodes and a plate full of children's pictures.

Mrs. Watson bustled into the house. She wore tight-fitted shorts and tossed her car keys up and down as she talked.

"Thank God we don't have to go to the public pool today," Mrs. Watson said.

"The girls would get lost."

"I've arranged with George at the club for a table. We'll swim and have soft drinks, then we'll have ice cream."

"Lizzy and Ellie have money," Win said.

"They don't have to pay when I take them," Mrs. Watson said.

"They have money," Win said with peculiar authority.

The woman stared at Win and her gown: fragile and untouchable as a china doll; bright colors and shining black hair and a face of quietness.

"We'll be back at two," Mrs. Watson said.

Before Win could wish them a good time they had vanished and she was again with the house. Ned had restored the living room. Oak floors, laid at an angle, had been refinished. Cut glass surrounded the doorway and there was a crown of stained glass over each window. Win turned on the room air conditioner and rocked in a maple rocker.

The dominant object in the room was above her, an oil painting of the clipper ship *Arcturus*. Sailors the size of mice hauled line; their terrified eyes were bulging excrescences of oil. Upsurging pillars of water attacked the ship, but, oddly, the insistent elements didn't for one minute forestay the detail of masts and rigging. Win bought it for a thousand dollars. The frame alone was worth eight hundred, the salesman told her. Win rocked back and forth past the brass title: *Arcturus in Heavy Seas*.

At eleven she went upstairs, changed into a skirt and blouse and wrapped a small red ribbon across her head. Most of the drapes in the house were drawn. The only air conditioner not on was in the attic.

The doorbell rang. Win said, "Yes," to it, but not loud enough for anyone to hear. Walking faster, she hurried to the door.

"I'll be ready soon. Only a minute," she said. "I have to check the back door and see that it isn't open. The heat, you know." She stepped backward. "Maybe it would be best if you didn't come in. We can leave in a minute."

Johnny Inglebretson whistled a flat note. He wore gray poplin shirt and pants with plain oxford shoes. His fingers worked the edges of his billed cap like an old nun with her beads.

Win left the front door slightly ajar for the children.

"It's not as hot as I thought," she said.

"I'm glad you hurried," Johnny said. "My carburetor's been acting up. Afraid I might stall in your driveway."

Johnny owned the Gambles store, selling hardware and paint and lawn mowers. He had never been married. He was shy but efficient in his work, so his store was busy, respected. Courteous to a fault, he often blushed at the simplest of things. His fellow businessmen kidded him for his parsimony; he lived like a miser, banking his money and never in the least way giving evidence of financial success.

"It would be a scene if your car broke down," she said.

"I was worried."

"It's too much, all the worrying we do."

He drove a six-year-old car that had no chrome. It was rusting around the doors. When they were out of town, Win opened the window and put her face directly in front of the onrushing air.

"Where are we going?" she asked.

"For a ride."

"I have a special idea. Drive out towards Ned's farm. If you turn on a road before it, there's a big, long field and there's never anybody around. We could go for a walk."

"Sure it isn't too hot?"

"There'll be a breeze."

The town was behind them. Win moved over and sat next to him. She put her arm around him. "I like to sit like this. You shouldn't be so nervous. It's natural."

"I just wonder sometimes if people see us."

"I wondered that myself last week, then do you know what I thought of?" She finger-painted a patch of dust on his dashboard. " 'What do people see?' I thought. A car comes down the road driving at us. They see us like this. What do they know? Maybe they think there's a dog sitting over on the other side of the seat and I have to sit here. Maybe they don't think the worst all the time."

"People see us at church and the movies."

They had met at the Baptist church. Each sat alone for a long time, quiet worshipers, slowly coming together through brief encounters and an increasing awareness of the other's loneliness. They were embarrassed when they began sitting with each other during services and prayer meetings. Johnny was responsible for special occasions and called upon Win to help prepare coffee and buy doughnuts and cookies. When she kissed him the first time, playfully, after an evening service, he recoiled in fear. She waited a full two months before kissing him again.

"They'll have to think what they will because we're both so quiet, none of us would tell them."

"People just think we're quiet." Johnny slowed for an unmarked intersection.

"You're the shy one! I was in your store one day and you stuttered when you talked to this woman. That's how shy you are!"

"I forgot to order a special garden sprayer. I told her I did. I'm not good at lying."

"Did she ever get it?"

He was looking for a road sign. "What?"

"The sprayer."

"I called long distance and had them send it air freight."

He was lost and asked her for directions. She pointed toward a narrower road. There were cornfields on both sides. Weeds hadn't been mowed on the roadside.

"About half a mile there's a lane. There's a small shed. We can park the car behind it. No one in the world would find us."

"We hope not."

"There you go again. I started it. Remember? When I had nightmares about Ned killing us. I shouldn't have told you. We both thought we'd be killed. Now I think he's like the other people. He wouldn't think the worst. That's because we're so quiet!" She laughed and gave him a hug.

"Do you think he would?"

"Kill us?" She continued to laugh softly. "No. He'd just be mean. Loud mean, not hateful mean. He's like a box of wound-up springs. He might scare us. He wouldn't kill us."

"You sure?"

"If you're so scared, park the car further in the weeds," she laughed. "We'll get stuck and really be in trouble."

He hid his car behind a rotting shed. They faced a long edge of a field of corn. It was a hybrid variety and in late June was taller than they, much taller than knee high. Win had correctly forecast a breeze. Corn stalks moved in clusters as surfaces of the wind touched them.

Win led him into the field. They walked in tandem for a long distance into a world as dense as a jungle. If the rows hadn't been planted evenly, they would have soon been lost.

When they were clearly a good distance from civilization, Win ordered a halt.

"Are you sure this is OK?" Johnny asked.

"As much as I can know. I never see anybody here."

"What if we get caught?"

"Who's to catch us? The sheriff looking for Jesse James? If they see us, we can say we're out looking for rabbits."

"We don't have guns."

"They don't have guns in Africa when they look for animals."

"That's different."

"You're more of a kid than I thought." She touched a palm to his face. "I knew we should come here. I feel safe, don't you?"

"I'm not sure."

"Listen, then."

Standing quietly, they heard leaves move with patches of wind, here and there, in a circle around them. There were no other sounds.

Win began to break down stalks of corn, methodically, in a ritual. She bent them over as they came out of the ground and arranged the stalks and leaves like a mat. Johnny protested, telling her that she was guilty of vandalism. She paid no attention and continued breaking stalks until an area of ground the size of a small bedroom was covered with leaves.

"Now sit with me and listen to the wind again," she said.

Johnny sat next to her in a small depression between corn rows. The newly felled stalks smelled rich. Breaking the stalks had released the scent of milky sap.

"Do you know what I'm going to call this place?" she asked.

Johnny, more relaxed now, at peace in their hideaway, shook his head no.

"Taliesin," she said slowly. *"Tally-essen."*

"Is that a Welsh word?"

"It's a name. Know where I learned it?"

"I bet I know. From your dad."

"You're smart. Isn't it a nice name, Taliesin?" She said it twice over and he tried to say it but couldn't. "It means special place. That's what my dad said. 'Everyone has a Taliesin,' he said."

Win looked at him and smiled, so that he blushed. "I'll tell you a story and I'll tell it like my dad told me, except I can't remember the Welsh words he used. But I'll try to sound like him." She crossed her legs and put her head down, looking up at him in mock seriousness. " 'Everyone has a Taliesin. That's true, ye better believe it. You know how I learned about it? From the mines, for sure. From the bleedin' mines!' "

She laughed at herself. "Johnny, you remind me of my dad sometimes. You don't look like him, but you're the only person soft like him. You're the only other person I know would never hurt me." He opened his mouth but nothing came out. "The mines hurt him. Inside. People didn't know that about him. They thought he was a silly old man. But he wasn't. 'Aye, lass. To the frig with ye and fetch yer old man a bottle of that there medicine.' If he told me a long story, I'd have to go to the refrigerator two or three times. He never got drunk. 'Aye, love, it all began with a sparrow,' he said. 'You can learn a lot from a poor wee bird, ye know.' He was foreman of a crew at the time.

He told me he was the youngest foreman ever at that mine. It was his job to check all around before the crew left for the day. He had to look for equipment and count noses. One day all the men were waiting at the elevator shaft to go up. He heard a strange noise and told them to wait. He took a lantern and searched all around the area where they had been working. He heard the noise again." Her voice was so quiet Johnny looked about for an intruder. "He didn't see anything in the main tunnel, so he crawled into a narrow place. He said he was scared because it wasn't supported right and if it caved in he wouldn't have a chance. He was almost stuck when he heard the sound and saw what it was. A sparrow sat all alone. It was wet all around and the bird stood on a lump of coal. He reached for the bird and caught it without any trouble. Then he worked his way back to the main area and put the bird in his lunch basket. He kidded the men about it. Some of them didn't believe him and thought he took the bird down himself as a trick. When they got above ground, the late-afternoon whistle blew and scared the bird. It flapped its wings and went crazy in his basket. Lots of miners gathered around him. One of them was an old man, a singer. 'So ye found a bird there, did ye?' he said. 'And what might your plans for it be?' he asked. 'I'm going to set it free, of course,' Dad said. 'Don't be a fool, man, do the bird a favor and take it back down in the mine,' the old man said. The other men argued. 'There's no food or light down there,' one of them said. 'That's no place for a creature with wings,' another told him. The men got rough. One of them took Dad's lunch basket and opened it up, taking the bird and throwing it high in the air. For a moment the bird didn't open its wings, starting to fall. Then it flew away. The old man yelled at them. 'Fools. You men are fools. You did the bird a great harm,' he said. They laughed at him but he stared back. They became like little boys when they knew they did something bad. The old man's face was black with coal dust. He took a handkerchief and wiped his face. They were quiet and looked at the dark around his eyes.

" 'How many of ye have seen a feathered creature in a mine? How many?'

"No one answered.

" 'And do you think birds go around every day gettin' themselves five hundred feet below ground? They've got a union, too, you know. And how do you think that bird got there? 'Twas a thing of magic. Not an accident. Sure enough there were crumbs for it. It wasn't about to starve. Heaven knows it wouldn't go thirsty down there, that's the wettest mine north of Cardiff. It wasn't by accident. The bird had found its Taliesin.'

"Dad said no one had heard the word before.

" 'You see there's always been one damn fool or another holding his thumb over the people of Wales. And there's pitiable few of us that find our Taliesin. About as many as there are birds in that mine. A long time ago there were druids here, good magic people. Then the Romans came, then the Christians. Ever since the people of this country have been looking for a hiding place. Look at us! Which one of us wouldn't like to go off to a place where there was food and water and no one tellin' us to work every morning?' "

Win stood up. "See. This is our Taliesin."

"We can't ever come back, not after what you did to the corn."

"Johnny, Johnny. Relax. You're so fidgety. Can't you pretend? For now? It'll rain tomorrow and the leaves will get muddy and we wouldn't come back anyway."

"I'm afraid, Win. The more I think about what we're doing the more frightened I get."

"The preacher will help."

"Are you going to tell him everything?"

"I don't know everything."

"Think of Ned. We're both afraid of him. He has all the money. The people in town will side with him."

"When the time comes, we'll know what's right. That's not a worry in this place!"

"What are we going to do? You have nightmares. We can't make him go away."

"There was this book I read," Win said. "There was this beautiful princess from France. She was in love with a soldier. But her father made her marry this Russian prince. For money, you know. She went to Russia and the soldier came to America. Louisiana. Every day she hated it. So she thought up a plan with her maid. She pretended to get sick. Each day she got worse. The doctors couldn't help her. One day the maid told the prince the princess had died. They put the princess in a casket. At night, before the funeral, the maid let the princess out and filled the casket with baloney."

Johnny laughed.

"Maybe it was summer sausage. The princess hid out in the city. Then she left and came to America. She found the soldier in the woods. He still had her picture. Since he waited for her, they got married."

"You have such farfetched stories. Either your dad or the books. I like to hear you tell them."

"You look better, now, Johnny. Relaxed. Lying there like you owned the field, little shed and all. Who knows? Maybe the shed is Taliesin for some wee animals, the rabbits and creatures like that."

Johnny lay back with his hands beneath his head. Win coaxed him into removing his shoes. He protested, and when his right shoe was off his big toe stuck through a hole in his sock.

"Look at the poor thing," she said of the toe. "Caught in the open without a thing on." She sat next to him. He smelled cold cream on her hands. "But you don't need worry, Johnny, when we're here, no one cares if there's a hole in your sock. Certainly not I. My mother used to tell me that patches were like medals on a uniform. We never had any money. My dad and his stories made up for it. I'll probably spend the rest of my life telling you things he told me."

Win played with his face, teasing. Then she unbuttoned a lower button of his shirt and put her hand under his belt.

Johnny twisted away from her.

"Win. I worry about us. Doing things."

"Johnny. We've known each other for three years."

"But here?"

"You're touchy because we've never done anything in the light! We've been like frightened kids, afraid in the night."

"It still bothers me that you're married. We're Christians. Saved by the word of God. What does God think of us?"

"He loves gentle people. He can't look too harshly upon us. But Ned and I! There's no gentleness there. It's a sin not to be gentle."

"We're not man and wife."

"Johnny! Johnny! The day will come when we'll gird our loins and take spears in our hands and do what we must. Until then God understands."

"How can you say what God does?"

"The scripture says that there was the word and the word was God. Like Taliesin is a word. God is a word. Maybe that's all God is, Johnny. A word. Look at us! The sun is out, bright the way He intended it. The smells are good. There's a little shed back there, home for little things. You're lying there with your big toe stuck out like you were proud of it. You're afraid to have me touch you in the light! That pleases me. You know so little about women. You were thirty-five before you even touched anyone and that's because I forced my way on you."

Win reached around her waist and untied a cloth belt. Unsnapping a catch, she let her skirt drop to the ground. Again as quickly she slid off her underpants, which left her on her knees, naked from the waist down.

Johnny looked the other way, frightened.

Win reached her hand again through his shirt and rubbed the lower part of his stomach.

"Look at me in the light," she said softly.

Johnny slowly turned his head.

"Look at me."

Her skin was near porcelain in color; white with the slightest wash of gray beneath. She was thin, standing on her knees, her body slightly twisted to the right. Her left pelvic bone jutted out and created a small shadow, almost sadly, as if she were malnourished. Johnny's head and eyes lowered, looking at her as instructed. The very lowest part of her abdomen was smoother but had a slight bulge, from childbirth. Black hairs then burst outward in profusion like the hair over a dark terrier's eye. Johnny looked at folds of her body that began at her inner thigh and continued to her vaginal lips in some geometric order, as if the large folds and smaller wrinkles were fashioned like waves near a coral reef. He looked at her womanness, the anatomy she revealed so quickly. He looked at her in childlike ease, silently, for a long time. The hairs which protruded boldly at the top separated, yet remained intertwined. The wrinkles of her body met where the two bulges of her lips lay together, slightly to one side. He looked beneath her, where curving lines passed out of sight. Win continued her pose, her back arched and upright. She was like a perched hawk, watching every movement of his face.

"Johnny, my little boy, Johnny," she said. Her voice was tender, thick with the resonances of a tongue spoken in a country where miners with coal-dust faces emerge from darkness and gather in modest churches and schools to sing hymns and arias in anguished consort with their pagan forebears, who, they all know, wandered in mystic freedom through once-ripe valleys that have become tired villages and heaps of slag.

Johnny's hands were trembling. He couldn't speak.

She touched his groin. "That's the way you should be."

He blushed.

Win delicately pulled his shirt from his pants, unbuttoning all the lower buttons and laying the sides apart. His hand reached to stop hers as she undid his belt. She slapped it as she would a child reaching for a forbidden cookie. "Lay still." She opened his pants enough so that his penis was exposed, erect and lying upward toward his belly, its underside looking like a winter-killed dead fish. She stroked it with a single finger so softly that her touch could have been an extension of the breeze that guarded their privacy. Johnny's entire body shook in a fine tremor. She continued to stroke him and softly say his name as if it were a song. A drop of white appeared within the slit of his penis. It remained, caught in the sunlight like a clouded jewel. Win touched the drop and smeared it over the flared end. Two more drops appeared and she spread them about in a circle.

"This wetness, it's part of our softness," she said. With that she took his hand, folded all fingers but one into his palm. She took his remaining finger and put it at the lowest part of her vaginal opening. With a steady hand she brought his finger upward so that it separated her lips. She fixed his finger on a particular spot. "Now look, Johnny, and feel." She held his finger. He saw her stomach mucles contract. Then he felt a warm thin liquid come from her and wash across his finger to wet her lips and hair. "See how I get wet?" she said. His hand was bathed and she was wet throughout her groin and along her thighs.

"Feel me now."

He rubbed his hand until it was as wet as she.

Win reached to touch him again but she was an instant too late. What had begun with a drop shot from him in bursts, colorless clots catching in the hairs of his stomach before washing down his flank.

"Close your eyes, now, Johnny. Close your eyes and feel the sun on your face."

Sunday, July 4

Ned began his celebration of the nation's birthday sitting on his deck reading about asthma. He sat in his bathing suit with his feet propped against the railing, listening to a program of patriotic country music on station WHO. Willie Ralston was about to finger-pick the national anthem on the flat-top guitar. On the lawn below him the children were filling the plastic boat with water to make a swimming pool for two screaming neighbor kids.

Asthma, the article said, was an IgE medicated allergic phenomenon affecting the lungs.

"Dad," Ellie yelled up to him.

"Ya."

"The little kids are getting wild. Roger took off his clothes and tried to bite the canoe."

"If it will survive white water, it'll survive Roger."

"And he did worse things."

"He's too little to do anything that bad."

"Well, he's trying," Ellie said.

"Send him home," Ned yelled.

"I can't. His mother is paying me to watch him."

"Sounds like you got your money's worth."

"Dad! Will you yell at him?"

"Roger. Shape up," Ned yelled.

"Thanks," Ellie said.

Ned read about a new drug, cromolyn powder. He had used it, but, more importantly, he had bought a hundred shares of Syntex, the company that made it. He bought at 120. The stock immediately split and dropped to 45. Ned was waiting for the rest of the profession to learn about it. The drug's mode of action, the article said, was to degranulate the mast cells in the bronchioles. It apparently did that whether Syntex was at 120 or 45.

He carefully read the admonition: *Status asthmaticus is always an emergency and should always be treated as such.*

With that bit of knowledge safely locked in his head he raced downstairs, ran to the water-filled boat and jumped into it with a splash. He bit the hull, chased Roger, caught him, and threw the child in the air—twice for good measure.

The kids copied Ned's boat-jumping trick, taking turns jumping and splashing. Lizzy tried it knee first, slipped and dunked her head, getting water up her nose.

"Come on," Ned yelled. "Can't catch me."

He ran from them in crazy circles until he had a good angle on the boat, like an A2 Skyraider sighting in on the deck of an aircraft carrier. With the kids following behind, he took an olympic run and jumped feet first into the boat, creating a huge splash. The boat slid three feet on the grass.

Roger jumped on him, jamming a heel into Ned's groin.

"Roger!" he yelled before the pain doubled him up.

"I told you he isn't behaving," Ellie said.

Ned rolled out of the boat onto the luxurious warm grass and let his pain subside. After a deep breath he said, "Maybe we better take it easy around the boat. Somebody might get hurt."

"We were," Lizzy corrected. "You started the jumping."

They heard a horn honking. Ned assumed a pose of dignity in his swim trunks. A '59 Chevy pickup drove past his Mercedes onto his lawn. Darrold Toombs and son, Wilbur, got out and hurried toward Ned. Both wore patched overalls. The boy was Ellie's age. Darrold was narrow in the eyes and the child's face was vacuous, bleached out. They looked like characters from the movie *Deliverance*. The man carried a folded newspaper as if it were full of nitroglycerine.

"Mornin', Doctor Ned." Darrold opened the newspaper. "Look what Wilbur just passed."

An eight-inch roundworm was stretched between a K-Mart ad and Ann Landers' nose.

"That's good," Ned said. "He doesn't have it anymore."

The boy was shy and turned his head.

Lizzy crowded close to Wilbur. He wasn't dressed for the Fourth of July.

"Don't you think we ought to do something about this right quick?" Darrold said.

"You're right, Darrold. I'll call up the druggist and get him down to the store. You drive on down there and he'll have the medicine. I'll have to look in the book to figure out the dose, but it'll be ready when you get there."

"Thank you, Doc," Darrold said. "I was sure this was nothin' to fool around with."

He handed Ned the newspaper and hurried his son away.

The pickup almost hit Ned's Mercedes as they hurried away.

Ned walked disconsolately to an overflowing garbage can and dirtied his hand when he shoved the worm beneath a rotten grapefruit and coffee grounds, beyond the reach of Roger's curiosity.

Inside the house, Win sat by the air conditioner, cutting asparagus tips. "Are you going to the Jensons' today?" she asked Ned.

"It's the Fourth of July, isn't it?"

"They said we should dress up."

"Are you going?"

"It might be nice."

"I thought you didn't like parties."

"I wasn't brought up with bankers, you know."

"Neither was I, stupid. Are you going to dress up?"

"I have a nice dress."

"Good. I'm glad you're going. You can drive me home if I drink too much beer."

"That doesn't worry me."

"Why are you going? You told me you don't like talking to those women."

"The kids want to go. The pool, you know. I'll have a fine time."

"I'm going in my swimming suit. I don't have any checkered pants."

"You could go in your underwear, Ned Owen, and there wouldn't be an eyelash raised for a second."

She looked at him, from quarter profile, her lips precise, intent, a twist of the Celtic.

"Right now I'm going to the parade. You coming, Win?"

"I might sit here by the air conditioner. Like my uncle in the fruit cellar. I might do other things. You never know, Ned."

"What the hell, Win?" Ned ran upstairs, put on a shirt and sandals and a straw hat with a red band he bought in Missouri.

When he passed her on his way out, he said, "You haven't gone with me to a party in three years. Are you sure you're going?"

"I'll have my party, too."

He drove to the parade with Ellie, Lizzy and Roger. It was near a hundred degrees, a perfect Iowa Fourth of July. Spring Falls had a business district with two main streets which intersected three avenues named after tribes of the Plains Indians. The place hadn't seen a teepee or a wickiup since 1924, when a group of Mesquackies were run out of town for doing a ghost dance on the corner of Cherokee and Second.

A boy scout with white gloves manned a roadblock.

"What number is your unit?" he asked Ned.

"We're not a unit."

The boy pointed to the Mercedes.

"Just looking for a place to park."

They found a spot at the beginning of the parade route next to a popcorn machine.

"Just think," Ellie mused. "He thought we were in the parade."

"We can't be in the parade. We're not old enough," Lizzy said.

Roger spilled his popcorn.

The Spring Falls band led the way with a loud drum cadence. Ned caught the eye of Melissa Norris, who had been in his office for poison ivy in an embarrassing place. Melissa blushed as she looked past the polished bell of her trombone.

The mayor rode by with his family. Too shy for his own good. No roaring crowd for this Caesar.

The Seventh Avenue Baptist Church had six children pulling a toy wagon holding a papier-mâché firecracker. Two students carried the banner, EXPLODE FOR JESUS.

They were followed by a flat-bottom truck aflutter with banners and flags. It advertised the Woodburn Grade School Tiniklers of Greater Des Moines. Thirty kids were packed on the truck, some snapping Philippine dancing sticks together as the others danced between them holding beach balls, jumping ropes, hula-hooping, snake-dancing.

The next band was the most forlorn group of miscreants Ned had ever seen. The Saddest Band from the Smallest Town in Iowa.

The Shriners arrived: clowns, motor big-wheeled tricycles and the tipsy truck. Ellie grabbed Roger so he wouldn't get run over. Behind them was the Danver

County Democratic float, a John Deere tractor pulling a hayrack with the Central Committee and state representatives.

Jane Roberts, chairman, yelled, "Come on, ride with us."

Ned threw the kids aboard and climbed up himself, catching a splinter in his left elbow.

The girls began waving like beauty queens.

Roger threw straw.

Ned stood, waving his hat.

"What you runnin' for, Ned?" a voice yelled.

"Governor."

They passed the Astro Theater, which was playing *The Sting.* They saw Darrold Toombs leaving the drugstore, prescription in hand.

"We'll have to get you on the float more often," Jane said.

"It's good for my practice," he said. "A lot of Democrats in this town."

"I always thought your politics were pure."

"They were."

Ned worked his way to Lizzy and Ellie, waving his straw hat at the crowd.

"Happy Fourth of July," Lizzy yelled to the crowd.

"Dumb. You don't yell that," Ellie said.

Children clapped.

"It worked," said Lizzy.

"Happy Fourth of July," Ellie yelled, louder than her younger sister.

The parade ended in a pool of sweating bandsmen, exhausted Shriners and the unsinkable Tiniklers of Greater Des Moines.

Ned gave a war whoop as he dismounted.

The kids thanked him.

They walked nearly a mile in the heat back to the car. By the time he got home Ned felt as though he'd endured the first phase of a nuclear attack.

Win was on the phone.

The kids grabbed her, telling her about their adventure.

"Take Roger home before we're forced to explain to the county sheriff," she said sternly. "His mother came for him more than an hour ago."

"Let's go to the Jensons'," Ned yelled. "I need a beer!"

Ned snuck his 280 SL past an Eldorado at Two Golf View Park, home of Arlen Jenson, executive vice-president and son of the president of Midwest National Bank.

They walked around the house. Ned perked up when he heard a sound. There was a band on the patio, a Bluegrass band.

Arlen and Darlene Jenson greeted them.

"Good to see you, Doctor. I took your suggestion and hired this band."

They were playing a fiddle tune which sounded like "Gray Eagle" to Ned. A group of three children listened.

"They're good," Ned said.

Arlen put his arm on Ned's shoulder and turned him toward the lawn. "We have a tent for the A-rabs," he said, "and the kiddie pool is full of beer. I always wanted a swimming pool full of beer."

Ned looked at the people. No one would dare show up in anything less than their summery best.

Ned yelled, "Yahoo."

Arlen was impressed.

"Listen to that." Ned turned to the band. " 'Foggy Mountain Breakdown'!"

"I hope more people go up there and listen," the banker said.

Ned clapped when the song ended. The fiddler bent forward and waved his bow.

Ned was ushered toward the guests. He walked toward a huge blue-and-white striped tent. "For the A-rabs . . ." Nearby was a tall willow hiding several people. Arlen gave Ned a beer from the kiddie pool filled with blocks of ice and Schlitz. The real pool was hidden behind wire fence and ivy.

Ned was introduced to people he already knew.

They owned the Astro Theater, Vanderwaal's Department Store, the IH Implement Agency, Niebuhr Chevrolet–Cadillac, *The Danver County Inquirer*, Hoyt Insurance, Loess Realty, The Captain's Wheel Restaurant and the Midwest National Bank of Spring Falls.

Before he had time to react, his arm was being clutched by Ralph Loess, who, in the bright sun, looked like a ticket taker for a freak show.

"Doctor," he said with ingratiating vigor. "Congratulations!" He waited for Ned to respond.

Ned didn't.

"You really hit that hippie hard, huh?"

"You heard about that?"

"All over town. A college kid told me, then I heard it at Rotary. Did you really bust the guy's nose? He was a druggie, huh?"

Ned was pondering the legal possibilities when he saw something through an opened flap of the tent. He turned, rudely, from Ralph and looked.

It was a hot summer day and the prevailing wind was about six knots. Barely enough to lift the flap to the woman's thigh.

Ned blew at the flap in his mind's eye. Up. Up.

A hidden waft of warmed southern air picked up the edge of the tent gently and let it float back to its tether.

Ned saw the leg. A woman's leg with a dainty piece of gauze.

"Excuse me," Ned said to Ralph.

He strode across the summer green in his swimming suit, flapping shirt, sandals and Missouri straw hat.

"There's my doctor," Gail said to the couple with her.

"I see you can walk," Ned said, pointing to the bandage.

"It's doing very well." She pulled the tape and showed him the wound.

"Looks good. What are you doing here?"

"No storms today so I thought I'd come. The Meyers brought me. They found me stringing up a hangman's noose." She introduced Ned to the couple. "And what are you doing here?"

"Talking to people wearing silly clothes." He pointed to Ralph, who wore a blue coat, red pants and a luau shirt.

"I like your outfit much better."

"You look pretty good yourself, Professor."

"Aha! You've learned respect."

"You want to go and listen to the band with me?"

"Great."

"I'll get some beer." He left on the run.

About Gail were the quiet murmurings of the party; small clusters of sun-brave people conversing, a group sitting awkwardly beneath intimidating branches of a huge willow, the splash of children jumping into the swimming pool. Ned returned with beer.

"I love that tent." Gail excused herself and she and Ned wandered toward the band.

"A real country-and-western band. It's not the Boston Pops but it's nice."

"It's Bluegrass," he corrected.

"What's the difference?"

"Bluegrass is special. Not hokey. They don't use electric instruments. And they don't play stupid songs. Most of the tunes come from old folk songs."

"I didn't know that."

"Listen for a while. You'll hear."

They walked to the band and stood behind some children. The band played "Down Yonder." Children clapped. Ned gave a real hog call. Gail tapped a foot and moved her head from side to side.

"Play another fiddle tune," Ned yelled.

"We was gonna play 'Bonaparte's Retreat,'" the fiddler said in a shy voice. "Let Bob here pick a little on the banja. I get a lick o' fiddlin' near the end."

The guitar started with a fast chord sequence before the

dark-haired banjo player picked a melody with lots of runs and slurs.

Gail leaned against Ned, caught with the song. He leaned toward her.

The banjo stopped with a flourish, and the fiddler, now with audience, drew his bow to a slower beat, turning the song into a minor key with forced double stops.

She touched him when the tempo changed.

The banjo picker ended the song with a wild flourish.

"God damn, that's good," Ned yelled. Gail and the children clapped.

"Thank you," said the fiddler.

"Hot out today," the banjo player said.

"You guys get paid for this?" Ned asked.

"It's a gig. It's all right," the fiddler said.

"You get fifty bucks?" Ned asked.

"Thirty-five."

"Too damn hot for that kind of money," Ned said. He took out his billfold and gave them twenty.

"You like fiddle tunes?" the leader asked.

"That wasn't a bribe."

"We know. Just wondered if you ever heard of Curly Ray Cline."

"Sure."

"He's got a record with this tune. 'Kentucky Fox Race.' "

Gail looked curiously at the proceedings.

The fiddler struck a pose. Then, before playing, he relaxed his arms and said to his cohorts, "For twenty bucks a tune I'd damn near play anything!" He jumped into "Kentucky Fox Race." Ned began stomping his feet and did a quick pirouette, almost tripping.

Suddenly there was quiet, the song was over and Ned leaned on Gail, out of breath.

"Thank ya, folks. We're gonna take a little break now but we'll be back shortly," the fiddler said.

Ned expected to find everyone staring at him. Turning, he realized his *danse bucolique* hadn't raised an eyebrow.

"What a group!" Gail said excitedly.

Ned was about to reply in agreement when another voice, unseen, talked to him.

"Doctor Owen. You have a patient in the Emergency Room."

He pushed a button and stopped his page radio.

"I'm sorry, I have to go to the hospital," Ned said.

Gail looked at the crowd. "Mind if I go along?"

The only way he could extract his car from the parked cars was to turn sharply and drive across the banker's lawn.

"Nice car," Gail said.

"Ya," he replied.

"It's a Porsche, isn't it?"

Without his sunglasses, the streets of Spring Falls were as leeched as faded Ektachrome. Hot air rose from the asphalt and made the world seem brittle. A string of fire-crackers exploded serially in a back lawn, the explosions echoing from houses and the soft bark of oak trees, in-nocuous. The city was quiet from the holiday; he heard the distant whine of traffic on the Interstate. Ned looked at Gail. She held her head back, sniffing the summer air.

He stepped on the accelerator and made a teen-ager's entry into the Emergency lot.

"Here we are." Dust curled about them.

A nurse greeted him and paid no attention to Gail. "It's Mrs. Eilers. Mandy. Having a lot of pain. She's in the first cot in the trauma room."

Mandy Eilers was fifty-two years old and obese: five feet four and two hundred twelve pounds. She was Danver County's visiting nurse.

"Got you away from your kids, didn't I?" she said be-fore wincing.

She pointed to her right side, high up.

"Same place as always. It's those stones for sure."

Ned asked questions. What brought on the pain? Did

she vomit? Any blood? Any blood in the stool? Black-colored stool? Weight loss?

"No. It's my gallbladder. Had it X-rayed in Minneapolis ten years ago. They wouldn't operate because they said I was too fat. Gave me six months to lose a hundred pounds. I lost seven." She winked at him. "Some people are just destined to be fat."

He checked her blood pressure, then examined her chest and abdomen carefully, rolling folds of fat to find landmarks. He thought he felt a mass in the region of her gallbladder. After ten years she was likely to have a big, infected stone-filled bag.

Ned pulled her lower lid and looked at her eyes. No jaundice.

"First of all, I'll get you a shot." He asked the nurse for a hundred milligrams of Demerol.

"Mandy. There comes a time, fat or not, when that thing has to come out. Your weight will cause a little more problem for us, but you're going to keep on having the pain until that thing comes out. And the longer it's in, the more chances you can have of getting bad infections in the belly and other things that give us all ulcers."

Mandy asked the nurse to leave.

"I don't have cancer, do I?"

"No," Ned said.

"My mother had cancer of the liver and died right after the operation."

"You've got stones in your gallbladder. They could cause a lot of trouble if they stay there, but you don't have cancer." He was totally reassuring.

"Heck, then, an operation ain't nothin'. I would'a had that done a long time ago if they would'a done it."

"Well, we'll put you in the hospital and check your blood and recheck with X-rays. I'll talk to Dr. Markham tomorrow and we'll schedule you next week sometime. I want you here so we can give you medicine and make sure there's no infection before we operate."

She felt better. "Come here. Just one thing." She laughed with her fat eyes. "My daughter thinks you're cute."

Ned and Gail drove back through the outskirts of town.

"Where did you learn about Bluegrass?" she asked.

"From records. I like fiddle music best."

"Do you go to hear many groups?"

"I listen to records. My name got on a club list and I get two records every month."

"Do you like other music?" she asked.

"Bach."

She named other composers. Did he like them?

He said no.

"Just Bach."

"And Bluegrass."

He stopped the car on a small rise that looked out upon a long valley.

"That's the French River. If you look carefully, slightly to your right, you'll see some hills. Covered with trees. That's where my pond is."

Gail saw them.

"Are you married?" he asked.

"I got my degree and my divorce the same day."

"I am."

"I know that," Gail said.

"I'd like to show you my pond. There's a little beach, then it's all surrounded by green. Bushes on two sides and a tall row of trees on the other. By late summer the water's so warm and full of moss it's like taking a bath in Aveeno."

"What's that?"

"A special oatmeal, for bad skin."

"You should call it Oatmeal Pond."

"Don't knock it. I might bottle the water and sell it as patent medicine."

"Or turtle soup."

They looked at each other. Ned put his fingers to his hairline.

They returned to the party. It had an odd resemblance

to a chess board; the tent and tree standing as royal
figures and the guests and children poised like pawns and
rooks and bishops. The band had packed up and gone.

"I'd like to meet your wife," Gail said.

"She's swimming with the kids," he said.

"Ned. Ned!"

A man ran toward him from the swimming pool. He was
tall and blond, running with a slight waddle in his hips.
He wouldn't have appeared so awkward except for the fact
that he was the only person dressed plainly. He wore long
gray pants and a dull blue shirt, appropriate for picking
leaves in the fall.

Ned laughed at him.

"Ned, I've got to talk to you." His voice was begging.
"You've missed twice now."

"For Christ's sake, Johnny, what do you think I do for
a living? If I had your job, I'd play tennis all day long.
I can't say to my help, 'Watch the store, I'm going out for
two hours.' "

"You could call me. Twice I waited over half an hour."

Ned introduced Gail to Johnny Ingelbretson. He owned
the Gambles store and played tennis.

Johnny was upset and nervous. He was balding pre-
maturely and combed long strands of thin blond hair the
breadth of his skull. His chin was recessed and malformed,
knoblike; it was thickly creased with a fissure which ran
at an angle, as though his chin were an accessory,
screwed on improperly.

"For five dollars I'll play you right here." Ned pointed
at the lawn.

Johnny snickered.

"Five bucks," Ned demanded.

"Be serious, Ned," Johnny said.

"You want to play, here we are."

"We need a court."

"Gail can be the net. She can get on her knees and hold
out her arms. The first person to hit her on the head loses
the five bucks."

"Do you want to play tonight?" Johnny asked. "I can get a court for eight."

"Sunday. At eleven."

"I have church."

"You want me to give up medicine to play but you can't give up church." Ned turned to Gail. "Johnny and Win are Baptists."

"Sunday at seven," Johnny said. "It won't be hot then."

"OK," Ned said. "But for five bucks."

"You know I don't gamble."

"You bring the balls, then. And bring good ones, not the kind you sell in your store. Bring Wilsons."

"All right." Johnny agreed and left.

They watched him return to the pool.

"That was an interesting exchange," Gail said.

"Ah, no, that's just Johnny. Damn Baptist like my wife. He played on the tennis team for some Baptist junior college in Missouri. He's made it his life's goal to beat me."

"You always win?"

"If I want to," Ned laughed. "He's such a setup. I usually have fun with him. One time I soaked a tennis ball in water overnight. I kept it in a can until after we'd warmed up. Then I got out the wet ball and served it to him. It hit the court and stopped. I told him I had a new top-spin serve."

"He can't be that gullible."

"One day I told him he was foot faulting. That's when your foot goes over the base line when you serve. Every time he served I yelled, 'Foot fault.' By the end of the game he was serving from two feet behind the line."

"Why doesn't he beat you?"

"He has no timing."

"Would you like to get together with me?" Gail asked. "I'm not that good at tennis but maybe we could eat at my place or something."

"Can professors cook?"

"I can try like hell."

"Good."

"I'll call you tomorrow. OK?" Gail leaned over his shoulder and kissed him on the cheek. She touched him, slightly, with her wet tongue.

"Call me at nine-thirty. Tell Ann you're calling long distance and she'll get me to the phone right away."

"Perfect."

Thursday, July 8

Ned drove past Denby Manor, squealing his tires as he sped down the narrow road to the Raffensberger house. He stopped, slammed the door and rang her bell twice.

"You're an hour late," Gail said.

"Then I'm early."

"Come in and tell your story to my pot roast."

"One of your students is to blame. She took a hundred aspirin. She couldn't take the pressure from your class."

"Not one of my students!"

"She was scared to death of the big test."

"I don't give tests."

She led him through the living room, where her earthly possessions were spread out with the best instincts of a practiced itinerant. They walked past her 6 x 10 Sarouk rug, princely red with poppies of black and navy and delicate angled tendrils. Upon it was a white leather beanbag chair, her portable Zenith record player, thirty albums and her books dealing with the depression.

"It sounds like she took a lot."

"A hundred aspirin will cure any headache."

"Was it a suicide attempt?"

"She tried something. She succeeded in messing up the Emergency Room. Bad."

"Why did she do it?"

"American Civilization got to her."

"I could have saved her," Gail said.

"I did."

"It sounds like you helped her mess up the Emergency Room. Did you pump her stomach?"

"No. I gave her ipecac—makes her vomit. Three basins full."

"That should whet your appetite. We are having pot roast. My dad is a gourmet cook, he writes articles for magazines. I don't share his enthusiasm but I know three or four things—pot roast basted with butter and beer. Are you hungry?"

"Starved."

"After watching someone vomit three basins full?"

"She's sitting up, crying, happy. No problem."

"She's happy?"

"Laughing."

"Why?"

"She understands life, now."

"I'd take a hundred aspirin for that knowledge." Gail struggled with a wine cork. "Back to the original question. What drove her to it?"

"Roger Dietrich. He's a foreman at the furniture plant. She was in love with him, but he didn't get a divorce like he said and she found herself without Roger."

"My course wouldn't have helped her. We don't discuss love affairs. Unless they involve presidents—like Roosevelt and Lucy."

"Who?"

"FDR had a lifelong affair with a woman named Lucy Rutherfurd. It was terrible when he died, he was critically ill and they rushed her away from him so Eleanor wouldn't find out. Lucy heard the news of his death over the radio."

"Did she take aspirin?"

"She was too tough. A good woman."

"How did he die?"

"He had high blood pressure. His ankles were swollen a lot. He had a lot of chest pain a month or two before he died. I think a stroke got him."

"That's too bad," Ned pondered. "Today there's medicine to handle high blood pressure. They didn't have it then. He probably would have lived a lot longer."

"I never thought of that. If Roosevelt had lived, he wouldn't have let the French have Vietnam. Truman didn't know this and let the French have their way. What do you give for high blood pressure?"

"Diuril, reserpine, Aldomet, Guanethidine, Apresoline."

"Roosevelt would have lived longer with those drugs?"

"Probably."

"Damn."

"You're right," Ned said. "Ho Chi Minh asked for independence in nineteen forty-six. He went to Paris and they refused him. They answered him by shelling Haiphong. So he told the French he and his men would be like a tiger in the jungle, jump on the back of the elephant from trails, over and over, until the elephant bled to death."

"You know a lot about some of our history."

"I read a lot about Vietnam when I came back. I was an army surgeon there. I came home, grew my hair long, marched with the kids. Spring Falls hippie doctor! T. B. Travis, one of our doctors, still hates me. He thinks I'm a Communist."

"You had peace marches in this town?"

"Good ones. I gave speeches."

"Wasn't it odd—your being a doctor and all?"

"Best advertisement I could get."

"That's what kept my marriage together—peace rallies. Willy P-3 and I were good together marching. After that, we had nothing to talk about."

They ate her pot roast and potatoes as the oak trees outside joined the darkness. It would be dark when they finished; the summer grass would deepen in color until light was gone and the sound of insects filled the void.

Gail apologized for not having brandy—her father's recipe didn't call for beer at all. He asked for more.

They sat at either end of a long table. Between them were two candles and the bottle of wine.

"I'd love to hear one of your antiwar speeches."

"I told people it wasn't the Democrats who started wars, it was schoolteachers."

"You did not."

"I can't remember what I said. I remember arguing with the preacher at Win's church. He's really dumb. He didn't like the war but worried a lot about the red menace. I told him it wasn't nice to kill people. He said something about original sin. I almost gave him the finger. I told him syphilis was like original sin. But it went away with a shot of penicillin. 'Peace is like penicillin,' I told him. He got mad and said I was mocking the Bible. I let him know if he ever needed a shot I was available."

"Peace is like penicillin! Christ, what a metaphor."

"I never used it in a speech."

"Too bad."

"Why did you get a divorce?"

"Simple. Willy P-3, William Peter the third, smoked a pipe and thought I was part of the furniture. Next to his African fertility statue I was his favorite thing. He really got off on that statue."

"Do you still hate Iowa?"

"If I could get some material on Senator Brookhart, it might be tolerable. His library and writings seem to have been lost by his family. Brookhart was a Republican populist who gave big business hell in the Senate hearings after the depression. One of those—I'm lifting a William Carlos Williams phrase out of context—purest products of American soil. A real son of a bitch. Good, like your Senator Harold Hughes."

"Hughes is Welsh, like me. But the preachers got him."

"He was neat. I heard that when he was governor, he was pulling for money for the university and said, 'You can't buy half a Beethoven string quartet.' That's class."

"Don't worry about class," he said. "You want to see something special? Now?"

"Sure."

"Do you have some beer and a blanket?"

"Where are we going?"

"You've already seen it from a distance."

"Oatmeal Pond!"

Before he could answer, his pager went off. Ned pushed the reset button and went to the phone. The conversation was brief.

"What was that?"

"The hospital. Two-West wants a laxative order."

Candles were extending the light of a passing sun. For a moment they didn't talk. They heard the sound of summer night things. Ned scratched his chin unconsciously. They looked at each other with wine-tempered curiosity.

"Wouldn't it be nice," she pondered, "if that fiddle player and the banjo player were outside the window serenading. It would be so natural for this house, this summer."

Ned stared out the window at the darkened grass.

"What would they play, Ned?"

"There's a tune called 'Soldier's Joy.' It's a square dance tune, a reel."

"We could close our eyes and imagine dancers on the lawn."

"Let's go to the pond."

"Do you have a telephone out there?" she asked.

"At the pond?"

"In case that thing goes off?"

"Screw this thing," he said. "Do you have a portable radio?"

The purr of his Mercedes echoed from curbs and shuttered houses as he drove out of town. A reticulum of coral and thin clouds remained over the sunset. The moon was rising, nearing its final quarter.

"I see what you were talking about," she yelled over the wind rush. "This is extraordinarily nice."

He drove past farm fields, then turned onto a road which followed the French River. After a while he turned and crossed an old plank bridge that went *thump thump thump* as he crossed. They were isolated with frogs and crickets and other beeping things.

"Are we safe out here?" she asked.

"I hope so."

After the bridge they came to a small building. He pointed and said there were horses in it. Without warning, he turned into a thicket of dense bushes.

"Duck."

Leaves and branches scraped the car. Looking up, she saw a blur of greenery obscuring the moon's light.

Then it was quiet.

They were driving on a pasture, creeping over small branches and lumps of earth. It was clear and almost bright enough to see the green of the meadow. Ned stopped the car.

Behind them were the bushes and the river. Ahead were simple hills—small, covered with an occasional stunted tree.

"It's beautiful," she said.

Gail put a hand on his shoulder and turned toward him. He hesitated for a moment, then turned to her and kissed her, putting his left hand on her breast for only a moment.

"Let's go." He took her arm.

They walked the length of the meadow without speaking. He helped her over an old fence and they moved up a hill.

"It's not scary at all," Gail said.

She didn't know where they were going. Up the first hill, down a small draw, moving to their left and to the summit of another hill.

A reflection caught her eye. Gail walked until she saw it completely. The pond lay in front of a row of trees. It was almost square except for a portion which extended to the right; smaller than a football field. From her vantage it looked like an amphitheater. He led her through a swath of thick grass and they arrived at a beach covered with sand.

It was a place unto itself. They looked in silence.

The trees behind were a wall of negative light. Thick and undergrown with stubble, they were visible against the skyline as parapets of a cathedral, isolated and protecting.

The water was dark with almost invisible ripples. It looked thicker than ordinary water, but not like oil or an unpleasant fluid. The smells of moist plants and the waterlilies added with the color to create an illusion of something organic and inviting, a new medium of nature. Odd and unpredictable surfaces of the pond caught the moonlight.

"Look!" Gail said. "Around the pond. Right above the waterline." Millions of weakly glowing lights outlined the edges.

"It's a kind of algae that glows in the dark."

"This is spectacular."

"Spread the blanket and we'll have a beer."

Ned tuned the radio to WHO: "Country Music, USA." He left her for a moment and put the radio up on the hill.

"It's your Walden. It must be good for you, Ned. It's a nice balance in your life."

"It's wilder than Walden."

"You like things a bit wilder, don't you?"

"I wasn't aware of it."

"Medicine subdues you. What would you be like if you weren't a doctor?"

"I'd probably be in jail."

"I'm serious."

"When I was a kid I saw things different. I thought

people were stupid. I knew I was smarter than most people; other kids couldn't do their schoolwork as quickly. I was always in trouble for doing stupid things. I'd drive my car crazy so other kids could see. One winter night I drove across lawns, making big circles and leaving tire marks in impossible places. When I was a sophomore in high school, I walked by the principal's office—I ducked down and knocked as hard as I could on his door. He came running out; I went running down the stairs and ran into my classroom. He stormed in and yelled, 'If I ever catch you doing that again, I'll throw you down the stairs and stomp on you.' Scared the hell out of me. I settled down in college. I went on a football scholarship but didn't play. Too small for the Big Ten. But I liked college."

Spread above them was the summer sky. Up on the hill Mother Maybelle Carter sang, "Will the Circle Be Unbroken?" He opened more beer, dropping the opener rings into the paper sack. Gail asked him if he had many girlfriends in college.

"Makes me mad, now that I think of it," he said.

"Why?"

He gulped his beer. "I was stupid. I lived in a medical fraternity and most of the guys dated undergraduate sorority girls. They were good looking but they were dumb. So I acted like a dummy. I never bothered to go out and find girls on my own. Besides, medical school is sort of like prison. You don't have the time. Once I had a date with the head of a sorority. She was nice looking and she was really smart. I think about her now and then. We had a good time, but I never called her up again because she was taller than I was. Christ, I was stupid."

Gail began to say something, then hesitated. She took the index finger of her right hand and rubbed it all around his nose, up and down across the bridge, on the sides. Very softly.

"You want to swim?" he asked.

"Is it cold?"

"It's good."

He stood and pulled her up. They undressed close to each other. When they were naked, Ned bent forward and lay his cheek to her breast for a second, an oddly formal gesture. Then he ran to the pond and dove, swimming wildly. Soon he was halfway across and invisible. He yelled for her to come.

She stepped to the water's edge primly, her body faintly lit by the moon. "It's warm and the bottom is squishy," she yelled. "Hey! I can yell as loud as I want and nobody but you can hear me."

Gail swam on her back to Ned.

"This is luxurious. I've never swum in anything like it."

Ned didn't answer.

"Is it deep?"

"Forty feet."

"Jesus."

"And it's full of barracuda." He reached down and touched her bottom.

Before she could respond, he brought his hands to her sides and slowly slid them to her breasts, smoothly, his hands lubricated by the warm, silty water, moving upward, wavelike, over each rib and then forward so that his palms felt the sides of her nipples. He moved his hands as if he was molding newly made clay.

Gail reached deep into the water, way down, between his legs until her hand was filled with him. She kneaded him firmly, her hand moving rhythmically with her breathing.

They arched their backs to stay afloat. He put his hands on her buttocks and drew her to him. She spread her legs and tried to put him inside her, but she couldn't.

"Let's go ashore," she said.

They swam side by side, touching frequently, breathing loudly. About them was a warm and private world of water with algae and croaking frogs and the sounds of their bodies moving in the water. Waves traveled to the far shore and were returned to them as the faintest of echoes.

They reached the blanket and stood, rubbing each other like gluttons, kissing, pushing their thighs and hips, biting ears.

"Let's slow down just a bit," she said. "At the rate I'm going it'll be over in a minute." She kneeled to the blanket and threw the clothes aside. His radio hung from his belt.

"What if this thing goes off, Ned?" She handed it to him. "I don't know."

Gail leaned her face against the calf of his leg, rubbing his thigh with both hands.

"Look at this!" Ned laughed.

The naked athlete and former quarterback took the radio in hand and leaned back, away from the pond. He threw the thing with all his strength into the air. It followed a high trajectory and hit the water in the middle of the pond.

All was quiet.

They were alone, the water stilled.

"Let's do it now," Gail said.

He moved slowly into her.

"Do it easy and as long as you can," she said. "Let's move like the water in the pond."

He did as she said. They moved slowly with each other, lifting and heaving as he would move all the way out, holding the position until they were in jeopardy, then pushing inward as far as he could, forcing her pelvis into the sand with a rocking motion.

Gail pulled her legs way back.

She felt him move more quickly, pushing deep, out of control.

"Come, please. I'll come, too," she yelled, then pulled violently on his back to keep him in her, to make him go deeper so she could push down on him.

She offered her last utterance of lovemaking and they lay together without moving, drained and unable to speak.

The next thing either of them heard was Roy Acuff

singing, "When whiskey and blood run together, did you hear anybody pray?" The radio sang to the night, as unheeded as a TV set after all the stations have signed off.

Ned sat up and opened another beer. She asked for one.

"If you deliver babies like you make love, you're perfect."

"I don't deliver babies anymore. Too busy for it."

"It's just as well. Your radio is at the bottom of a deep, deep pond."

"That's spooky, the way you say it."

"How much did it cost?"

"Three–four hundred dollars. That's OK. Hell, I make a hundred and twenty-five thousand a year."

"I'm glad I found that out after we made love."

"Why's that?"

"I've been used to poor graduate students." She leaned over and kissed the middle of his back. "Money makes it better. You were wonderful." She took a sip of beer. "Most first times are awkward. We were like old pros."

"We probably are," Ned said.

"We are," she whispered.

He reached for her. "Let's spend the night. Swim and make love. Drink beer and swim. Make love. And swim." He talked to the sky above.

When he awoke, the sun was almost risen. His watch said six-eighteen. His head was near her chest, one of her legs lay over him. He moved and she woke.

"We fell asleep," he said.

"Uh-huh."

The radio was giving morning news.

He lay his head on her belly. It growled.

"It's morning," she drawled.

They dressed slowly, fumbling for buttons and zippers, their feet sticky with sand. He reached for his page radio, instinctively, to check its tone control, then laughed at himself.

They made their way to the car. At the top of the first

hill, she looked back. The pond was smaller. The algae around it weren't lit.

She grabbed his arm and they moved like tired revelers through the meadow.

She thanked him for the night, then looked glumly ahead.

He drove into town, past a ramshackle tavern, skirting the business district, driving slowly; tired.

When they stopped at her house, Gail said, "I wish you could come in and sleep with me some more."

Ned drove home listening to rock-and-roll on KIOA. The town was waking. Workers headed for the day shift at the factory; he passed a milk truck. Scorching weather was predicted between songs. Ned turned down the radio and heard the quiet pneumatic noise of his tires against the streets. No one would be up at his house. A doctor's family, late sleepers. He drove into his driveway wishing he had the morning to while away.

He walked to the front door trying to remember his day's schedule, hoping he could sleep another forty-five minutes.

"Ned."

Win stood inside the doorway, behind a screen.

"We tried to get you. We paged you."

"I lost my—"

Her voice had lost its musical cadence. She spoke slowly. "I've talked to that girl four times tonight."

"What girl? What's going on? Is there an emergency?"

"The girl who took the aspirins. She wanted to talk to you."

"Didn't you tell her to call later?"

"She wanted to thank you."

"God damn it, Win. It's too late for this."

"Why didn't you answer your radio?"

He looked at his watch, then at the image behind the screen. "You know that wasn't important. Why did you wait up for me to tell me that?"

"I didn't wait up for you. I just answered your phone all night." She turned into the dark and the cool of the air-conditioned house.

Friday, July 9

Gail was put on hold. She held the phone for fifteen minutes.

"Hello, Professor."

"Hello, Doctor," she said. "You sound awfully alert. Did you take some speed?"

"I'm used to it."

"Don't tell me I'm one in a series. Hey, thanks. It was special."

Ned agreed.

"Did you get in trouble? I worried all morning about you. Was your wife upset? I would hate to hurt her."

"She was sleeping."

"I'm free for lunch. Would you like to come over?"

"You going to make it worth my while?"

"Did Napoleon Bonaparte ride a horse? I may go to the trouble of making you a cold beef sandwich. I'm still twitching from last night."

"It was too good," Ned said.

"What do you mean?"

"I never had such a good night."

"That's bad?"

"It makes me nervous."

"Ned. It's only a summer. I leave the tenth of August. I don't take aspirin when it's over. We can have it for a while if you want. I want it. Besides, what am I going to do all summer if I can't research the life of Wildman Brookhart?"

"I'll be over at twelve-thirty. If I'm lucky. I'd better get going. I have ten patients left."

"How many do you see in a day?"

"Sixty or more."

"How long does it take you?"

"Ten hours."

"How often do you stay over at the pond?"

"Once."

"We'll improve on that. See you when you get here." Sheryl led Ned to the microscope. "There we are. Trickies!" It was a slide with vaginal secretions from a female patient. Pale round objects with miniature tails wriggled madly under the microscope. *Trichomonas vaginalis*: little things that made women itch terribly. They caused a minor excitement of the office.

"She's really got 'em," Sheryl said.

"Makes me itch to look at them," he replied.

Ned returned to a man who was waiting nervously.

He was a Romanian professor visiting the college. He had a terrible sore on his hand. "Please. I worry about VD more than anything. It is a neurosis with me. Do I have it?"

"No," Ned said. "It's the bite of the Recluse Spider. Maybe you got it in that old hotel you told me about. I'll give you special penicillin for it. If you should have VD, the penicillin will take care of that, too."

"You please me greatly," the man said.

"You can tell your women friends you were bit by a vampire."

The Romanian became animated. "Dracula wasn't a

vampire, he was Vlad Tepes, the mad impaler. He impaled the Turks and the Turks impaled the Romanians. That was a long time ago. Now we worry about VD."

"In a socialist country?"

"Why not in a socialist country?"

After Ned and Gail had eaten a roast beef sandwich, they made love. Afterward, Ned lay back in a drowse. Gail asked him a question when his eyes were half closed.

"Is Des Moines as terrible as I think it is?"

"Worse."

"I have to go there to fight a computer. I'm dreading it."

"I'll drive you there in the Mercedes."

"Would you?"

"Sure. It's only thirty minutes, if I don't get picked up."

"Great. In return, I'll tell you about Brookhart's battle with rich industrialists."

Ned was yawning, fighting his tiredness from the night before. "Give me two days' notice. We can go some noon. I should be back by three or so."

"Are there other places we can visit?"

"In the spring we could have gone to the Tulip Festival in Pella. There's a threshers' festival at Mount Pleasant this fall."

"How about a Holiday Inn somewhere?"

"I know the best thing." Ned was awake, sitting. "We'll take off and head south with the top down, towards Missouri. If we have time, we'll cut over towards Shenandoah. It's nice there. We'll drive through those little towns that haven't changed much. No tourists. We'll drive around like we own the place. Do you have a touring hat?"

"I have an old hat with a wide brim."

"We'll drive up and down the hills and wave at the people. They make good hamburgers down there. The small-town bars are good, they haven't changed in fifty years. They smell like beer and sweat. We can say we're from NBC, studying small-town bars."

Ned crawled out of bed, looking for his clothes. She threw him his shirt. He was dressed after pulling on his boots. Gail walked him to his car, where they continued talking, leaning in the sun against a fender.

"Will it be hard for you to get away?"

"No."

"Please be honest with me, Ned. You won't get in trouble with your wife, will you?"

"Hell, no."

"Do you get away often?"

"Not much. She doesn't like to go places much."

"Is there a reason?"

"She's easygoing. A little lazy. She's happy where she is."

"This town is pretty conservative. What if people found out we went somewhere together?"

"They won't. Wouldn't matter anyway."

Gail stepped away from him, looking him up and down. He was slightly taller than she, his hair lighter. There was an ease in his manner; she studied his face. She concentrated on his upper lip, soft, almost pudgy; it was the first part of his face to signal emotion; puckish.

"That brings up something else, Ned. Are you known for this—going out with other women?"

"I wish I was."

"That means you don't misbehave? That's a dumb word."

"I work."

"You don't have a reputation? I only ask so I know what to expect this summer."

"You're the teacher from out East. Divorced. You're the one who probably has experiences."

"That's your view."

"I don't mess around. Not because I don't want to—I just haven't."

"I'm the only one?"

"Yes."

"My God. You're a virgin. Once removed, of course."

Wednesday, July 14

Johnny parked a block and a half away from the church, far away from a single street light.

"Why don't you park by the church?" Win asked.

"Someone might see us."

"Maybe you're right."

He stopped the motor and turned off the car lights.

"Should we do it?" she asked.

"It's your idea."

"I'm scared."

"Of the preacher?"

"What if he gets upset? Maybe we are wrongful."

"Then he can tell us."

"Let's sit for a minute," she said.

A car drove by. Win turned her face from the lights. "I know this is the right thing to do, but I don't want to. But we have to." She huddled tightly about his arm.

"Come on. He's waiting." Johnny opened the door, but she didn't let go of his arm. "Come on," he said. She followed him through his door.

Tom Waylen met them at the side door of the Baptist church. The door was only used in funerals, when it opened onto the rear of a hearse.

"Thought that was you," the preacher said.

They ducked inside and he closed the door.

"Rosalie is typing in the office, so we have to sit out here." The preacher led them to a side pew and they sat beneath a paper print of three women at Christ's tomb. The picture, framed without glass, revealed a crown of thorns, a centurion's spear and vases of anointing oil.

"Are you comfortable talking here?" he asked.

"This is all right," Johnny said.

The church was simple: no formal altarpiece; only another paper reproduction, this of Christ ascending to heaven. Bright green indoor-outdoor carpeting had recently been installed throughout.

"Your eyes tell of a heavy burden," the preacher said.

"I have to talk to you. Johnny is along because I asked him."

"I understand," the preacher said. He wore a striped sport shirt with a narrow tie decorated with a hand-stitched cross.

Win began to cry, lightly and without tears. She held her face in her hands.

"We've talked before of your sorrow," the preacher said. "We can talk again with the communion of Christian love."

"That's what I told her," Johnny said. "No reason we should be afraid of talking to you."

The preacher adjusted his tie and smiled, then grabbed her hands and lay them deep in her lap, holding them.

"I have a suggestion. Let us pray, here in the Lord's house. Let us ask God to move our tongues so that we may talk and with His love find the peace of Jesus Christ." He put a hand on the shoulder of each of them. They bowed their heads contritely as he raised his head and voice to beseech God.

"Dear Heavenly Father, Creator of All People, look down upon these Children of yours who come to this Holy Temple with pain and suffering. Deliver unto us the Love of Jesus and the Power of the Holy Spirit so that we might do Thy Work in accordance with Thy Teachings and Thy Way. Touch us with Divine Wisdom in this hour of need so that with Thy Holy Guidance we might understand the Mysteries of Eternal Love. I ask You to remember the good works of these two Christians who have made your house their house, in word and deed. Look back upon the prayers they have said to You, both in Fellowship of this congregation and in the privacy of their Hearts. Remember also, Dear Jesus, that Johnny here has devoted hours of personal labor in the repairs of this Temple and that Bronwyn has freely given her money to help buy our new carpeting. Blessed are they among Thy Children. They have confessed their sins and have taken up the Cross of Jesus Christ, Born Again into Thy Bosom and destined for Eternal Bliss. Hear our prayer and Asking. May these two walk steadfast the difficult road to Salvation. In Jesus' name, Amen."

"Thank you," Johnny said.

Win stopped crying.

"Well, what is it?" Tom Waylen asked.

"It's Ned," Win said.

"His swearing?"

"More than that."

"He struck you?"

"No."

"We've talked before of your fear of him. What has he done?"

Win was silent for a long time. Her eyes followed the green carpet around the pews.

"What does God say about divorce?" she asked.

The preacher pursed the muscles of his mouth. He looked at Win, then Johnny, then again at Win.

"Does he want a divorce?"

"I do," Win said.

"Tell me more."

"It bothers me to live with him anymore."

"Is there a reason?"

"Everything. He takes the name of the Lord in vain. He's always working, never at home. He's not a good father. He doesn't tell them stories or spend time with them. He didn't come home till sunup the other morning."

"He never would come to church, would he?" the preacher asked.

"He swears at the church," Win replied.

"I didn't know he was a heathen," the preacher said.

"He doesn't believe in God," Win said with certainty.

"An atheist?"

"Darn near," Johnny said.

"You have a problem, child," the preacher said. "Tell me what you want."

Win stood and paced a distance, her steps quiet on the carpeting. She walked back to them, standing behind Johnny, putting her hands on his shoulders. When she spoke, her voice was steady and confident. "I want a divorce. Then I want to be friends with Johnny. I trust him."

"Do you have plans of marriage?"

"Maybe."

"Have you followed God's ordinances?"

"Yes," she said directly to his face. Johnny looked downward.

"When you first came, I prayed to God Almighty for divine wisdom. We must now ask God again for that wisdom. Your burden is terrible, woman. Answers aren't easy."

"People are getting divorces. God must not condemn them," she said.

"The Scripture says of marriage, 'Let not man put asunder what God hath joined.'"

Johnny's eyes were clear blue, always sympathetic. He

looked in disbelief at the preacher; sadly. "How can people get a divorce, then?" Johnny asked.

The preacher began to speak, then lost his voice. He swallowed twice and looked at his hands. "Let me ask you about yourself and Ned," the preacher said. "How long have you been married?"

"Almost twelve years."

"Where were you married?"

"My hometown."

The air in the old building was humid and static. Johnny's fingers were sticky and he rubbed them as he listened to the interrogation. The preacher hesitated often, midway through his questions, as though afraid to continue.

"How old were you?"

"Twenty-one."

"Old enough to know better." He laughed.

"Not old enough," Johnny said.

His voice uncertain, the preacher nonetheless persisted. "Did you love him?"

She waited a long while before answering. "No," she said coldly.

"You didn't love him?" The preacher sat up in surprise. "Why did you marry?"

"He pestered me ever since I was in high school. He was older than me. Ever since I was a freshman he was after me. He never stopped chasing me. He came back on weekends from college."

"Didn't you try to get away from him?"

"I moved to Des Moines and got a job at Smulekoff's furniture store. But he bothered me there."

"Why didn't you tell him to leave you alone?"

"I told him so many times I thought I was a broken record. I told him I didn't love him. I was afraid of him. I guess I figured if I didn't marry him he'd do something to me."

"Poor child," the preacher shouted.

A tear came to Johnny's eye.

"I couldn't get away from him. He told me I was the prettiest girl he knew. He liked the way I talked. The Welsh. His family were all born here and didn't sound like that. He told me he never wanted anyone else."

"He wouldn't take no for an answer?"

"You know Ned. He says he's from poor people, too, but he's been spoiled all his life. His ma babied him, even when he was so wild. He'd get in trouble and she'd always side with him. His dad never spoke back to him. He was plain spoiled. Like the car he drives! He went looking for a car. When he saw it, he said he wanted it. I told him it wasn't any good because it wasn't a family car. You can't get the kids in the thing. He went and bought it against my ideas. He always gets his way."

"You didn't have to marry him."

"He wore me down. I finally said yes. He told me I could have everything. Nice things. I figured if he wouldn't bother me too much life wouldn't be much different."

"So you didn't carry love into the marriage?"

"I thought if I married him he'd stop bothering me."

"Did you try to love him?"

Without looking at Johnny, she said, "I prayed and prayed after the kids were born. I asked Jesus for love. But my prayers went unanswered. A few years ago I told him we should go on a trip. I thought that would help. We were going to go to Hawaii, but we ended up going to the Black Hills. It was OK, but it didn't help."

"What do you want from marriage?"

"Someone to be nice to me."

"Is Johnny nice to you?"

"He is gentle."

"Have you thought about just being friends? Johnny could help you in your marriage. Maybe he can be a tool of the Lord."

"I can't sleep the night through with Ned anymore. I

wake up in the middle of the night and go for a walk. He thinks I'm lazy because I'm sleeping so hard in the morning. It's because I'm up half the night. I just can't stand to lay next to him. His skin burns me."

The preacher sat back and looked at them. He undid his tie and wiped sweat from his neck, then wiped his fingers on his trouser leg.

"You want a divorce?"

"I told you. Yes."

"I don't know how you can do that if you were too afraid to tell him you didn't want to marry him in the first place. You have a family now and he's a famous person in town. He may not be a man of God but people look up to him. Maybe there is the spirit of God hidden deep in his soul because people say he is a good healer. To heal is a gift of God."

"People don't hear him swear. They don't see the look on the kids' faces when I tell them he won't be home before they go to sleep. They might as well not have a father half of the time. People don't know that about him."

"Is he as bad as you say?"

"Yes."

"I'm glad I'm not you," the preacher said.

"Why?" Johnny asked.

"He won't be easy to deal with. There's a lot of law in divorce and he'll fight hard. I can bet you that." The preacher wiped away more sweat from his neck.

"I talked to a lawyer. I know the law. I wouldn't ask anything from him. He can have the house and his money."

"He's a proud man. It will hurt him."

"If there was love in his heart for me, things would be different," she said. She reached for the preacher's hand. "I come to ask you God's thoughts on divorce."

He patted her hand and put it aside. "I'm looking with my inner mind for a vision, for God's guidance and wisdom," he said, closing his eyes. "Divorce. Ah, what a problem."

Johnny and Win looked at his closed eyes.

"The Scriptures are filled with parables and examples." He opened his tie and shirt. "You know we all came from dust. God reached down and grabbed a handful of dust and made man. From this He took a rib and made woman. They were given Paradise. But they listened to the serpent of Satan and ruined everything. To this day there have been plagues and scourges as witness of man's fall from God." He patted Win's hand. "So many scourges." He mused.

A very fat woman exited from a door near the altar.

"Wouldn't it be nice if we could go back to the Garden?" he asked.

Johnny nodded approval.

The preacher stopped talking and smiled at them. Neither spoke back. The fat woman flicked a switch, leaving them in near darkness.

"Rosalie. Bring me my Bible."

The fat woman brought him his massively worn book. He began leafing through it, pondering a page, then leaving it for another. He began to speak softly. "A vision is what we need. Some sign. As Moses saw the burning bush and as Aaron turned the Nile to blood." From one end of the Bible to the other, he sought a proper parable. After a great length of time, he put the book aside. "What are you going to do, Win?"

"I don't know."

"Do you have the strength?"

"That's why we came here."

"I'm not one to be talking against Ned," he said, patting the Bible. "Much as I know your suffering, I'm not one to throw the first stone. Yet life is a heavy cross for you, yes, a heavy cross." His voice gathered strength. "What you have told me makes me think that your marriage wasn't ordained in Heaven. It wasn't a gift from God. There wasn't love. So maybe God wouldn't think so bad about it if it went asunder. You know what I mean?"

"That's what we thought," Johnny said.

"If you break up your marriage, I think you should know that you are the servant of God responsible for a Christian education for your children. You are the mother, the giver of life. Your kids came from your womb. You must see that they follow in the pathway to Jesus. Ned has failed, as you say. In a divorce you have a great responsibility to see to matters of religion."

"She'll sure do that," Johnny said.

"Then God will give us strength?" Win asked.

"God will bless you, child. In Revelations it says that we must suffer three woes. Your divorce will be one of them."

"I don't know how to do it," she said.

"Can you talk to Ned?"

"No," she said. "I can't talk to him."

"Pray to God, then. Pray in the morning and pray at night. Ask God for a message, ask God for guidance. Only He can tell you what to do. Ask Him for a sign, yes! ask for a sign. When it comes, you will know what to do. Be vigilant! God will take care of you if you show Him your faith." He reached for his Bible and immediately found a passage from Psalms. " 'Behold, Thou desirest truth in the inward being; therefore teach me wisdom in my secret heart. Purge me with hyssop, and I shall be clean; wash me, and I shall be whiter than snow. Fill me with joy and gladness; let the bones which Thou hast broken rejoice. Hide Thy face from my sins, and blot out all my iniquities.' " He raised his head. " 'Create in me a clean heart, O God, and put a new and right spirit within me. Cast me not away from Thy presence, and take not Thy holy spirit from me. Restore to me the joy of Thy salvation, and uphold me with a willing spirit. Then I will teach transgressors Thy ways, and sinners will return to Thee. Deliver me from blood guiltiness, O God, Thou God of my salvation, and my tongue will sing along of Thy deliverance.' "

The three were alone in a darkened church that smelled of mildew and synthetic carpet. It was time to leave the sanctuary. Win stood, thanking the preacher. He escorted them to the door.

"Pray and look for a sign," he said.

Tuesday, July 20

Ned roared to a stop outside his office and ran up the three side stairs to the lab room. He filled a coffee cup, read a list of patients tacked on the doorway and talked while drinking hot coffee.

"Sheryl? Why did you put a question mark by Rosalie Sturn?"

"I didn't know if you could get through the others and have time to take off her cyst before you leave for the hospital."

Ned looked at his watch. "It's a quarter to nine. Let's see"—he touched his index finger to each name on the roster—"surgery is at ten-thirty. Give ten minutes for Bill Leaman to screw around with an extra IV and figure Byron won't be too mad if I'm a little late. He shouldn't be, he's delayed Mandy for over a week. Go ahead. Schedule her. Have her prepped. I'll need three cc's of Xylocaine and I'll suture with 4-0 nylon. It's not a big cyst, on her back, won't take long, it's not infected." He finished his coffee.

"What was that about Bill Leaman and the IV?" Sheryl asked.

"He went to an anesthesia conference and they recommended putting in an arterial line for major cases."

"Does she need it?"

"Nah," he said. "More screwing around. She's routine. Just more screwing around."

"Is that because of malpractice?" Sheryl asked.

"Hell, no. He'll get into more trouble using the line than he'll save by having it. He believes that everything the university says is gospel. Next week they'll change their mind." Ned put on his white coat.

"Can you see Lloyd what's-his-name, the horse dealer, first? He got his finger caught in a gate."

"Cow-kicked by a mule." Lloyd sat on the surgical table. He wore a seventy-five-dollar Stetson. "Look at this!" He held his injured finger in the air. "Damn."

Blood the color of old motor oil had collected beneath the fingernail. The base of the nail was separated from the nail bed by the blood.

"Light the lamp," Ned instructed. Sheryl lit an alcohol lamp and gave Ned a paper clip which had one curve straightened. A hemostat held the clip.

"Christ, Doc. What are you going to do?"

"Burn a hole in your fingernail."

"Wait a minute, buddy." He spun his hat around his head twice. "I'm a chicken, down deep."

"This won't hurt."

"You kiddin'?"

Ned took the hemostat in hand and held the end of the paper clip over the top of the flame. "Look the other way. It's hot, but after it goes through the nail the blood cools off the tip and you don't feel anything."

Lloyd protested, forcing Ned to explain the procedure again.

"OK. I'll look the other way. But it better not hurt!"

Lloyd faced the wall. Ned took the injured finger and held it firmly against the padded surgical table. When the end of the paper clip glowed red, he pushed the point against the base of the nail where the blood was thickest. The hot wire caused a sizzling sound and the burning nail smelled like burning hair.

When he smelled the burning nail, Lloyd turned his head, and when he saw the paper clip impaled in his fingernail, he jerked his hand violently. The clip had just passed through and blood poured out.

"My God. My God." The man waved his finger in the air. The paper clip was stuck in the hole. His finger and the clip looked like a broken machine fluttering in the air. Blood dripped onto the table and Lloyd's tan pants.

Sheryl looked on in horror.

"Put your hand down," Ned yelled.

Lloyd continued to swear, waving his hand hysterically.

Grabbing the man's hand in midair, Ned quickly pulled out the paper clip.

"Jesus Christ, Ned. You told me it wouldn't hurt. That was a Tasmanian son of a bitch." Lloyd looked at his finger. The blood was gone, making the nail as floppy as a flat tire.

"You weren't supposed to jump," Ned said. He left Sheryl to clean the mess.

Clara Lester was terribly fat. With Sheryl's expert help, Ned examined her. By the age of forty-five she'd given birth to twelve children, developed diabetes and suffered one heart attack. Her problem was that every time she coughed she urinated on herself, creating so much soreness she couldn't stand to wipe herself. The woman was on her back, one leg in a stirrup, the other held by Sheryl. Ned saw fields of fat. The farthest valley was red and gray and covered with spots of pus, green as a cat's eye.

Finished, he instructed Sheryl to fold Clara together.

Outside the room, Sheryl asked Ned what he was going to do for her. He mentioned soaks and antibiotics and special creams. When his coffee cup was warm, he asked, "What do you think is her problem?"

"The skin thing is from her diabetes, right?"

"What's her real problem?"

"She's fat."

"No."

Sheryl gave up.

"That's what happens to someone who spends their life eating and screwing."

"Do you think something dirty like that every time you see some woman's underside?"

There were three patients and a cyst to be removed from a woman's back before he was due in surgery to remove Mandy Eilers' gallbladder. He quickly looked in on Jess Brooker, checking the man's heart, prescribing digitalis.

Tom Nyall was back with his stomach complaint. A week before he'd developed stomach flu, which responded somewhat to routine medication. Three days ago the pain and nausea returned but they weren't severe. Tom was a tall, angular man who smoked heavily and had two previous episodes of ulcers. Ned carefully examined his abdomen. The findings were vague.

"I don't know, Tom. Maybe the flu set off your ulcer."

"It don't hurt like my ulcer. Feels like I still got the flu. Sort of off, that's all."

"We'd better put you in the hospital. I want to check your blood and get another X-ray of your stomach."

"Do I have to?"

"It would be best. I think you'll get over it, but the flu shouldn't last this long. I'll put you in just to be on the safe side. Ulcers sometimes can cause trouble. Bleeding, that sort of thing."

"OK. But let my boss know. He thinks I'm dogging it."

Ann called the hospital and made arrangements for Tom's admission.

Ned hurried. He saw a cross-country truck driver who had pulled his rig off the Interstate. He complained of weakness in his left leg. Ned asked questions quickly, humming at times, distracted.

"I felt this coming for the last year," the driver said.

"Take off your pants."

The man leaned to his right when he stood. Now that the pants were off, Ned saw that the right thigh was half the size of the left.

"Wait a minute. How long have you had this?"

"A year. Maybe more."

"Has your leg always been this thin?"

"That's why I came in. It's getting so I can't drive."

Ned stared at the thin leg. The muscles were wasted. Remaining bits of muscle twitched and fluttered as if the leg was possessed by another force, sad and malevolent. The man's reflexes were gone but he could perceive sensation in the leg.

"Put your pants on."

Ned ran out of the room.

"Ann. Call neurology at the university. I'll talk to anyone."

She reached one of the staff.

"This is Ned Owen in Spring Falls. I have a man you should see. He claims his right leg has been getting weak for a year. On exam he's got massive atrophy of the right quads. Maybe his left is going, too. Sensory exam is intact."

The neurologist asked several questions. Ned said examination of the eyegrounds was normal.

"Be glad to see him."

"Does it sound like ALS to you?"

"Good chance. I'll have my secretary make an appointment."

Ned returned to the truck driver and told him of his appointment at the university.

"They'll fix me up?"

"If you're lucky."

Ned looked at his watch. Sheryl caught him in the hallway. The nurse had prepped Rosalie Sturn for the cyst removal.

"What did you do with that new guy?" she asked.

"Sent him to the U."

"What's he got?"

"ALS. Amyotrophic lateral sclerosis."

"Is that bad?"

"Terrible."

"Did you tell him?"

"Not really."

"Why not?"

"He'll find out soon enough. He knows it's something bad."

"You don't like to tell people bad news, do you?"

"No."

"You're good at most things, though," she said.

He was due at the hospital in twenty minutes.

"What will you bet I can have this cyst out in eight minutes flat?"

"Your car."

"OK."

He injected Xylocaine about the lump on Rosalie Sturn's back, made a skin incision, dissected skin from either side of the cyst, grabbed the cyst with an Adson's forceps, which he gave to Sheryl with instructions to hold; as she pulled upward, he quickly pecked away at the tissue around the cyst. With a final flick of his knife, the oversized pearl flopped out and Sheryl held it for the patient to see. Ned closed the incision with two sutures.

"Ten minutes," Sheryl said.

"Your watch was wrong."

"Doctor! I just won your car."

"We'll take the stitches out in a week."

Ned checked into the hospital by punching his number, 110, on the electronic board. The operator spoke to him through an intercom.

"Dr. Owen. I have your new radio."

"I'll get it after surgery." He spoke into a metal box.

"Did someone really steal it?"

"No—"

"Darn," she said. "We were having the best time thinking of messages to give the thief. How'd you like to steal something and have it talk to you?"

He didn't answer. Byron Markham was waiting at the scrub sink.

"Morning, Ned."

"Hi, Byron."

"Two hundred and twenty pounds. That's what Mandy weighs. I weighed her yesterday. Thought I'd give you the cheery news. Let's scrub."

They put on caps and masks. After Byron had started the automatic scrub sink, he turned to Ned.

"Ned. I heard stories about you."

"About me?"

"And the circumstances surrounding the loss of one radio."

Ned concentrated on a soapy sponge.

"You told Win you left it in your locker."

"Did you ask her?"

"It came out in a phone conversation."

"I thought I'd left it there."

"Oh, come on, Ned. No one would believe that."

Ned watched Byron scrub.

"Win said you were out with the boys."

"For a while."

"This is serious, Ned!" Byron said. "The hospital is

buzzing. The case of Dr. Owen's disappearing radio. The stories are wild, Ned."

"Come on, Byron."

"All right! If you won't tell me, I'll tell you my theory. I have to defend you, you know. I think you got mad at it and killed it by driving over it with your Mercedes. That's what I've been telling people."

"That's as close as you'll get."

"That's as close as I want to get." Byron yawned.

The scrub nurse asked Byron if he would close the incision with wire.

"That's what makes a Steinway sing," he said.

Ellen didn't get it.

"Yes, yes. We'll use wire to close. It not only keeps her together without getting infections, it hurts Dr. Owen's hands when he ties, making him think twice about sending me fat patients."

"Dr. Owen, have you ever thought of referring your patients to a surgeon who is a little kinder?"

"He can't send them to anyone else," Byron chuckled. "I'm the only surgeon in town who accepts referrals from a Democrat."

A red light appeared on the scrub sink. They rinsed and entered the room, arms raised high.

Ellen gowned them and the circulation nurse tied them from behind.

Byron placed four white towels around the incision site before Ned and Ellen draped Mandy with three sheets. A small patch of skin showed beneath the drapes.

Byron reached for the sterile lamp handle, screwed it into the overhead lamp and positioned it so the light shone directly onto Mandy's skin.

Ellen handed him the knife. Ned grabbed a sponge.

"Excuse me," Byron said. "Tell them to be sure to get a hemoglobin on that next case and to let me know if it's dropped."

He bent forward, touched the knife to the skin and

made an incision that went through an inch of fat. Blood spurted from five vessels. Ned clamped bleeders and sponged.

Once the wound was dry, Byron continued until he reached the first layer of fascia. He extended the incision and cut another vessel. Byron swore mildly.

Ned was ready with a clamp in each hand when Byron cut through the layer of muscle.

"Strong woman." She bled briskly.

They quickly stopped the bleeding. Byron made a final brush with his knife at the midline and a large vessel bled.

"There it is," he said.

Ned held the wound edge so Byron could clamp.

"Pickups," Byron ordered.

Ellen gave each of them a long instrument. Byron grabbed the peritoneum, lifted it and Ned grabbed it near him. Moving quickly, Byron nicked the thin layer and exposed the abdominal cavity. Handing away the knife, he finished the job with scissors, first cutting toward the midline, then to the flank. Rolls of intestines were visible.

"We're in," Byron told the anesthesiologist.

The surgeon inserted his right hand through the wound, past intestines, pushing, groping.

Bill Leaman stood, looking at Ned. Ellen arranged hemostats and silk suture.

Byron reached downward, toward the pelvis. He felt the uterus and each ovary.

"Small cyst, probably nothing," he said.

Mandy's appendix hadn't been removed.

Byron reached toward her head, reaching for her left kidney and her spleen. They were normal.

The wall clock made a loud clunk as it reached eleven.

"Wait," Byron said, his voice slightly higher.

His hands groped in the area of the gallbladder. The

muscles about his eyes tightened; he moved his head forward, concerned.

For minutes he moved his hand slowly, looking with raised eyebrows, searching.

He pulled his hand from the wound. Thin blood covered his glove; he wiped it with a sponge. He looked at the clock. Then he looked at Ellen, not at Ned, and at Bill Leaman.

No one spoke.

Byron inspected the Mayo stand, looking at the neat rows of hemostats and sutures and retractors. He looked over it carefully, picked up a knife, raised it into the air like a native with a hatchet, poised his arm as if to throw it, thought better of it and set the knife down. Looking again, he picked up a Richardson retractor, a heavy piece of stainless steel.

The operating room door was open. Byron faced it, took a step, then threw the retractor the length of the hallway.

"Bitch!" he yelled. "Bitch."

Sweat erupted on Ellen's forehead.

Ned looked on.

The surgeon took a deep breath, exhaled. "Ned. Take your right hand and feel. She's got cancer, Ned."

Byron turned so that his back was to the table. He held his head down, muttering to the floor.

Ned reached his hand into the woman's abdomen, feeling the spongy resilience of the intestines. His thumb bumped against something firm. Twisting his hand slightly, he grasped the gallbladder. It had the consistency of wet potter's clay. Within it was an irregular mass which extended to the liver. Ribbons of the same substance ran through the liver.

"It's spread."

Ellen stood with her hands on the Mayo stand.

Byron didn't move.

"Her mother had the same thing," Ned said. "I told her

she would be back at work in a month. I promised her."

Byron turned to the table. "I'm sorry I did this to you, Ned."

"I thought I felt a mass the first time I examined her," Ned said.

"I felt it, too," Byron muttered. "I didn't think, Ned. I told her the same thing."

Byron reached for a Kocher clamp, gave it to Ned and took one himself. "We'll close now," he said.

Ned checked out of the hospital, pushing his number. The red light flashed, signaling a message.

He ignored it.

He drove out of the lot, to the edge of town and onto the Interstate. Cars and trucks passed him; he felt the rush of air, heard the noise.

He floored the accelerator. The rear of his car wavered and his tires made a loud noise. He held tightly to the steering wheel, but the acceleration had brought his car over the curb. Passing through eighty, he directed the car back onto the road. He kept his foot down, passing a van in the outer lane. He switched lanes to avoid a priest in a Buick. Wind tore at his collar; he was past the red line, 124 miles an hour.

He drove for ten miles, barely avoiding traffic. When he saw an exit sign, he slammed the brake pedal. His radial tires slid and the car began to waver. The rear end jumped. Suddenly his car began to slide back and forth. It turned completely around and he felt it go into the grass toward the oncoming lane. It was out of control.

He looked up and saw the blur of a speed-limit sign as the car slid. A semi was coming at him.

It honked its air horn and swerved just as his car came to a stop, its back wheels on the pavement. He shifted into first gear, drove back across the grassy median and headed for his office.

"It's wart day," Ann said. She'd made her weekly trek to the welding-equipment shop for liquid nitrogen.

"We have Ron Messer first," Sheryl said, handing Ned a large metal thermos filled with liquid nitrogen.

After five patients, he asked Ann, "Can I get away early?"

"It's a zoo."

"Tell them to come next week."

"Do you want me to?"

"No. Hell." He took a cup of coffee into his private office. Gail was at the college library.

"Do you want to go someplace this weekend?" he asked.

"The car trip?"

"No," he said. "Away. On a jet. I don't know where."

"You sound down. Is something wrong?"

"Byron and I opened a woman today. The one I saw on the Fourth of July. She kept asking about cancer and I kept telling her it was plain old gallstones."

"Did she blame you?"

"She won't."

"You must feel terrible."

"Let's go someplace."

"Any idea where?"

"Not yet. I'll look at some journals and see if there are any conferences."

"Why not get away from medicine completely?"

"I can deduct expenses."

"That's romantic."

"It's also an excuse."

"That's OK. Being a tax deduction isn't my bag."

"I don't have to go to the lectures, you know."

"Let's make it fun, huh?"

"It'll be fun," he said.

He treated three more patients with warts. He dipped

a cotton applicator into the freezing liquid, then held the tip of the cotton against each wart until it was frozen white.

When he called home, Win was there. He told her he'd be gone over the weekend.

"Is it important?" she asked.

"It's an important meeting."

"How long will you be gone?"

"Three days."

"That will make a nice trip," she said.

Wednesday, July 21

"But the pool doesn't open until eleven, Mom!" Ellie yelled.

"You can stay home, dummy, I'm going swimming," Lizzy said.

"You're both going swimming," Win said.

"Mom! We can't swim now. There's no guard. Besides, Kitty was coming over to play."

"I talked to the club. Sammy is there and will watch you."

"Can't I wait for Kitty? We can ride our bikes over."

"It's too far for bikes," Win said.

"Well then, I'm staying home."

"You can't," Win said.

"Why?"

" 'Cause."

"If Lizzy drowns, it's your fault," Ellie said.

"She can swim as good as you can."

"She can't do the crawl right."

"I can too."

"You're both going to the pool."

Ellie and Lizzy changed into their swimming suits and sat in the back seat of the station wagon as their mother drove them across town to the small country club. Win led them to the pool, where a boy of seventeen vowed to save them should they appear to be drowning.

From the club Win drove to the Super Valu, parking in the rear. The manager was happy to oblige her. The two walked to the rear of the storage area, where empty boxes were kept.

"The big one," she said.

He shoved a large empty box which barely fit in the rear of the wagon.

The box was almost as wide as the stairway to her bedroom. Its bulk made it difficult to maneuver. She stopped twice on her way up the stairs.

She and Ned each had a bedroom closet. Hers had been made smaller when Ned's deck was constructed. She used a hall closet as well.

She dragged the box into the bedroom, stopping at the closet door. Beginning at her right, she worked her way through the closet, hanger by hanger. With a first inspection, she found six cotton blouses, two denim skirts and four pairs of old slacks. She put these on the bed. Looking at the floor, she found an old pair of sandals and tennis shoes. These went on the bed.

Dresses and skirts and pantsuits were randomly placed without regard to color or history. The first thing she threw into the box was an organdy formal she wore their first New Year's Eve party at the country club. Like most things fancy, she never wore it again. They never went to another New Year's Eve party. The dress was rose, a wrong color for her. It looked like a strangled doll at the bottom of the box. Next was a blouse with lace-trimmed short sleeves. Win had worn it twice, once to coffee for the Rotary wives and once to a bridge party, where they learned to their dismay she didn't play bridge, nor did she care to learn. She had bought a flouncy skirt in expectation of their trip to Hawaii. She wore it three days in a row, at sundown by the side of the pools of the Holiday Inns in South Dakota. She dropped it into the box. The Baptist Church held its twenty-fifth anniversary a week after Easter in 1972. Johnny asked her to serve coffee at the picnic lunch after services. She wore a wool suit with shoulders far too big; the suit was a tweed with accents of green. It hung on a special wooden hanger. She threw the suit and the hanger into the box.

She'd been so fat when she carried Lizzy! So fat she was shy. She wore a maternity dress of striped poplin, large as a sheik's tent. She put it in the box without pause. Last Christmas she'd agreed, after some pressure from the preacher, to be a chaperone for the youth choir on their yearly trip to Des Moines. She wore a dacron dress which she stained with mustard at a lunch counter of the department store where the kids sang. When it fell into the box, it slid over the tweed suit and nestled snakelike in a corner. When Lizzy was baptized, Win wore white: the first white dress in the box. Because Ned was a Democrat and because the president of the college liked him, Ned and Win were invited to Denby Manor along with twelve other people to quietly celebrate the American withdrawal from Vietnam. For such an occasion she drove to Des Moines and spent a day. Sheer black with sheer black underthings! Making such a sound slithering into the box. Empty hangers rocked along the closet rod.

There were two notable women's shops in Spring Falls. They catered to the college trade and to the wives of the business community. Win's bills were sent to Ned's office. She bought her clothes quickly, sorting through the racks with little indecision or wasted words. She never learned the names of the clerks. There were several dresses she never wore; one was purchased for a fund-raising dinner for Fred Harris, another was to be worn at a PTA

style show, and another, and more, hung, unworn, aban-
doned for this event or that. When they were first married,
she had made it a point of honor never to be poorly
dressed—a doctor's wife, after all. She learned to wear
casual things to her church. These she also dumped unquestioningly into the box. She worked slowly, but main-
taining a rhythm, never hesitating to ponder if this or
that piece of clothing belonged in the box. Her world
beyond the house was the church and the swimming pool.
When she came to her swimming suit, she threw it in as
well.

After emptying the bedroom closet, she opened her
dresser drawers and gathered her slips and underwear in
bundles, dropping them into the box.

The box had accumulated a fair amount of weight.
She dragged it out of the bedroom and pulled it to the
hall closet. As if they were of special significance she immediately grabbed every winter coat. They were the first
from the hall closet to go. The coats were bulky and she
had to arrange them so as to make room for the other
things. When Ned was elected president of the county
medical association in 1975, he responded by inviting the
society—eighty members in all—to a party at his house.
Win splurged and wore a cashmere body dress. Sweaters
and special lingerie were stashed above it. She reached
up and they cascaded into the box, some things spilling
onto the floor. The box was filled to the top now, yet there
still was half a rack to go: a cocktail skirt worn at a party
after a medical meeting in Iowa City, a velvet vest for the
Markhams' anniversary celebration, things she'd forgotten
completely. She had to force them into the box.

When her closets were empty, she found all her dress
shoes and tucked them around the sides of the box, bend-
ing the cardboard.

She eased the box down the stairs, standing under it
and letting it slide slowly. She had to move the sofa and
an easy chair to get it across the living room. When it sat

on the porch, she realized how difficult it would be for her to lift it onto the tailgate of the station wagon. As a solution, she backed the wagon to the porch. She got inside the hot car, struggled for a while in futility until a bottom corner of the box rested inside the car, then, sneaking out through a side door, put a shoulder to the box and worked it into the wagon. She forced the rear door closed with a slam.

She drove on the outskirts of town, avoiding the business and college districts. Turning onto a service road near the Interstate, she drove past a service station until she came to a small lot.

She backed the station wagon to the Goodwill box, which was square and taller than her car. A truck came twice a week from Des Moines to pick up.

The ground around the Goodwill collection depot was dusty. Win opened the tailgate. Her box was jammed. After a massive effort, she freed it so that it slid onto the ground, spilling half its contents.

The door of the Goodwill box was at the top and wouldn't stay open, so she had to reach up, fumble with the clothes and guide them. She put several bundles into the box, looking about frequently to make sure no one saw her, but the only people within sight were motorists on the Interstate.

The metal door made a banging sound each time she released it. Now and then an article of clothing would get stuck and she would have to fight to release it. Though a lot of her things were covered with dirt, she didn't bother to brush them. They went into the box, dust and all.

The heavy metal door on the Goodwill box made it impossible for her to hurry. She fought it each time she made a donation. She tried folding things together, but different materials slipped, forcing her to continue putting small batches in, one at a time. She put each offering on the door, then let it slide into the box, like a seal dropping into the quiet of the ocean from an offshore rock.

She put in the winter coats.

Her fancy underwear had become matted and dirty from being scattered about in the dust. She flipped each article, one by one, into the box.

The empty cardboard box was bent and dirty. She pulled at one of the flaps, struggling until it tore. She put it into the Goodwill box. Bit by bit she tore the cardboard apart, putting each piece into the metal container. Sometimes she found herself with a piece no larger than her hand, but took her time. The cardboard box had been dismembered haphazardly, but eventually all its fragments were out of sight, sharing the same darkness as her clothing.

She drove away from the Goodwill box, and it was soon alone on the empty dirt lot. Patches of earth around it were marred with scratches and footprints as inscrutable as the sands of a public beach at sundown.

Thursday, July 22

"Gail. This is Ned." He was calling from his office desk. "How does San Francisco sound?"

"Great."

"I found a conference. On sex. Participants are supposed to bring their spouse or a companion. They want a fifty-fifty ratio, males and females."

"It sounds boring. What do they talk about?"

"Orgasms. Masturbation. Wait a minute." Sheryl interrupted him, holding two syringes for his inspection. He pointed to the smaller one in her left hand.

"For Christ's sake. Is this for real?"

"Does it make any difference?"

"Do you see patients with orgasm problems?"

A child screamed in hysterical and violent protest in the next room as Sheryl drew blood for a lab test. "They go to Des Moines for that."

"Why don't we forget the conference? We can go to San Francisco and deal with orgasms on our own level."

"You want to go to Wichita for a conference on collagen disease?" His desk was littered with the journals and pamphlets he'd scoured.

"God, Ned, you're hung up on going to a conference. I'll go. Anywhere. But don't deduct me, OK?"

"I'll pick you up at eight-thirty in the morning."

"Should I duck when we drive out of town?"

"Hell, no. I'll honk the horn all the way to Des Moines. To hell with everyone!"

"I'll be ready."

Ann told him there was a call on the other line. The hospital.

"Tom Nyall looks worse, Dr. Owen. His tachycardia is up to a hundred thirty and he just doesn't look good. Do you want us to do anything else?"

"He didn't look that bad this morning. Is he complaining of more pain?"

"It's moved to his right side."

"Poke him on his back. I'll wait. Go poke him right under the ribs behind." He waited for her.

"Doctor. He's not tender there, but his belly is distended. I don't think he looked like this an hour ago."

"Is he still running a temp?"

"It hasn't dropped. Thirty-nine point seven."

"What time is it?"

"Quarter to two."

"Byron should be in the hospital. Page him and have him look at Tom. I don't know what the hell's going on." He hung up.

"Is that serious?" Ann asked.

"Don't know."

"It won't mess up your trip, will it?"

"I hope not."

"Sheryl and I will die if you don't go."

"Don't say that."

"What?"

"Die."

"Oops. I wasn't thinking."

Sheryl grabbed Ned's arm. "Do a quick pelvic so I can free up the third room. Melody Jenson."

"Who?"

"You heard me."

"What does she want?"

"The pill."

"How old is she?"

"Sixteen."

"Oh, Christ. Do I have to?"

"If you don't, let me know quick so I can use the room."

"If her old man finds out, I'll never get another bank loan."

Melody sat draped on the end of an examining table. She was a tall girl with a long chin.

"Hi, Dr. Owen."

"Hi," Ned said. "What's going on?"

"I want to go on the pill."

"You need it?"

Long blond hair fell over her shoulder as she nodded.

Ned felt her thyroid gland, listened to her heart and lungs, examined her small breasts and felt her stomach. All normal. He waited outside the examining room as Sheryl prepared Melody for the pelvic exam.

Ned sat on his exam stool. Thin pubic hair lay on a flat mons veneris. Her labia were long and sharply demarcated, like the edges of baby calves liver. He inserted a speculum with ease. The skin over her cervix was delicate and the opening was perfectly small and round, covered with a thin secretion. When he inserted his fingers inside to check her uterus, the heel of his hand rested against her thin buttock.

Melody smiled politely.

Finished, he began to explain how to use the pill.

"I know," she said.

He wrote a prescription. "Say hello to your folks."

"Be delighted," she said.

Ned ran to a phone and called the hospital. The nurse reported that Tom didn't look any better. Byron was due any minute.

"Get him up there. My wife's cooking steaks tonight and I'm leaving town tomorrow."

"Dr. Markham said he'd come," the nurse said.

"Bug him for me."

He went to the lab room, calling in Ann and Sheryl. He made them sit and poured each a cup of coffee before he poured his own. "Ann, did you get me the money?"

"A thousand in fifties. It's in the desk. Locked."

"Why don't you stay at the conference longer?" Sheryl asked.

"Can't."

"Poop. You're addicted to this office. Maybe if you stay away you'll get unaddicted."

"Doctor? Do you know what we're going to do tomorrow when the office is empty?"

"Leave?"

"No. We're going to take off all our clothes and run all over, screaming our heads off. Whooopeeee!" Ann said.

"I'll stay around for that."

"You can take your clothes off in San Francisco," Sheryl said.

"Sheryl!" Ann giggled.

"Who knows what might happen to Doctor once he gets out of this burg?"

"Think of it! An empty office. This place will be like a morgue. It's usually so hectic," Ann said.

"You two would hate it if it wasn't."

"We're not as crazy as you," Sheryl said.

"I'm glad she was the one who called you crazy."

"Where else can you have as much fun as here?"

"Movies."

"A dog fight."

"This is the most fun place you've ever been," he said.

"Sometimes," Sheryl said.

"It beats the checkout counter of the Super Valu," Ann said.

"Fooey. This is the best place in the world," he said.

Byron called and asked Ned a series of questions. Ned informed him that Tom Nyall worked at the feed elevator. He had a history of ulcer disease, had contracted the flu a week before. He got better with antacids and Compazine, then his temperature came back. On previous examinations there was some mild upper-abdominal tenderness, but nothing marked.

"Any other pain?"

"Not really," Ned said.

"He a boozer?"

"Nope."

"He's sick. I'm like you, I don't know. But I'm getting some films of his belly. His urine is clear, so I don't think it's renal, a pyelo or a stone. Looks to me like he's got peritonitis."

"From what?"

"Maybe he had a low-grade regional enteritis. Did you ever get a barium enema on him?"

"No. But he hasn't had any lower GI symptoms."

"I agree. But he's sick, Ned. I'll call you back."

"You think he's that sick?"

"Definitely."

"I was going to San Francisco tomorrow."

"I'll take care of it."

"If we have to do anything—"

"I'll get you in San Francisco."

Sheryl handed him a chart. "OK. Ready to eat your words? Gladys. She wants a refill on her Valium, Seconal, Elavil, and she wants to talk about her skin condition." Sheryl directed him to a room. "Tell her what a fun place this is."

Gladys Mullendorfer waited on a chair with her hands folded.

"I know you're going to be mad at me," she said, wringing her hands and sighing deeply. Gladys looked at the wall when she spoke to Ned. Her face was fat but not uncomely—a bit cherubic. "I sat up all night and worried," she said. Before Ned could speak, she continued: "Walter came home in a dither about his work, you know he has to smell that terrible chemical stuff and now and then it burns his nose and he's afraid of getting cancer or impetigo from it, so he was all upset and naturally it frightened me so I didn't say anything, you know you can't speak to Walter because he gets upset so easy, well just as I went into the kitchen Alfred comes home and tells his dad he sassed the teacher, you know he's almost a grown man, Alfred, and he says—"

Ann interrupted. "Doctor, your wife's on the phone. She says she has to talk to you."

Ned walked to the phone. "Any word from Byron?"

"No. I'll get you right away when he calls," Ann said.

"Hello. What's up?" he asked Win.

"You're coming for supper, aren't you?"

"Might get hung up with a case."

"You have to come. The kids want to see you."

"I'm not going to Africa."

"What was that champagne you liked?"

"Almaden. What's going on?"

"It's time for champagne," she said in her Welsh voice.

Gladys continued to explain to Ned that she was doubly upset because her son was thinking about joining the army in a year. "How can he do good in the army if he doesn't even help around the house? Last week I told him to weed the garden and he never touched it."

"How much Valium do you need?"

"Can I get a hundred?"

"And Seconal?"

"Fifty. And I need my Elavil."

Ned had heard a story, perhaps apocryphal, about Gladys—that she had had a daughter, a toddler, who died a pathetically grotesque death. An accident so horrible it made *Time* magazine.

Helen Revson returned to be checked for her pneumonia. All that remained was a smoker's cough.

Ned was looking into a baby's ear when Byron called.

"I'm scrubbing now, Ned. He's got an acute belly. Can you get here straight away?"

"Be there in five minutes."

He yelled for Ann. "I have to go to the hospital. Now."

"What about the rest of the patients?"

"Anyone that can't wait?"

"I'll check with Sheryl and leave a message at the hospital if you need to see anyone. Hey! How about when you're gone? What about calling in medication for patients?"

"Give 'em anything."

"Hey, wait." Sheryl caught up with him. "What about Katherine Kay?"

"The baby? Call in some Ilosone. Hundred twenty-five milligrams. Hundred fifty cc."

Byron had scrubbed. Tom Nyall was asleep and draped.

"Short scrub will do," Byron shouted to Ned.

When Ned was ready, Byron gave him a suction tip. "When I put the tube in his stomach, there was a lot of pressure. Be ready to suck. Anesthesia? You ready?"

Bill Leaman nodded.

They made a lower-midline incision. The patient's belly was rigid. Ned looked at Tom's head; it was covered with sweat.

"We have a hypothermia blanket to get his temp down," the anesthesiologist said.

"OK. Be alert, Ned. You take a pickups and I'll take one. Get your suction ready."

Byron made a small nick in the peritoneum. It looked like used Saran Wrap. Pus seeped out of the wound.

"Suck!" Byron yelled.

Byron extended the incision with scissors.

Ned pushed the suction tip into the incision. The tip was perforated with rows of small holes. As it slid across the intestines, pus was sucked out and shot through the plastic suction hose. It traveled to a quart-sized container near the anesthesia machine.

Byron took the suction tip from Ned and moved it all about the belly.

There was pus everywhere. Tom had generalized peritonitis. The smell was intensely foul.

"I don't understand," Ned said. "I thought he had the flu."

"Hold on, Ned. We'll take a look." Byron checked the suction container. It held half a quart of pus. When he'd suctioned as much as he could, Byron began to slowly touch and check, looking for a cause.

"Would you believe?" His forehead was wrinkled as could be.

"What?"

"Appendix."

"Crap," Ned yelled. "I missed it cold."

"Look. See here. This piece of garbage used to be his appendix. It all started here."

Ned swore and stomped his feet. "Why didn't I think of appendicitis?"

Byron took the suction and removed more pus from the lower abdomen.

"I feel lousy. How could I be so blind?" Ned moaned.

Byron took a hemostat and clamped it across the stump of rotted tissue that had been an appendix. He ligated the stump and inverted it into the large intestine with a purse-string suture. Ned held the circle of silk outward as Byron dunked the stump out of sight, tied the knot and removed the clamp. Byron let Ned complain and moan.

"We'll leave him open. I'll put some stay sutures in and

we'll gradually close him. He'll have two drains. We'll get cultures on the pus. I'll cover him with Keflin and Garamycin until we get cultures back. He'll do all right, Ned."

"I feel bad."

"You've said that ten times already," Byron said caustically.

"I thought he had the flu. Look at this."

"I failed to point out, Ned, that he ruptured this at least two months ago. He walled off the infection, then it began to break out of the cavity. That's when he felt like he had the flu."

"He never acted like an appendix."

"Of course not. He's a hard-working man. He probably had a little catch in his side and let it go. He never let you make a primary diagnosis."

"I still feel bad."

"Never feel bad about something you can't see. You can't make a diagnosis unless you have facts in front of you. He threw you a curve."

"I wasn't thinking."

"You did the right thing. He looked sick. You put him in the hospital. When he looked sicker, you did something about it."

"You want me to stick around tomorrow?"

"You're going to San Francisco."

"I can stay."

"Take off, Ned. You need the break. I can handle anything. Take off."

Ned assisted Byron as they put drains on either side of the abdomen. They fashioned a closure of sorts with vaseline gauze and thick wire-support suture. Tom's vitals were markedly improved after the operation.

Ned changed clothes and found Ann waiting outside the operating suite.

"Your money. You almost went off without it." She handed him twenty fifty-dollar bills.

"Hey, thanks. Does anyone else need seeing?"

"Nope. Sheryl and I told them you have pneumonia. Besides, your wife called twice to see if you were coming home."

"Nothing else to do?"

"Doctor! You're done. Go home. We took care of you." She laughed.

Bronwyn Owen set their dinner table beneath the spreading branches of an oak tree. She set the table with linen and silver goblets and mismatched plates. Between the table and the garden was the barbecue, a present on her thirtieth birthday. The garden was weedy—only the tomatoes had a chance for survival. The sun was rushing to illuminate the moon, or so an old Celtic myth had said; its copper light touched yellow to trees and the house and outlined mosquitoes. A barn swallow appeared from nowhere. Couched oddly in weeds about the tree's trunk was a bottle of Almaden Extra Dry, wrapped in an old dishcloth.

Ned came to a panic stop in the driveway and honked his Maserati air horns.

The elbows and faces and dangling hair of Lizzy and Ellie appeared from a stairway window.

"We can't come out," Lizzy said.

"Not till you're done eating," Ellie explained.

"Can I have your lobster if you don't eat it all?" Lizzy asked.

And Ellie would have his steak, if he didn't eat it all.

Ned walked to the back yard. He could smell the fire. When he passed the house, he looked and saw four things: To his left was the garden and its weeds. Next he saw the charcoal pot, backlit, its gray smoke rising upward, commingling with leaves and branches. He saw the oak tree hovering over a bottle of champagne. Win stood between the tree and the fire, facing him. The ebbing daylight outlined her as a thing of darkness. He couldn't see her face or her arms. There was a halo of saffron around her dark hair, an uneven and changing trick of the evening, as if she were alive with freed sunspots—dancing and bright for a moment, then slipping into the shadow of a quieting horizon.

"You're right on time," she said. She was dressed in old slacks and a faded blouse.

"I forgot we had those goblets."

"I hid them after that Pakistani intern drank all our wine the night of the interns' party. He said he was a rich king."

The coals were ready.

"I'll start the food if you open the bottle. Save the cork for Lizzy."

They sipped champagne made drier by the silver goblets, slowly, over the coals and the smell of the barbecue.

"San Francisco is a pleasant city for a conference," she said.

"It should be."

Win held her goblet to her face, higher than her lips and nose, so that he saw only her eyes above the silver. Her pose created a mask like that of a veiled woman in a bazaar, adding mystery to eyes already dark and secretive. "I should tell you not to go, I should tell you to stay here this weekend." If she lowered the chalice, he could see her lips. "And you should be telling me things. But we're not like that. So nothing gets said and nothing gets told and we don't know, finally, we don't know, Ned Owen."

She turned from him toward the fire. Glowing coals were reflected from her goblet. She walked to the fire. When she turned again to him, her face was fully visible and she laughed.

"The first time I ever heard your name my mother told it to me with a hushed voice. 'Ned Owen,' she said, 'Ned Owen was taken to the jail for his hell raisin', and he'd be there yet if the judge had his wits about him.'" Win drank a full draught. "For a year I thought Ned Owen was one word."

Win and Ned sat across from each other. Darkness

arrived as an unnoticed shadow which had run halfway up the side of their house. Their goblets were full and their plates so crowded with lobster and steak there wasn't room for salad.

Two figures stole from the house and perched like gargoyles on the fenders of the Mercedes.

"Tell me about the Welsh," Win said, not to his face but to an emptiness on the horizon. She sniffled, looking into an emptiness beyond the oak tree, a darkened portion of the summer sky. "Do you believe those things about the druids and the bonnie rats?"

He didn't answer.

"One thing I know. In Wales they outsing nightingales."

Before they were finished eating they were attacked.

Lizzy and Ellie hugged Ned.

"Mother wants us to give you a special, special hug."

"That's what I'm doing, stupid."

Ned hugged them back.

"Dad. The bunny-rats will get you." Lizzy laughed.

"They can't," Ellie said. "He's a doctor."

FRIDAY SATURDAY SUNDAY
July 23   24   25

Gail and Ned made love like people who had arrived in paradise—lazily, with leg stretching and false passes and childlike touching; sybarites; skin conscious, languishing.

They left their suite at the Hyatt Regency, descending in a glass bubble past sun-drenched terraces of Babylon. After a taxi ride they arrived on Mount Parnassus, home of the University of California Medical Center. It was mid-afternoon and they had missed a good portion of the conference. The woman at the registration desk took Ned's check as payment for the meeting and suggested they enter the auditorium from above, quietly.

"What have we missed?" Gail asked.

"Heterosexual behavior and masturbation," the woman whispered.

The auditorium was dark. A movie was in progress. There was a city street with early Beatles as background music. Two figures approached, hand in hand. Ralph and Franklin. They were lovers in Chicago. Both worked and were productive. They shared household duties and the problems of apartment living. They were in love.

Mary and Alice lived in a houseboat on Lake Washington in Seattle. They sat side by side on their dock, looking at sailboats. Mary kissed Alice gently on the cheek. On the lake a Cal 26 was tacking. Alice touched Mary's knee. A red, white and blue hot-air balloon floated grandly above Lake Washington. Mary undid Alice's brassiere snap. A child in a Sunfish sailed by. Alice leaned back. A sea gull took wing. Strands of sunlight walked across the lake. Mary began to tickle Alice's belly button with her tongue. Mount Rainier stood in the distance. "Clair de Lune" became louder. The gold-and-black spinnaker of a gilded antique flew open. Mary put her hand in Alice's pants. Sails on a Hobie Cat 16 flapped as the skipper put it in irons. Mary told Alice she loved her.

Auditorium lights brightened.

"The next movie," Gail said, "is Mary and George and a Doberman pinscher."

There was a group conference. The moderator urged the participants to utter their gut-level responses. Most of these made Ned and Gail laugh. A timid woman who said the content was provocative was assailed by a man who informed her it was all pinko. Noticing the new arrivals, the moderator looked up at Ned and Gail, asking them for an opinion.

"Very nice, thank you. We're from Iowa," Gail said.

Ned began to giggle.

"It's four forty-five. We'll adjourn now. Be here promptly at eight for our last visual input. Tomorrow morning is practical clinics and counseling techniques."

As Ned and Gail entered the corridor, they were stopped by a couple in their mid-forties wearing gaudy and expensive clothes. "Iowa!" the man said. "We're from Minnesota. Neighbors." They introduced themselves as Steve and Jan. He was a psychiatrist.

Steve and Jan suggested they all eat together at the Blue Fox. By the time they arrived, Ned and Gail were having difficulty joining the conversation. Steve ordered *escargots* and champagne and recommended either the Long Island duckling *flambé aux cerises noires* or the *bœuf*.

"And a bottle of Chateau Margaux, sixty-seven," Ned said.

"Ah, you know wine," Steve said.

"We're from Iowa," Gail replied.

Through the courses of *escargots* and wine and *bœuf* and duckling, Steve and Jan told them about their experiences. Sex conferences were important to them, professionally and emotionally. This one was good, Steve insisted, because there were a lot of rednecks in attendance.

"They say the crudest things," Jan said. "I never knew what 'cornhole' meant until some old man said it after a session in Houston."

Ned ordered a bottle of Chateau Haut Brion. "We're celebrating."

"The American Dream," said Gail.

"The program tonight will make you dream American," Steve informed.

Later, Gail was successful in an attempt to avoid sitting with the couple from Minneapolis. She excused herself and hid in the bathroom as long as she dared. Then she and Ned ran to the upper entrance of the auditorium and sat in a corner. *Potpourri*, the movie, had begun. Three projectors filled the room with light, aimed at three screens. There were nude men and women on beds, on beaches, in showers, in pools, in theaters—giving and getting pleasure in every possible way, with every possible mechanical device known to humanity since the Marquis de Sade. One, two, three and four people at a time, filling the screens with moiling, dripping, oozing, churning flesh. Labia and penises and pelvic thrusts and *coitus interruptus* and *coitus praecox* and anguished, flesh-starved faces with groaning so primal it appeared as though all humanity were a twisted ball of flesh groping to reach light from a captive womb.

Ned rubbed his knee against Gail's thigh; she blew softly on his face.

"Let's go to our room right afterwards," he whispered.

"If we can hold out." She kissed his cheek.

The second movie began without intermission. It was an evening in London. Richly attired couples exited from Rolls limousines and entered Covent Garden. The marquee advertised *Sleeping Beauty*. The camera revealed a tittering, jeweled audience. The orchestra played opening strains. There were quick cuts to the ballet corps. Tension mounted with the music. Princess Aurora rose from her bed; Prince Florimund leapt. The camera moved in closer as the Prince and Princess joined in a pas de deux. He held her. She freed herself for a *bourrée*. The Prince executed a daring grand jeté. The camera moved closer, closer, closer and cut to the title: *Ballet of Sex*.

"Here we go again," Ned said. "A quiet night in the big city."

"It isn't over yet, Ned."

The camera moved to a large bedroom of a country estate. Long windows were open. Flowing, white diaphanous curtains were lulled with a sotto voce breeze. A huge bed occupied the center of the scene.

Gail and Ned began to play serious thigh games.

The music quieted. It was very idyllic. A bird chirruped.

Gail rubbed a finger on the back of Ned's hand.

A modern-day prince and princess entered from opposite sides of the room. They were naked. They faced each other, full profile.

She touched a breast with a gentle hand and moved it downward to her flank. He imitated her.

They looked at each other languidly.

"Are you erect?" Gail whispered.

"Shhhh."

The dancers met at the foot of the bed, slowly reaching for each other, and embraced with long caressing movements across their backs and buttocks. They touched each other's genitalia.

When they were on the bed, the camera slowed. Close shots revealed delicate massaging and wet skin kisses. He explored her vagina with a finger. A very close shot revealed a bead of moisture on her labia. She caressed his penis with both hands. She kissed it. At times the motion stopped for a still shot, like the stopping of a flower in the process of unfolding.

"Let's run out of here and get the first cab," Gail said.

"Let's do it in the glass elevator," Ned replied.

The ballet of sex continued as the prince moved his entire face in her groin until it was soaked and then they joined, male and female, kissing madly, writhing— Then it was over.

"Let's go," Ned grunted.

They got up and moved to the aisle, then hurried to the upper door of the auditorium. As they were running down the hall to the nearest exit, they heard a loud shout.

"Hey there, Iowa! Wait for us."

Jan and Steve ran after them.

Gail swore.

"We thought we'd lost you," Steve said.

"I have to call the hospital. I left a pretty sick person there."

"You have someone covering, don't you?"

"Sure. But it's important."

"That's easy. Come on up to our room for a drink and use my phone."

"No, thanks," Gail interrupted. "We're dead. We've been running all day."

"Where are you staying?" Steve asked.

"Hyatt Regency."

"We're at the Hopkins. Right on the way. Why don't you share a cab, have a drink, make your call. We insist, we're starved for good company. Just one drink."

The Mark Hopkins smelled of a different kind of luxury than the Hyatt Regency—older, a different kind of money.

The psychiatrist's room was littered with paraphernalia: tape recorders, camera cases, film cassettes, speakers, tripods, unfolded maps, a portable bar. It also smelled of incense.

With the serving of drinks, Steve said, "You don't think we got you two up here just for drinks, did you?"

Neither Gail nor Ned responded.

"How about a little movie to burn the snow off your roof?"

Jan was setting up the equipment.

"We're social people. Do some photography ourselves. You ready?"

"I guess," Ned said without emotion.

"That's the spirit that launched a thousand ships."

Suddenly they were watching a movie called *Sundown at Tamalpais*. Ned hurried his drink. The movie began in San Francisco, showing a shaky view of Coit Tower, from bottom to top. Steve laughed. The ocean appeared. Steve exhaled with excitement. The camera found a pine tree and examined it from bottom to top. The camera explored the floor of a forest: pine cones, weeds, a rusty beer can. A path led upward, upward.

Jan walked between the projector and the screen. She was naked from the waist up.

Two naked people crawled up the path, the camera catching them from behind. They crawled meaningfully on their hands and knees. The camera jerked.

Jan sat next to Ned.

The naked couple crawled over a rock. Turning, the camera revealed the smiling faces of Steve and Jan.

Jan put her hand on Ned's thigh.

"Debark! Debark!" Ned yelled as loud as he could, his voice fracturing the reverie of the movie. He grabbed Gail and they ran wildly out the door and down the hall. A quick look told Ned that none of the elevators was near their floor, so he ducked through a door and found the service stairway. Gail held his hand, her heels producing an uneven staccato which bounced off the stairwell. At the bottom, Ned pushed open a steel door and they were outside, out of breath.

He led them through an alley and they found a well-lighted street alive with the noises of San Francisco.

"That was a great escape," Gail said, leaning on his shoulder.

"It sure makes me realize I'm from Iowa," Ned mused.

"I knew they wouldn't seduce us. We're too moral."

"I'm still horny, aren't you?" Ned asked.

They walked up the street. Ned stepped backward into an unlit doorway and pulled her against him, rubbing her back, pulling up her dress.

"I have an idea," Ned said.

"What?"

"Follow me."

They walked fast for two blocks until he found a dark alley.

"Let's go." He led her into the alley.

"Are you sure?"

At the darkest spot he kissed her, then turned her around, pulling up her dress.

"Ned! You're a madman!" She jumped away from him, smoothed her dress and ran toward a lighted street. "We could be murdered here."

They rode a cable car to their hotel.

They slept amidst luxury and splendor akin to the praetorian elegance of ancient Rome. It is certain no magistrate of Caesar's court ever awoke seventeen stories above San Francisco Bay in bed with a professor of American Civilization. Ned woke before her and spent a long time looking at her, at her body breathing quietly.

When she awoke, she was startled to see him staring at her.

"It happens when you're in a strange bed," he said.

"You scared me."

"Once in Vietnam I got drunk at this outfit's bar and they bedded me down in an old French building. When I woke, there was a Vietnamese woman standing over me yelling, 'Bac-Si, Bac-si. Doctor, doctor.' I thought I'd been captured."

"You have been captured."

San Francisco Bay was gray water and clots of fog and fishing boats with wakes like long-tailed comets.

"How much are we paying for this place, Ned?"

"A hundred and fifty bucks."

"A night?"

"Yup."

"Christ!"

"It's deductible."

"I know, I know."

"Besides. I've never done anything like this."

"Don't you go on trips with your wife?"

"Not really."

"Ned— I feel I should say something and get it out. As nice as this is, something makes me nervous. What if your wife found out? What would she do? I hate to put a damper on things, but I feel vulnerable. Women can do some pretty terrible things. Your wife wouldn't strangle me or anything?"

"She might."

"God. Really? She's vindictive?"

"I'm kidding. Nothing will happen."

"You sure?"

"Absolutely."

"I just don't want to be strangled." Gail was dressed in a white lace nightgown. Her hair was loose and uncombed, falling over her shoulders. Ned followed her as she wandered about the suite.

"I'm the one who's supposed to feel guilty. Not you. And I feel great," Ned said. "I should have done this a long time ago."

Furniture in the sitting room was grouped around a polished coffee table, facing a gaslit fireplace. Everything was done in red, expensively. Gail sat down in a brocade chair. "Why haven't you?"

"You didn't come to town."

"There. I'm guilty. If your wife throws a fit, I'm to blame."

"She wouldn't know how to throw a fit."

Gail's face became that of the professor: wrinkled brow, raised finger, steady gaze. "Maybe that's the problem with your marriage."

Ned wasn't in an analytical mood. "She's a quiet person," he said easily.

Again the professor, Gail corrected him. "I think you mean passive." She paused. "That's how I explain your attacking me. Passive women don't allow it." Her point made, she relaxed.

"I didn't attack you."

"If we continue like we have on this trip I'll be sitting in a bathtub all week recovering."

"That's a good idea. The bathtub."

"Why don't you want to talk about your wife and your marriage?"

"Why?"

He led her to the bathroom, where he consummated the act he'd attempted in the alley the night before.

A little past noon they found themselves adrift on the Embarcardero, surrounded by tourists, sea gulls, shrimp vendors and a graduating high school class from Osaka, Japan. Forty kids with Nikon cameras swept by with the grace and precision of a group of nuns at St. Peter's Square.

They took the ferry to Sausalito. From the upper deck they witnessed a miracle of transportation: All forty students from Osaka were adsorbed onto surfaces of a cable car; their blue-and-white uniforms made the car look like a beluga whale at term.

When they were abeam of Alcatraz Island, Gail said, "There are two deep and lingering questions I have to ask. I'm a curious person, you know. Most of my curiosity, at least professionally, is aimed at the dead and famous. You proved this weekend you're not dead, and I hope not too many are aware of your fame. Two questions, Ned. First. How in the hell did you know which wine to order last night?"

"It wasn't a matter of knowing anything." Ned paused. "You want a simple answer. Hah! There isn't any. And I didn't do it to impress anybody. I ordered the most expensive wine on the list. I've never done that. I've never thrown money away like that before this weekend. That's how I ordered the wine."

"You have an expensive car."

"I need that."

"Then I'm honored. I've never been with anyone who has thrown money around like that. It was fun."

A tight-hauled sloop, the *Merry Pan*, sailed nearby.

"The second question," she said, "is about you and your wife. You said you never take her anyplace. If that's true, how does she survive? Don't you go someplace with her, even with the kids?"

"She's from poor people. She never had anything and doesn't expect anything. I had to force her to buy what's in the house."

"Poor people want things, too."

"Not her. You know where she came from?"

"No."

"A real shack. My dad was a carpenter and we didn't have much. He was a union man, a laborer, really. But I lived in a mansion compared to the place Win came from. It had one room which was part kitchen and part living room and bedroom. Then there was a cold room on it, kind of a porch. The porch had a stoop and that's it. The place didn't have a sidewalk, only two long plank boards that covered a wet spot on the lawn. Her folks were older. Her old man spent all his life on the stoop, drinking beer. The cold room was lined with beer bottles and always smelled of beer, even in the winter. He was a coal miner in Wales and a champion soccer player. There was some accident in a mine and he left Wales and came to Iowa, where there was some mining back then. I never figured out how they lived. He never worked and I don't know of any pension. Her mother did odd jobs, but that wouldn't buy the beer he drank. He was funny, very Welsh. They all have a sense of humor, but the mines twist it and you have to know a Welshman like him to even know he's being funny. He always talked rough to me, like—" Ned attempted a Welsh accent—" 'Hey kid, how's about a round with the fists, I don't like the look in ye eye.' The worst thing he ever did was tell me about the bonnie rats. One night I brought her home from a high school dance. It was cold and rainy. When I walked her to the door, he was sitting in the dark, drinking beer. I didn't see him.

" 'Aye, lad,' he said like a dog growling. I jumped. 'What'd ye jump fer? Afraid of something?' I didn't say anything. 'I'll tell ye something. It's nights like these that the bonnie rats come out.' It was spooky because I couldn't hardly see him. He had been drinking. 'They come through your attic, you know, the bonnie rats. And they'll get you if you don't take care. They like nights like this. You listen when you go home. If you hear anything movin' about up there, pay heed for they's bonnie rats and they'll wait till you're sleepin' to get you.'

"I didn't sleep at all that night. For months I heard those damn bonnie rats."

"Sounds like he had bonnie rats in his brain."

"He was a sad old fart. Win loved him. He was gruff and sounded mean to me, but he talked to her and told her all kinds of bullshit about Wales and the singing there. He was different with her. That's why she doesn't care about fancy things. She won't admit it but she likes the sound of her voice and she reads *Reader's Digest* books and says things out of the books with a Welsh accent to sound like him."

"Was he psychic? Is his story prophetic?"

"He was putting me on. It was his sense of humor."

"That's a heavy sense of humor. There's something almost wishful and ghoulish in that story, sort of like, 'It's out there, kid, waiting to get you.'"

"It was the beer in him. And the Welsh. I'm third generation, so I'm not like them. At least with the words. A college friend knew all about the Celts, the Irish and the Welsh. They love life in a peculiar way—they like mystery and words. He was pure Welsh."

"Why did you marry her?"

"I liked the way she talked. And she was pretty."

They shopped in Sausalito, and when they were done, they drank beer from ceramic mugs.

It was while they were walking back to the ferry that Ned spotted a helicopter.

"There's something you've never done," he said.

"There are a lot of things I've never done."

"I swore I'd never do it again. But I changed my mind," he said. "Let's go."

There was a helicopter painted like a bee sitting by a sign advertising its rental.

"Where are we going?"

"Over the Golden Gate Bridge."

"And then where?"

"To the park."

They hurried to the landing pad. Ned told her it would be neat to land in the center of Golden Gate Park. "When we land, I'll show you how we got off helicopters in Vietnam. Right before touchdown at the LZ the team leader yells, 'Debark, debark,' and we jump out."

"You yelled that already."

The pilot had different ideas. "There is no way in hell I'll set this thing down there."

"How much?" Ned opened his wallet.

"More than you think."

"I want to show her how it was in Vietnam."

"I'll drop you off on Seal Rocks. The park, no."

"You don't dare," Ned insisted.

"There are little kids, old ladies and college dropouts messing with each other in the grass. It's not only illegal, we might kill somebody."

They flew between the buttresses of the Golden Gate Bridge and over terra cotta roofs of the rich, floating over the city with the intimate perspective offered by the helicopter. Gail shouted over the engine noise, "They should call this helicopter the *Muhammad Ali*—float like a bird, sting like a bee."

The pilot suddenly made a dizzying downward spiral, as though the thing were out of control. They felt a jolt and were motionless atop a five-story building: St. Joseph's Hospital.

"That's as much Vietnam as I can come up with, buddy. Jump out and you can deal with the sisters down there. Fake a heart attack. I'm gettin' the hell out of here."

Dr. Ned Owen informed Sister Mary Alice that he was on a tour of Bay Area hospitals. The sister cooperated fully, giving Ned and Gail an hour-and-a-half tour of the hospital.

In the taxi to Golden Gate Park, Gail cornered Ned. "You're a pushover. I thought we'd never get out of there. I'm beginning to wonder about you. You refused to be seduced by a very nice couple, but you couldn't say no to a nun."

"I couldn't think of a way out."

"You could have told her we were doing Vietnam landings on her roof."

"That was pretty good. Just like the real thing."

"What if we would have crashed, got knocked unconscious and woke up with a bunch of nuns around us? We would have sworn we were in heaven."

"That's one place I don't worry about."

There were little kids, old ladies and college dropouts messing with each other in the park. Ned and Gail walked hand in hand.

"I had my first peace rally here," Ned said. "I was on my way home from Vietnam. Lots of people that day; seventy thousand, I think."

"Willy P-3 was great at rallies. He kindled me! He knew all the facts and the latest atrocities."

"I loved the peace rallies," Ned said. "Too bad we can't do something like that now. The most fun I had was shocking the other doctors. That was great."

"We're really a warped people," Gail mused. "I agree with you. The good old days! Our youth! And here we are standing on sacred ground wanting the damn war back. God forbid! Let's go eat. I have an idea. We'll have drinks at one place, hors d'oeuvres at another, main course someplace else and dessert at one of those rooftop restaurants —I think there's one in our hotel."

Dessert was French chocolate cake and ice cream in the Equinox, the revolving restaurant atop their hotel. They spent twenty minutes plotting the course of their helicopter flight. Gail interrupted Ned mid-sentence.

"Did the peace rallies make you horny?"

"Not at all."

"They did me."

"My pond does that to me."

"Remember that night! That was simply beautiful, Ned. I doubt if I'll ever spend another night like that. This trip has been great, but the pond. Remember the pond! Just think, Ned, we already have a history. No matter where we go or what happens to us, we have that."

They sipped cognac until the city lights were slightly ablur. The glass elevator took them to their room. After they had made love and before Ned was asleep, Gail asked, "Do you like cathedrals?"

"Never saw one."

"I'll take you to one someday."

They had planned a walk along the wharfs before their flight, but it was cold and rainy next morning. Ned ordered breakfast brought to their room. They ate leisurely, quietly looking at the bay through the rain.

"Two weeks and summer school is over," she said.

"Too bad you don't like Iowa."

"That isn't the problem. Iowa doesn't need me. Not at least Cathlin College. I'd stay if they had a job. They don't and they couldn't afford me anyway. I'm over-educated."

"Do you teach much history?"

"In a sense. The trend is to analyze American history and culture psychologically. That's what I'm doing with the depression."

"I'd like to know about San Francisco. The history."

"I can make up a history for you. Give me three facts and I'll expand it into a story."

"I want to know the real truth. What it was like when it was discovered."

"There wasn't a street or a building here."

"I want to know what it smelled like."

"The hell you aren't Celtic! The mystery of the earth! People didn't write about smells in their journals."

"That isn't what I mean. What did they think when they found the place?"

"They probably said, 'Let's put the Oakland Bay bridge here and the Transamerica building there and Coit Tower up there.'"

"You're no help."

"I'll research it for you when we get back."

They arrived in Des Moines at four-fifteen. Ned drove on back roads, explaining that it was past mid-summer because the corn was tassled and fully grown.

"Out east we look at a calendar."

He dropped her off and headed home. Win's station wagon was in the driveway; he parked behind it.

"Hello! I'm home. Kids! I'm home."

Their inflatable canoe barricaded entry to the living room. He stepped over it. Upstairs he dropped his suitcase and threw his coat on a chair.

"Hello," he yelled down the stairwell.

He called the hospital. There were no messages for him.

When the sun had almost gone, he became aware of a quietness in the house. He looked out the kitchen window. The station wagon was still there. He called the hospital again, asking if his wife had left any message. The operator said no.

As darkness penetrated the house, he made a tour. "Kids! Where are you?" He checked the bedrooms, the TV room, the basement. He walked to the front door, stooped to move the canoe. There was an envelope inside it. For him.

It was Win's stationery, perfumed. There were three pages written in her small, protective handwriting. They told him that she had taken the children, she was leaving. Johnny was with her. She would wait awhile before telling him where she had gone because she was afraid of him.

> *Don't ask me to come back because I can't. After the town hears about it it would be impossible. I will take good care of the kids. We're used to getting along without you. Johnny is nice to them.*
>
> *I couldn't ever corral you. I knew when we got married I would be alone but I didn't know how alone that would be.*

Ned read it over, several times.

When he had looked at it enough, he yelled, "Noooooo," loud enough to fill the house. He kicked the canoe, sending it crashing into a table lamp. The light bulb exploded.

Slowly, he walked to his deck and looked across the fields. It was a clear night, balmy and moist.

After some time, he walked through the empty house;

the early silence had grown immeasurably with the dark.

He had started crying before he called Gail.

"She left, Gail."

"What?"

"She took the kids."

"Where'd she go?"

"I don't know. She just took the kids and their clothes. She left the station wagon."

"Are you at home, Ned?"

"Yes."

"I still don't know what's going on. Your wife left—she wants a divorce?"

"She took off and said she wouldn't tell me where because I might get violent. She's right. I would hurt him bad. I'd hurt him." He was crying openly now, and swearing.

"God, Ned. I'm coming over."

His answer wasn't coherent.

"Where do you live?"

Ned's lack of sleep wasn't noticed by Ann or Sheryl. They welcomed him back and asked about his trip.

"I'm expecting a call from Amos Beardsley."

"Are you being sued?" Ann asked.

"He's just calling."

Ned walked into the lab and drank two coffee cups of water. His hand shook as he put down the cup. Mrs. Sorenson was waiting with her fourteen-year-old son, Tad. The boy's asthma had worsened since he went to camp. He was brought home early.

Ned listened to the back of the boy's chest. To counter his tiredness, he asked brief questions.

There were some wheezes in the chest, the sound of pigeons cooing; a shot of epinephrine and an increase in his medication would take care of it.

Ned put a note on the chart, stopped it halfway through and stared at the wall.

"We had a bad go-about with the people at the camp,"

Mrs. Sorenson said. "The camp counselor said Tad got sick because he wouldn't participate. They made him run an obstacle course. By the time he could get to a phone he could hardly breathe. They told us it was all in his head."

Ned looked at the boy's chart.

"Will you write a note saying it wasn't in his head? Tad will feel better and we can get a refund from the camp."

"Sure," Ned said. He left the room.

Amos Beardsley didn't return his call until after ten. Ned closed the door to his inner office and took the phone.

"Now what is this business, Ned?"

"Win left. She took the kids."

"She go on a trip?"

"She left me—the house. She ran off. With Johnny."

"This isn't the truth and you know it. Are you getting back at me for that speech I made at Rotary?"

"She left. I'm serious. She took off."

There was a pause. "Did she file?"

"File what?"

"For divorce?"

"Hell, no. She never talked about divorce."

"Where'd she go?"

"She left a note and said she wouldn't tell."

"Is this the truth, Ned?"

"What do you think?"

"OK. Why didn't she tell you?"

"She thought I might get rough, I guess. And she's right. If I find Johnny, I'll bust his nose. I'll do worse, the son of a bitch. She took my kids."

"Whatever you do, Ned, and this is legal advice, don't hurt anybody."

He scratched the top of his desk with a letter opener. "I can't. Right now."

"Hold on and calm down. That's the first thing."

"Then what happens? I want my kids back and damn quick."

"That may prove difficult—if you don't know where they are."

Ned was insistent. "I want you to find them for me."

A man of action, often impatient, Ned was accustomed to working rapidly, analyzing information, categorizing possibilities, then acting directly without delay. His practice consisted of young and active people, working men and women, farmers, children. He preferred to care for acute illnesses and injuries, infections and fractures and lacerations, problems which, even if complex, could be tackled with immediacy and corrected. Chronic illnesses bored him: the elderly slowly dying of senility, bodies decaying from incurable causes. To compensate, he had learned an easy bedside manner with these people, talking of families and joking, treating them with a style as much as with medicine.

"Wait— I can help, but I'm a lawyer. How can I find them if they're lost?"

"That's why I'm calling you."

"Have you called the police or the sheriff?"

"You're the only person I told. I don't want people to know about it. And don't call our locals, either police or sheriff. Corky Furman couldn't do anything if he tried and I don't want the sheriff to know."

"They're our law enforcement people. We got to start somewhere."

Ned couldn't think for a moment. He had never been comfortable with the mainstream of society; however benignly, he had been a delinquent as a child. He had shied away from the self-assured in medical school who worked unquestioningly and with confidence toward a future of status and money. He lived in Spring Falls, working diligently, yet he wasn't a part of any club or group or circle. He had felt kinship during the Vietnam protest days when he joined students and faculty in the comfort of action and rebellion and cause. He was a part of them.

"Look, Amos. I almost didn't even call you. I thought about it a lot last night. I want to know one thing. Is what I say to you confidential? Can I say the truth?"

"Just like yourself, Ned. I wouldn't come into your office and expect you talkin' about it."

Ned toyed with the letter opener as if he was going to throw a dagger, then grabbed the blade in his hand and shook it as he talked. "Carlisle Butis would laugh his ass off about this. He's worthless as a sheriff; besides, he still remembers the day I was with the students when they gave him the finger. He still blames me. He'd laugh his ass off. Understand?"

"He thinks more of you than that, Ned. No one in this town has a bad word for you, including Carlisle."

Frustrated, Ned became frantic. "Can you call the FBI for me?"

"Hold on, Ned. The FBI won't get messed up with this."

"She kidnapped my kids. With Johnny!"

"I'm not sure about that. Kidnapping. I'd have to think about that for a minute."

Ned dropped the letter opener on his desk. "What else is it?"

"They're her children."

"They're my children," Ned screamed.

"The law is funny about these things."

"It's simple. She kidnapped my kids and I want them back."

Ann knocked persistently at his door. He told her to come in. "I'm sorry, Doctor. But it's a mess out there. The rooms are full, the waiting room is full and you have to put an IUD in Kathie Humphries."

"I'll be out in a minute." He waved her away. "Amos. You're a lawyer. Call the FBI and state police."

"I can check with the bank and see if he transferred accounts."

"Don't call the bank! I don't want anybody to know. Arlen Jenson—his wife—I don't want them to know."

"What if the FBI can't help?"

"Call them. They have a missing persons bureau. They can get police to track 'em down."

"Win isn't a criminal."

Ned stared at a black-and-white photograph of himself hanging on the wall. It was taken on a tennis court; he was standing in front of the net, posing with a racket in his hand like a pro ready to hit a winning volley. Aggressive. "She kidnapped my kids."

"Maybe I should look for some precedents. I don't do this every day, Ned."

"Get her back. Soon."

His desk was orderly. Every day Ann brought the mail and the two hurried through the paper work: answering insurance company requests, completing physical exam forms, sorting through junk mail and unsolicited journals. Ned looked at his desk as though he could find an answer beneath a stack of medical journals or within some patient's file. His only picture of his children was a small Polaroid print, poorly focused, tacked on the wall. There were no answers in his office. He phoned Gail.

"I've been waiting all morning," she said. "Did you have any luck?"

"I talked to the lawyer. He said he'd try and help."

"Did he have any good ideas?"

"No."

"It might be simplest to call around. Surely somebody knows what's going on. Ned, I keep pushing away thoughts that I brought this on you. I feel terrible. But I don't think she left with this guy on a whim. From what you say about her it doesn't make sense. Somebody in this town should know what's happened. Two people can't keep that many secrets quiet."

"I don't want to call around. I want the FBI to find them and bring them back. All I want is her and the kids back."

"Do you love her that much?"

Ned was about to lean on his elbow; her question stopped him completely. He didn't answer or move. He was thinking of an answer to another question, one that needn't be asked. It upset him that Gail didn't understand something so very simple: It was quiet in the house without the children. "We're a family. They're my kids."

"What if the FBI can't help? Then you'll have to break down and start checking things out yourself."

"That's why I called the lawyer."

"I have an idea if he knew anything he would have let you know."

"That's what he gets paid for."

"Where do you think she went?"

"I don't know."

"Maybe we should start with why she left. You were so upset last night I didn't want to get into it. I kept thinking I was the reason. Do you know why she left? Did she seem unhappy, did she talk about leaving or getting a divorce?"

It didn't take much to perceive obvious flaws with his marriage, yet his judgment had been faulty; none of the clues pointed to Win's leaving. It didn't make any sense to him at all. "She never said a thing. She seemed happy to me."

"Not even a hint of dissatisfaction?"

"Not much."

"And this man Johnny. What about him?"

"You met him on the Fourth of July. He wanted to play tennis. He's a simpleton. He runs the Gambles store."

"That's the person! There was something petulant about him."

"He's a dope."

"Why would she run off with someone like that? He doesn't have anything. He's not as good-looking, as smart, as alive. He probably doesn't have as much money. Were you mean to her, Ned? Did you yell at her?"

Ann knocked again. She entered without permission,

laden with charts and messages. "Doctor, I hate to push you, but things are a complete mess out there." She dropped the pile of papers on his desk. He took little notice. "Doctor, please," Ann insisted.

"OK. I'll be right there."

"Ned, I don't think talking to that lawyer is enough. We should sit down and work through this. You seem to think it isn't real, like she's a person who attempts suicide but doesn't go through with it. Maybe there's something going on and she's really going to do it—go a long ways away, hide out. Hey! You told me she talked about Wales. God. She wouldn't pull that number, would she?"

"No. How could she?"

"You should be doing a lot of things, Ned. Calling people. Checking your hometown. People might know something there. Did she ever work? Maybe she went someplace where she worked before. Ned, you need to know some facts."

His impatience and her prodding made him irritated. His voice became sharp and defensive. Everything was simple and logical in his mind except the reality itself. Gail asked questions like an outsider and he didn't want to admit his worst fear: of again becoming a delinquent, an alien, a cripple in the eyes of his patients and, worse yet, in the minds of the self-assured who ran the city. His reply was simple. "I don't want people to know. I can't call around."

"So what if people know?"

"Not here. Not with me."

"Is it because you're a doctor? People understand, Ned."

"I'm different. I don't play games like a doctor."

"I know it hurts. I'm sorry, Ned. But you shouldn't be working today. All you did last night was talk about your kids. If they mean that much, you should take off work and get busy finding them. I'll do everything I can to help."

"I can't take off work. The waiting room is full now. What would they do if I left?"

"They'd probably survive quite well. If they're terribly sick, another doctor can see them; if not, they'll wait."

"I can't leave."

"You have to. You don't have a choice."

Sheryl interrupted him this time. She waved a packaged intrauterine device and beckoned with a finger. "Hang up the phone. You've talked longer today than you do in a year. We'll put in this IUD, then I'm going to put track shoes on you. We've got twenty patients scheduled and it's ten-thirty already."

"I'll call you back, Gail."

"Leave if you can."

He hung up and Sheryl pulled on his arm. "Doctor, you were talking to a woman. You can get in trouble doing things like that. By the way, how was San Francisco? Foggy?"

Ned inserted an IUD into Kathie Humphries' uterus. His hand shook as he pushed the plunger of the 10 cc glass syringe when injecting Xylocaine into the cervix. He told her she would feel pain. Her cervix was clamped with a tenaculum, a long clamp with two sharp pincher teeth. It pierced her flesh and blood oozed from the puncture sites.

"Here." Sheryl put a uterine sound in front of his face.

He sounded the uterus for depth, then slid the piece of plastic and copper into the womb. Kathie complimented him. It didn't hurt much at all.

Ned worked as fast as he could. He did well until he saw Kristen Waylen, daughter of Tom Waylen, pastor of the First Baptist Church. Kristen was a thin child, pretty, pale, the skin of her face lacking the flush of vitality. She had a sore throat.

He looked at her with a face so somber as to be disconcerting to the child. He asked questions quickly. How long? How sore? All the time looking, staring through the

child, eyes out of focus. Her father's church was for poor
people, the Baptists. It smelled of poverty like an old pen-
sioner's house. Looking past dried wax, he saw gray ear-
drums. Her mouth wasn't reddened, but there was green
mucus coming from her sinuses. He swabbed the mucus
and put it into a glass tube. He remembered the water-
spotted picture of Christ above the altar.

"It's probably not strep. It's your sinuses. Have you had
a cold?"

Amos Beardsley phoned at eleven-thirty. Eight patients
remained.

"Any luck?" Ned asked the attorney.

"I called the regional FBI office. They can't help."

"Why? They get involved in kidnapping."

"It's not kidnapping. It's called a family squabble. They
won't take sides."

"What she did is illegal, isn't it?"

"Sort of. But not really."

"That's crap, Amos. Bullshit. She stole my kids. That's
illegal."

"The law says they are her kids. Possession is nine tenths
of the law. She's got them."

"She took my kids and she's with another man. What's
that called—when you're married and you live with someone else?"

"Bigamy. That's being married to two people. And how
do you know that Johnny isn't merely driving her someplace? That's legal. I don't think Win would up and take
off with another man, Ned. Not Win. And Johnny isn't
the kind to join in on something like that."

After his return from San Francisco, well past midnight
and after reading Win's letter many times, Ned had
torn the pages in half, crushing them in his hands. Later,
during a moment of calm, Gail, aware of the need for
evidence, retrieved the pages, smoothed them and folded

them carefully. He had obligingly put them into his bill-fold, behind larger bills, the pages creating a thick bulge. Now he said, "You can look at the note she left."

"When was it written?"

"I don't know. Before she left."

"Then you don't know how long she's been gone."

"I left Friday and got back Sunday. Sometime in be-tween."

"They could be almost anywhere."

Ned turned toward his window. Outside, two men in overalls and caps advertising the same brand of seed corn were talking, pointing in earnest at something or someone out of Ned's vision. "Isn't there a missing per-sons bureau?"

"People aren't technically missing after a few days. And they usually look for people where foul play is implied. You know, if life insurance is pending or something like that."

"How do I find her then?"

"Like I said. Start asking. Somebody's got to know something, Ned."

"You mean you can't call somebody and get them look-ing?"

"You could hire a private detective, but they'd begin asking people the same questions as you and I."

Ned looked at his watch, stood, and paced the floor as far as the phone cord would allow. "I said I don't want that. To me it's simple. They took off in his car. The car has a license plate on it. Somebody can tell the highway patrol to look for them. Once they catch them they have to come home."

"Do you know they took his car?"

"They didn't take the station wagon."

"Maybe they flew. Did you check the airlines?"

"I didn't check anything. That's not my job. That's why I called you."

"Ned. I can check local airlines. I can call the highway

patrol in this state. But they've had at least two days and could be anywhere. What if they flew to Denver, got in a taxi, bought a car and took off for Utah? Who do we call, Ned?"

Ned grabbed the chipped plastic handle of the letter opener, felt its dull edges and, for an instant, had the letter opener been a knife with a sharp edge, would have cut the phone cord. "If they were sick, I'd know what to do. If I couldn't do it myself, I'd know who could."

"Ned, this isn't a simple legal problem. Until we know more there may not be a legal problem at all. Right now it's a detective job. I can help, but you have to help, too. Call your hometown. Have someone there look for his car. Talk to people she knows. And get off your high horse."

"You call the highway patrol. I'll check with you right after lunch."

The last patient was a nine-year-old boy with pain in his lower abdomen. If it was appendicitis, Ned would have to operate over the noon hour. He concentrated as best he could. "Take him home. Don't give him anything by mouth. Watch him for three hours. If the pain is still there or if it's worse, bring him back to the office."

Gail offered to bring him a ham sandwich; he refused. He briefed her on the morning's events.

"That lawyer isn't going to do you any good. A smart lawyer knows the information you want. I think you're right; there must be a way of finding people. She's taken the most American solution: Leave your problems and go somewhere. It used to be out west. We have a basic freedom—split and leave everything behind. Do you have any idea where on God's green earth she may have gone?"

"No."

"Then we have to do like the man says and start looking ourselves. You don't want people to know. How long do you think it will take people to find out? There are probably people who know right now. They won't keep quiet. This isn't like Nixon and the White House gang. People won't clam up for party loyalty or political power. They'll talk."

"Why do they have to know?"

"Why are you so afraid? A terrible thing happened. You didn't do it. She's guilty. You and the kids are innocent. People can figure that out. Is it being a doctor? Is that why?"

"I was a rebel when I was a kid. I don't know why. I was in trouble a lot. In a small town you're pegged for life. At least I ended up in medical school. When you're a kid like that, you learn something. You're different, not like the banker's son. Other people have their place. For me it was knowing that if I did something wrong people would say, 'We knew it all the time.'"

"What you're saying is nonsense. You're not a kid anymore. This is a different place. I'm sure people love you. They'll support you."

"You don't understand."

"That's not true. I do. I deal with people all the time, alive and dead. You're not so different from them. The problem is, Ned, you don't know the truth—or you won't face it." Gail suddenly brought her hand to her forehead. "Wait a minute. That story about the bonnie rats. Either her old man laid a curse on you or you're living out some self-fulfilling prophecy. So you were a bad-ass kid. You aren't now. Look. You have one hell of a problem. Finding her may only be the first. You may face a divorce and that's rough even without kids. You're going to need help —from if you'll take it. From other people. Is there anyone else besides me you can talk to now?"

"About this?"

"Yes."

"No one."

"You don't have a single friend you can talk to?"

"Not about this."

"That's not right. How long have you lived here? What do you hide from people?"

"My patients are my friends."

"You can't talk to them. I think you give too much and hide too much. I don't understand a damn thing about your marriage and why she left. Did you ever talk to her, confide in her?"

"I don't have any big secrets to talk about."

"You do now. You've got some debts to collect from the people here. You'd better start now."

"I can't."

"Then you're stuck waiting until she decides to contact you. She's holding all the cards."

Ned's office was located at the end of the business district, a four-block section facing Denby Street. The solid block of buildings was built between 1889 and 1929. Had they survived fires and postwar face lifting, the area would be a historic monument. The Gambles store was located in a building which was three stories tall and crowned with Grecian stonework dating from 1903. Fancy brickwork outlined each upper-story window. Ned parked his car and walked along Denby Street to the store. As he approached, he saw windowpanes reflecting patches of dust. A hanging sign and ad posters cluttered the storefront. A sign on the door was visible from across the street. When he saw it Ned crossed the street, dodging a car. Paint was cracking on the old wooden door. The sign was askew, suspended on a string. CLOSED.

His first call was to Byron. The surgeon was checking out of the hospital.

"You got a few minutes, Byron?"

"Probably more than you, my friend."

"I've got something serious to talk about."

"You usually do."

"I got trouble," Ned said. "Myself. I need to know something. Do you know anything about Win and Johnny? Do you know if they have been seeing each other?"

"I know what I've heard."

"Tell me."

"They're friends. That's about it."

"Where did you hear this?"

"From the nurses. Listen. I haven't heard much."

"What did they say?"

"Every now and then I hear something. Not much. They go for walks together. Someone said something about them going to church together."

"Is that all?"

"I heard they go to movies, to the matinee."

"When did you hear this?"

"Every now and then I hear something. Not lately."

"Why didn't you tell me?"

"I never paid any attention to it."

"They took off together. With the kids."

"Oh, no. That's terrible." Byron stopped talking and there was a silence. "I don't know what to say—Ned—how on earth—?" Again he paused. "I feel terrible about this. Ned"—Byron's voice became composed and direct—"You can't practice medicine at a time like this. My schedule isn't bad this week. Why don't I take over for you? You shouldn't be in the office. I'll see your patients. I won't be as good as you, but it'll give you time. You need time to straighten things out."

"I'll take care of things. I can handle it."

"You have to respond to people. How can you do that?"

"I'm doing it."

"I don't make it a practice of worrying about other people's lives. But I'm keeping my schedule light. I'll come over and work in your office any time. Okay?"

Ned's first afternoon patient had been waiting over an hour. The man had lacerated the back of his hand on a rough piece of metal. Though it wasn't deep and didn't involve a tendon, the wound was filthy. Ned would have to trim the wound edges. He injected local anesthetic and asked Sheryl to get the smallest scissors she could find. Small bits of skin along the wound edge were tattooed with dirt and rust. Ned trimmed them away. The cut was shaped like a bent twig. Ned didn't talk to the man.

"He's doing a good job," Sheryl told the patient.

"Dumb thing to do. I wasn't looking," the man said.

When all the soiled flesh was gone, Ned played with the wound edges to see how they would come together. He asked for medium-strength surgical nylon. "Tell Ann to keep it light this afternoon. Have her cancel as many as possible."

"We'll try, Doctor."

After caring for the wound, he called Amos.

"Go ahead and check around. I don't care. Check with Corky and Carlisle and the bank. Do what you can."

Ann went over a list of patient requests with him, mainly phone requests for medication refills. He okayed them. "Can you cancel many appointments?"

Ann shrugged. "I'll try. But you know—I'll try. People aren't that easy to talk to."

Gail apologized for letting the phone ring so long. "I was looking through my stuff for an address."

"I took your advice."

"Which advice?"

"I told the lawyer to check around. I called Byron, the surgeon I told you about. He says that Win and Johnny have been doing things together for a long time."

"What is the lawyer going to check?"

"Local police. The bank."

"That's good. Johnny owns a business, doesn't he? If he's skipping town, he has to do something with that."

"I'll find out."

"Ned. I'm going to call this guy who was my attorney out east. I think he deals with this kind of thing a lot. He might have some advice. The more I think about this the more I worry. Since the women's movement a lot of women have run away. A lot of them don't show up for a long time. It's hard to completely disappear but it can be done if you're smart enough and desperate enough."

"I don't know what she's up to."

"You won't until you talk to her. In the depression a lot of people took off and became hobos. Young women did this, too. One girl was riding under a freight car in the cold. She couldn't hold on and was killed."

Ned laughed. "That's the kind of reassurance I get from a teacher."

"I'm sorry. That was heavy."

"We know she isn't a hobo."

Ann was able to cancel eight appointments. Even with that they were behind schedule. Ned did the initial exam on Monica Alden before doing a pelvic exam. She asked that he look for bumps on the left side of her vagina. He left the room and Sheryl moved her into stirrups for the exam.

Ann caught Ned in the hallway. "There's someone I think you should see right away. I'll put him in your office."

Arlen Jenson, the banker, sat waiting. Ned closed the door.

"I came over as soon as I could," Arlen said. "Amos called me and asked me to check some things about Johnny. He told me what happened."

Ned looked at the man in his madras sports coat.

"According to our accounts, Johnny took two thousand dollars out of a savings account and bought traveler's checks for that amount. I gave that information to Amos. Then I came here. Ned, this is a bad thing for you and I want you to know I'll do everything under my power to help. I told Amos, 'This is a good community and we take care of each other.' I can't believe this happening to you, but I guess it must have. If Johnny really means to leave for good, he'll have to move some money sooner or later. He had a respectable account with us. I told Amos and I'm telling you that it's illegal for me to give private banking information but there are some things I can hedge

174) Anthony Owen Colby

on, like where money goes, account numbers, nature of any transaction. Amos told me you didn't want anyone to know. I appreciate your concern and I'll keep my mouth shut. My wife and I have a lot of respect for you. You put a lot of energy into this small city. You're your own man and people appreciate that. I won't keep you any longer, but I want you to know I'll do anything, including looking sideways at some minor legal technicalities. And if there's anything you need—money, loans, use of our equipment, access to our credit research service—for whatever reason, you ask."

The banker left. Ned remained in his chair, doodling with a pencil. He was deep in thought when he heard Sheryl's voice. "There you are! I knew you were hiding somewhere. We left Monica in the stirrups half an hour ago! You'd better be super nice to her because she thinks she has something yukky."

Ned identified Monica's venereal warts and treated them with podophyllum. He removed his gloves and told Sheryl that he wanted to talk to her and Ann when the schedule was completed.

They finished at six. "Get some coffee and come on back to my office."

He told them what had happened.

"Oh, Doctor, I'm sorry," Ann said. "We knew something was wrong, but not anything like that. And I'm sorry for bitching like I did. I didn't know— You know how people are used to coming in. We've spoiled them."

Sheryl's face was as sad as Ned's. "Did she give any warning?"

Ned shook his head.

"She doesn't seem like a person to do that," Sheryl said. "That's dumb. If I had a setup like hers, I wouldn't give it away. Excuse me, Doctor, but I can't understand a woman doing that."

"Should we close the office?" Ann asked.

"What do you mean?"

"Why don't we close for a week? People will get along.

Doctor, we'll take care of things here. Oh, you must feel terrible."

"Let us take care of things," Sheryl said.

"What would I do if I didn't show up?"

"Sounds like you have lots of things to do."

"I can do it here. I'll go nuts if I sit around that damn house. I'm not used to not having people around. I'm better off here."

"You sure?" Ann insisted.

"Keep the schedule light. That'll be enough."

"Do you want us to come over and help at your house?" Sheryl asked. "Why don't we come over? At least we could keep you company. I can't cook but you know that."

Ned stopped off and bought beer and cigarettes on his way to Gail's. When he arrived, she put a frozen pizza in the oven and they drank beer.

"I called Syracuse and spoke to my attorney. He suggests you consult another attorney. I asked him if he knew any in the area and he recommended a woman in Des Moines, Emily Hart. He met her at a workshop and said he was impressed. I couldn't get in touch with you after the call, so I went ahead and called her office. I made an appointment with her at eleven-thirty tomorrow morning. They will change the time if you can't make it. I think you should go, Ned."

"Do you think it will help? Amos seems to know what to do."

"Which isn't much, is it? Maybe she won't help, but you're up against the wall."

"Did I tell you? I talked to the banker. Johnny took two thousand out of a savings account and bought traveler's checks."

"Were you embarrassed talking to him?"

"He was very nice. He offered his help. It's good business for him to do that."

"What did he say?"

"He came over to the office. He said he was sorry. He said his wife and he respected me—I'm my own person."

"Look, Ned. That was a very kind gesture. That's more than good business. I'm sure he meant what he said. Give some of these people a chance. You underestimate them."

"I'm different from them."

"So am I. Born that way. So what?" They were sitting at the dining room table. Gail moved her chair next to him and took his hands, stroking them softly, touching his fingers, each individually. While she was doing this, she looked at him, his impassive face which stared at the beer cans on the table. Taking one of his hands, she lifted it to her mouth; she kissed it and rubbed the back of his hand against her cheek. "I know exactly what you're talking about. The chairman of my department is straight as a bird. He was shocked when I swore. So what? You're a very private person. In your office you're a performer—more than you are everybody's friend. We all have myths about ourselves; they're important. Herbert Hoover believed himself to be a great humanitarian because of the Belgian relief fund. A lot of people think of him differently. You think you're a destructive kid while every piece of evidence"—she pointed a finger to the sky—"every single piece of evidence says that Dr. Owen is a healer and a softie, not the child terror from a small coal mining town in Iowa. And besides that, you're smoking."

"I haven't had a cigarette in ten years. Other than making me a little dizzy, it tastes like I thought it would. Damn."

"I smoke in binges. Once every three or four months I go three or four days and usually burn out my lungs. It's my manic-depressive gig."

They forgot the pizza until the crust was burned. Ned ate two pieces and returned to beer and cigarettes.

"Is there anything you're supposed to be doing tonight? Do you have to call the lawyer?"

"Nothing to do but drink beer. He'll call me if there's any news." They moved to an open porch and drank in silence for a long time.

His radio went off and he made a phone call.

"Was that the attorney?"

"Poison ivy."

After a visit to the bathroom, Ned had an idea. "I want to make a visit. There is someone who might know something. The Baptist preacher. You want to come along?"

"I'll go for the ride and sit in the car."

Tom Waylen lived in a small house near the furniture factory. It was past sundown when Ned arrived. The night was clear and humid. In the far distance there was a bank of clouds and occasional heat lightning. Gail sat in the car as Ned knocked.

The preacher came to the door. Ned asked if they could talk outside.

"Do you know what happened?" Ned asked.

"No," Tom Waylen said kindly.

"Two of your church people took off together. Johnny and my wife, Win."

The preacher's head dropped. He didn't speak.

Tom Waylen and Ned stood on the sidewalk. A porch light outlined them; Tom was taller, but with a soft and noticeable belly. Ned was bent forward, moving his hands from his thighs to his face to his chest, like a baseball coach giving signals in slow motion. Their voices carried well into the night. Gail had no difficulty hearing them. She smelled the leather of Ned's car and freshly mown grass—smells of comfort which now defined her role as spectator, captive in his car.

"Do you know anything about it?" Ned asked.

"No—"

"They took my kids, too."

"Where?"

"Hell only knows, Reverend."

"I didn't know this."

"What can you tell me about Johnny and Win? Everyone says they sat side by side in your church holding hands. That right?"

"Of course not. They are among the saved, the children of God."

"Must be a good religion they got, runnin' off together with my kids. They're saved all right. They're lucky to be saved from the FBI right now."

They had moved in a semicircle, exchanging places, Ned now closer to the house and Tom nearer Gail. They stopped talking for a moment and Gail looked upward to the sky, full with stars.

"Are you sure of what you're saying?" the preacher asked.

"I want to know what you know about them. Did you know they had a thing going? Did you tell you about their plans?"

"They were good friends who sought the peace of Christ together, Ned. They are like lambs, innocent children. Life wasn't easy for either of them. I know that much. If they left, it was in fear."

"Fear of what for God's sake?"

"You."

"Bullshit!"

"God's ways are difficult."

"You mean you think what they did was good? Is that what you preach in that church of yours?"

"I have talked to your wife. She bore a heavy cross. I know you're a good man, but you refuse to worship God. You curse in front of your own children. You leave the burden of their rearing to her. You respect money more than God's laws and the family."

Ned stepped closer. The preacher stepped away, onto the grass. Gail was ready to jump out of the car. "You son of a bitch! You bastard! You're a two-bit Jesus peddler. My wife runs off with this nincompoop and you praise God and blame me. They've been playing stink finger in the back pew of your church for years and you never bothered to tell me this before. She never bothered to tell me anything. That woman took off, man, she ran away with another man. That's sin! You say there was trouble in my house and you didn't bother to let me know. If I didn't have to fix you up, I'd bust your ribs right now."

"You've been drinking."

"Not enough."

"When you sober up, you might listen to reason. That woman carried a burden."

"I may never sober up, 'cause if God's word is being spread around by assholes like you, there ain't a chance in hell for someone like me."

Tuesday, July 27

Ned parked his car, removed a bottle of Maalox from his glove compartment, took two large swigs to ease his heartburn, stowed the bottle and found his way to the new attorney's office.

Emily Hart was tall, wore a tailored jump suit and offered Ned coffee. He lit a cigarette. As he smoked, she outlined the facts as she knew them.

"You had no warning?"

"No."

"She hadn't mentioned dissolution—divorce?"

"No."

"She left with your children and another man with no indication of where she went?"

Ned showed her the note.

The attorney donned huge eyeglasses and read. Sitting back, toying with her glasses, she said, "I think we have trouble."

Ned sipped his coffee.

"Your children are how old?"

"Eight and ten."

"What are their names?"

"Lizzy—she's eight—and Ellie."

"Elizabeth and Eleanor? Very British."

"Welsh."

"Are you first generation?"

"My wife is."

"She's in a very select minority. That's neither here nor there. Tell me, what are we going to do?"

"I don't know."

"Perhaps, then, I should tell you what you can and can't expect from me. That's only fair. I am an attorney. I can represent you in all formal legal matters. I am modestly experienced in situations like yours. I have uniformly found these predicaments difficult, emotionally draining and frustrating. You may spend a lot of money for a result you won't like. Let's back up a minute. Do you mind telling me what you want? If you could have your wish, this moment, what would it be?"

"To have my wife and kids home."

"Not only your kids?"

"Sure."

"In other words, you don't want a divorce?"

"Why should I?"

"You don't find fault with your marriage?"

"Not that much."

"Your wife seems to feel differently. If I read the note correctly, she seems to be quite lonely and afraid. You, obviously, don't share her feelings. Did she seem lonely and afraid to you?"

"Not at all."

"Let's look at a few things. You are a doctor. I presume you have a busy practice. How busy are you?"

"I work from ten to fourteen hours a day."

"Weekends?"

"Four to six hours a day, I suppose."

"That's a lot of time spent away from home."

"I'm in and out of the house. I'm not really away."

"Your wife doesn't seem to agree."

"She has plenty to do. She used to work and didn't like it all that much."

"Perhaps her work wasn't as enjoyable as yours. What did she do?"

"Sold furniture in a large store."

"Sounds less rewarding than medicine. But there's something I want to get at: Here's a woman who left home —that's a big step—and she never voiced complaints to you?"

Ned lit another cigarette. "No. Oh, maybe, but not much."

"I'll give it to you as best I can. Your situation is one in which your wife never dared communicate discomfort or negative emotions. I don't know why. To solve her dilemma she took this drastic action. This indicates a very poor prognosis, quite frankly. A lot of women in her situation would have demanded a long vacation or taken a job or solved the problem in some other way. Your wife left and burned all bridges, kaput. I would be surprised if your wish is ever a reality. You may get your children, with a struggle. But I doubt if that woman will ever come back. Am I being overly harsh?"

"I don't know."

"My powers of prediction are human, not occult. Let's talk about what we can do today. First of all, her taking the children is legal; it may be underhanded, but it's legal. Your friend who called said you termed it kidnapping. It isn't. How can you get them back? Until this thing is settled, either by her return or by dissolution, your only option is to do what she did—take them. If you locate her, you can take the children and kidnap them back. Your children are at the most difficult age. I would think that they aren't happy with your wife's action, but on the other hand, they probably won't like being kidnapped by you, either. That puts you in a very awkward and delicate position. The law always tries to choose the best situation for a child; a couple in your situation rarely does. Children are de facto property, to be used, transported and manipulated for one or the other parent's psychologic or neurotic needs. Not pleasant, but true. Be advised! You're damned if you do and damned if you don't. Any remedy comes at great cost and pain. Would you like more coffee?"

She interrupted the session for a minute. Ned followed her movements silently.

"There you go. Our coffee bill in this office is huge. Deductible. So you're faced with the proposition, to kidnap or not to kidnap. You'll no doubt struggle with that for a good, long time. Our other problem is finding her. This will depend on how badly she wants to remain hidden. From your note it appears she intended to do this temporarily. That could be one week to a year. I need the following information. If you don't have it, you can call me with it. Do you know her social security number?"

"No."

"Her age?"

"Thirty-three."

"I'll need a picture, color preferred. On the back, list her height, weight, identifying marks such as scars, previous surgery, the like. Any measurements would be helpful. Are you aware of any close friends who she might seek— friends away from your hometown?"

"No."

"Has she ever openly daydreamed about one place—like the beaches of Florida—romantic or scenic places?"

"When I was in Vietnam, she took the kids to the Holiday Inn at Sedalia, Missouri."

"I'll check it out. I want you to think carefully of any place she might choose, for any reason, to go. She left with another man, correct?"

"Yes."

"I need his social security number, a picture of him with

the same information. Did your wife take money or traveler's checks?"

"I don't know."

"Check this out immediately. Oh, I need pictures of your children. This man owned a store, or did he lease it?"

"I think he owns it."

"What kind of store?"

"A Gambles store."

"If he plans to sell it, he must, I think, go through their main office. Most franchise contracts have that stipulation. I'll locate the main office and ask if his store is for sale and if so, how I might contact him. I think this is our best bet. Unless he's willing to take a sustained financial loss, he'll be selling the place. The second he makes his move, we'll locate him. On the other hand, if he doesn't move, we're stuck."

She answered a phone call and took a note.

"You might wonder why all the questions. I use a private service, the Runaway Wife Locator Bureau. It's a fairly new outfit, to meet the needs of recent social changes. A lot of women do like your wife. Many, unlike your wife, leave the children. The service uses social security numbers along with a private detective service. They've been quite successful, though, realize, it takes time. Our best bet is this man's store. As far as cost, we're in for a minimum of one to three thousand dollars. I presume you're willing to pay this?"

"Yes."

"We'll go ahead, then. I'm sure I forgot a few questions. Can I call your office if need be? Fine. My last bit of advice is this: Prepare yourself for the worst. Your wife left you no option to do otherwise."

Late that afternoon Ned and Gail drove to a truck stop on the Interstate. Returning, Ned stopped and bought a bottle of Scotch. He asked Gail if she would join him at his house. She refused.

"I have this thing about houses right now, especially houses I didn't choose to live in. I'll get over it someday. I feel much more comfortable at my place."

Halfway through the bottle of Scotch and after one pack of cigarettes, Gail asked, "Where do I fit in, Ned? In a couple of weeks I'll be done and supposedly headed for Brown University. Actually, I don't need to be there until after the first of September. Do you need me here— do you want me here?"

"You're like me," he said, "if you don't have work, you go nuts. You can't give up your job."

"Who's going to take care of you?"

Ned held the Scotch bottle high. "Johnny Walker."

"You've been done in by one Johnny; two is too many."

"Who says I need taking care of? I haven't so far."

"Liar! Such lies you tell about yourself! You're a little baby. With lots of baby-sitters. Every time I call your office I hear a voice taking care of you. I'm sure it's the same way at the hospital. If your damn wife had stayed, there wouldn't be a problem. Ned, why in the hell—fill my glass halfway—did that woman leave you? Was she mentally disturbed? Depressed? Is she a latent tramp?"

"She says she was lonely."

"Aw, shit. Lonely. I'm lonely half the time, but I don't cut off my arm to show it. Some philosopher said something profound about loneliness, but I forgot what it was. Scotch-induced amnesia. You really don't know, huh?"

"Maybe. I got so busy I guess I forgot."

"Forgot what?"

"What it was like before we got married."

"You should remember that easily enough."

"It's easy to forget," he said.

"What is it you're saying?"

"It always made sense for me to marry her. Ever since I met her. I never thought much about other women. She was the opposite from me. I always wanted to be nice to people, but I didn't act that way—not until I grew up, I guess. She was always kind to people. In a special way. Never selfish, especially the way she talked to people. She used to enjoy talking to people a lot. She made them feel at ease, she talked about what they were doing, made them feel good. She seemed better than other girls, not awkward or silly. It's probably because her folks came from Wales. Sort of like being royalty, the real thing. Her old man wouldn't give an inch to anyone. Talking to him was like petting a mean monkey through the bars of a cage. She was so proper! She refused to be a cheerleader because she didn't want to jump around in front of people." Ned finished another Scotch. Almost as an aside, he said, "But she never wanted to marry me."

"Jesus Christ, Ned! Now you tell me!" Gail pushed her glass away, angered. "Then you knew she'd do this all the time?"

"No. I knew it made sense to marry her, but she kept putting it off. She thought I was too wild, but that was because I knew I wasn't. I thought that if she didn't marry me, she wouldn't marry anyone. So I sort of forced things."

"In other words, she married you because she couldn't think of a way to tell you no?"

"She was also pregnant."

"That's a hell of a way for a marriage to begin. Didn't you wonder right away if it would last?"

"No. I knew she'd settle down. I got the big house and we had the kids. She didn't seem to mind."

"She didn't tell you she was unhappy?"

"Maybe, in her own way. She's a different person. Always seemed happy just fooling around."

Gail filled her glass again.

"But she took off. With this clod. I want to know something. Did she like sex?"

"She liked to play around a lot before Ellie was born. She didn't like to talk about it, though. Then she changed. Sex seemed to scare her."

"Did you ever hurt her?"

"No, but she would sometimes lay without moving, like she was afraid."

"Do you think it was a good marriage?"

"It wasn't bad."

"What did the lawyer in Des Moines say?"

"She told me to expect the worst. The old military theory: Expect the worst and you'll be grateful for anything."

"Why did you take up with me?"

"What?"

"You heard me. You came after me like a starved cat. You may respect my mind, I'm not sure, but it was my body that pulled you away from your doctor world. You were hungry, friend. So was I, but with good reason. Did your wife ever attack you?"

"No."

"In a good relationship the woman should attack, at least now and then."

"You didn't attack me."

"Oh, yes, I did! Without pretense. Did you honestly come to my house for pot roast?"

"Not really."

"Am I bothering you?"

"A little."

"I have to know. I'm learning some things. I have to know. I'm part of this damn thing now. What's Johnny like? He seemed whimpery to me."

"He could be backed away from anything. If the sun was out and I told him it was raining, I could get him to say it was raining in ten minutes."

"Insecure. Is he smart?"

"He went to college for two years."

"Is he fun to be around?"

"For a laugh."

"If he bears the joke?"

"The best time I ever had was when I told him Bobby Riggs and Billie Jean King were starting a semiprofessional league for tennis. He was ready to sign up."

"He's gullible as well." The bottle was empty. "Look in the kitchen. If I don't have Scotch, I know there's beer."

He brought back three cans.

"I'm floating. At least I don't have class until eleven. What time do you have to get up?"

"Seven."

"I hope your first patient has cataracts."

"Why did you say that?"

"It sounded right. Here's mud in your eye." She stood, wobbling a bit. "Let's go barefoot and sit on my rug. I'll play a raga. If you like Bluegrass, you'll like the sitar." They took off their shoes and she rummaged through her records. "I'll play this side." She played the record and waited until the sitar and tabla were playing wildly. When the rhythms and melody were fast and compelling, she began to dance on her rug. She danced slowly, her toes playing against the nap of the rug. She danced a circle around Ned, at times almost losing her balance, aware of her feet, moving them against the softness of the rug. "When I get married again," she said, "this rug will be my wedding bed, and when I die, they'll wrap me in it before they lay me in the cold, wet earth."

"What if you die on the Sahara?"

"So what?"

"It's not cold and wet there."

"It will be someday, said Kurt Vonnegut. The world will turn to Ice Nine." She danced until the end of the record and put on Bach's *Second Partita for Piano*. "This is for people who are too lazy to dance."

She patted her beanbag chair so they could lay their heads against it, side by side.

"I think I'm right about your wife and that guy."

"What do you mean?"

"I figured her out."

"What?"

"Why she ran away with him. It has to do with sex." She caught his big toe between her feet. They stared at the ceiling as Glenn Gould rushed through the andante.

"There is a struggle in a woman that isn't easily resolved. It's a struggle between the devil and the angels. Hey, the preacher would like that! It's like—being raped or raping someone. No, that's not it. Women aren't by nature as passive as people think. That's more like it. In the old days they played out their aggressiveness by 'ploys.' Remember Shakespeare? Women went around devising ploys of one kind or another. This really meant they were horny. The chemistry between your wife and you was wrong. All women like sex. You scared her, so she hugged the angel in her. Angels live on the South Pole. Frigid. Kept the devil away. Understand? Let's split another beer."

Ned struggled to the refrigerator and found two cans. He lay back and she continued.

"I bet I know what happened. She met Johnny, this weak, sniveling, impotent, inadequate dude. A patsy. She couldn't be afraid of him. He was like a puppy dog. So they took up with each other, friends. They went to prayer meetings and held hands at Godzilla movies at the Astro. Like a couple of nymphets. All innocence and propriety. Then the devil-person—how's that? a neutered devil—slowly warmed the cockles of her ovaries. Wait a minute. Do ovaries have cockles?"

He didn't answer.

"She took another look at this creature and knew he couldn't rape her. She was the stronger person. So she seduced him, like a child playing with a baby's cock. She stroked it and played with it until her powers made it grow and get big. It didn't attack her, she made it dance to her tune. That's a heady experience. The devil had his day, Ned."

He didn't reply. She looked to see if he was awake. There was a tear in his eye as he stared through the window.

"I'm sorry. That was cruel. We shouldn't talk serious when we drink so much."

They lay quietly for a long time until the sound of

his radio disturbed them. Ned went to the phone and after a long silence said, "Put him in intensive care. Monitor him and give him lidocaine for PVC's. Give him oxygen and seventy-five of Demerol q 3. Call me if his vitals change."

He returned to her oasis.

"Was that important?"

"Sounds like this guy had a heart attack."

"Shouldn't you go?"

"No— If he gets in trouble, they'll call me."

"Are you afraid to go because we drank so much?"

"He'll be all right."

"Being with you and that radio is sometimes like being around a time bomb ready to go off."

Wednesday, August 4

Ned woke with a hangover. It was past seven, almost eight. He reached to his night stand and found the Maalox. The pain in his stomach made him stop completely for a moment; it irritated his stomach muscles and penetrated to his back. He drank from the bottle, then lit a cigarette. Halfway through the cigarette the pain returned, so he dropped the cigarette into the opening of a beer can and heard it go out when it hit the bottom. He had stayed up late for a storm which lasted past three. The morning was bright and sunny, the humidity being the only reminder of the night's rain. He walked onto his deck in his undershorts. A line of beer cans on the railing offered evidence of his slow retreat from the storm.

He shaved and debated whether or not he should take aspirin. It would help his head but hurt his stomach. He took three. There was a spot on his trousers above the right knee. He didn't have time to find another pair.

He walked over the pile of clothes which had accumulated between the bedroom and the bathroom. As he walked out of the house, his stomach hurt and he was more aware of a headache.

He checked into the hospital, punching 110. The board recorded the number. There were no messages.

He had walked halfway to the elevator when he met T. B. Travis, who was leaving the hospital.

"Hey, I want to talk to you," T. B. Travis said. His voice was like that of a child's recovering from croup— high pitched and hoarse. He wore his black suit and black tie and Rotary pin. He was sixty, his hair was crew cut and black, and his mouth puckered involuntarily in a twitch. Ned had privately accused the county coroner of necrophilia.

They were the same height. Ned wore tan and no tie, no jacket.

"I don't quite know how to say this"—T. B. Travis searched Ned's face as if there were a hole somewhere, which if looked through would free his tongue—"but, ah, well, ah, I've been gettin' some calls at night from patients of yours when they couldn't get a hold of you."

Ned concentrated on breathing slowly, hoping it would calm his stomach. He stared at T. B. Travis' tie; a nosegay of lint clung beneath the knot.

"Hasn't been an awful lot, but there were enough." Travis again explored Ned's face. He labored with his words. "You probably know I got plenty to do on my own."

The operating room nurses and aides walked past them, looking.

"You got family troubles, I hear." T. B. Travis' face didn't change. "I won't make that my business. And I don't mind seein' some of your patients."

Ned's stomach prodded him and he looked at his watch.

"Just one thing," T. B. Travis said. "About you and that car. Sheriff tells me you drive pretty fast, huh? Well, ah" —again he fought to be articulate—"I just wanted to warn you. Don't go drivin' that car so foolish, huh? You could get yourself killed pretty easy." His voice finally caught its cadence. "I can see some of your patients and I never complained gettin' up at night, but I don't need another man's practice. Huh?"

"Sure," Ned said and continued toward the elevator.

Ann greeted Ned at the door of the office. Her face was animated, not searching Ned's but searching from within for words. "Doctor"—her voice approached a croon—"remember that little boy in Holland? You remember him? The little boy. Had to put his finger in the dike. Well, you know what really happened, don't you? Are you catching on? You aren't. Well, I feel like that little boy. All week I sort of put my finger in the dike, but today I goofed. The water pushed my finger out." She looked for a response. "What I'm trying to say is, I'm sorry. The schedule is a mess. People are too good at talking me into things. Just wanted to let you know, OK?"

Ned saw two children who had been treated for a week for ear infections. The second child continued to have a collection of fluid behind one ear. His next patient was Ada Pritchard, his hillbilly lady. She was ninety-seven and had spent her youth in southern Missouri. Once a month she visited. He took her blood pressure from an arm so thin he had to hold the cuff with one hand. Then she slowly unbuttoned the very top button of her dress, like an old curator. Ned dropped the bell of the stethoscope through the opening. He listened a full minute.

"Well. How is it, young man?"

"Good."

"I'm not any worse?"

"The same."

"You sure, young man?"

"Yep."

"Then I guess I spent my money wisely," she said.

As she struggled to button up, she looked at him with sharp eyes. "Say, you ain't lookin' so good today. You know that? Heh, heh, heh. Probably workin' too hard.

When you get to be my age you know better than to ruin your health with foolishness like that. What you need is to get that good-lookin' nurse o' yours to give you a good rubdown with liniment. That'll fix you." She laughed to herself.

Ned was writing a prescription for a man with chronic undifferentiated schizophrenia when Ann shouted and ran the length of the hallway.

"Doctor. Hurry! To your phone." She yanked the door to his examining room open and yelled again, "Hurry."

Ned got up and followed her to his back office.

"The phone." She pointed.

"Hello."

"Daddy. This is Lizzy. Hi. Hi. Ellie and I figured how—"

"Hi, Dad. This is Ellie. How are you? We figured out how to call you. We miss you, Dad. Here, Lizzy wants to say hi again."

"Hi. You didn't call us, so we asked Mom and she said it costed too much but Ellie talked to a big kid who told us how to call free if you say it's OK. Your secretary said it for you. I want to tell you I found a real turtle in a park. We put it in a box and saved it for you. Ellie wants to talk again. Are you coming? We're having a nice trip."

"Dad. How come you didn't come along? Mom says you can't come. She didn't tell us until after we left. Why can't you come?"

Ann stood over Ned. He couldn't answer.

"Are we going to live down here?"

"Where are you?" he asked.

"Galton—Goldenberg. Something like that."

"What state?" He held his hand over the phone, yelling and waving to Ann. "Get a map, a–a–a an atlas. The one you keep up front. Hurry." Ann ran up the hallway.

"Ellie. Can you spell it? Where you're at?"

"I just saw it once."

"Are you staying there?"

"We stopped at a Stuckey's. The phone is by the bathroom. We tried earlier, but Mom said it cost too much but I know you don't mind."

"Is your mom there? Can I talk to her?"

"She's with Johnny. His car broke a hose. We told Mom she should have the station wagon. It wouldn't break."

"Can you ask somebody the name of the town? Let me talk to Lizzy and you find a grown-up who can tell you the name."

Ann returned with the atlas.

Lizzy took the phone. "Oops. The turtle pooped in the box. I fed it part of my hamburger and it ate it. Next time we stay at a Holiday Inn we're going to make it swim. I'm going to scare people with it because some people are afraid of turtles, but not me. I petted it and its head turned sideways and it tried to talk but it couldn't. You'll like it. Are you working today? Mom said you couldn't come because you work so much. That's OK. We'll wait for you."

"Are you all right? You haven't been sick or anything?"

"I cut my finger. It was messy but Johnny put a band-aid on it and made it better."

"Is your mom OK?"

"She's silly. She says we're going to have ducks and a billy goat."

"Do you miss me, honey?"

"Sure, silly."

"I miss you a lot."

"Here comes Ellie. I'll talk to you later."

"Wait a second, Lizzy. You call me any time now that you know how to do it."

"I'll call and tell you if the turtle can swim. Here's Ellie."

"Hi, Dad. It's Gatlinburg. Tennessee. That's where we're at."

"How do you spell it?"

"I don't know. I just asked this man and he told me."

Ned wrote a name as close as he could from her pro-
nunciation: Getlingberg. "Tennessee, Ann. Look for it.
Have you ever heard of it?"

"No, Doctor."

"I miss you, Dad. This is a nice trip and Johnny bought
us stuffed dolls dressed like farmer girls. But I want someone to chase me around like you do and tickle me. Remember the parade we were on and pretended we were
queens? I told Mom about it when Lizzy started waving
at people first."

"We'll have another parade when you get back."

"Are you coming soon?" Ellie asked.

"As soon as I can. Are you staying there tonight?"

"I don't know. If we are, can you come?"

"Yes."

"We better go. I see Mom walking down the road.
She'll get mad at us. Bye."

"Wait, Ellie. Call me again." He was too late. She'd
hung up.

Ann couldn't find Gatlinburg on the map. Ned quickly
looked and failed to see the name. He told Ann to keep
looking as he dialed Amos Beardsley.

"This is Ned. The kids called. From Tennessee. Getlingberg."

"You mean Gatlinburg?"

"Something like that. You know where it is?"

"Right above the Smoky Mountains."

Ned relayed this to Ann.

"What can we do, Amos?"

"Did you talk to Win?"

"No. The kids called collect."

"Are they staying there?"

"I don't think so. Just stopping for repairs."

"I don't know what we can do," Amos said.

"Well, Jesus Christ, somebody in this goddamn town
better start figuring out what to do." He hung up and
found the sheriff's number. A deputy answered. He told

Ned the sheriff was out for a while, maybe having coffee at the Captain's Wheel or maybe he was at the fire station looking at the new truck.

"Call him on your radio."

"Might not do any good."

"Try it, this is an emergency."

"You need an ambulance?"

"I need the goddamned sheriff."

He called Emily Hart in Des Moines. She was at a pretrial hearing. Gail's phone didn't answer.

"Ann. Get in your car and drive around and see if you can find the sheriff. Bring him back right away. Hurry."

Sheryl begged him to see some patients.

"What do we have?"

"Lots, the place is full."

"OK. But you stand outside the room and when you see Ann, you get me, understand?"

"Sure. Let's get going."

Gary Nisley had a rash over his chest. There were numerous flat and scaly circles. Gary drove a hopped-up muscle car and wanted to race Ned.

"This is a type of fungus. *Pityriasis rosea.* It'll go away if you leave it alone about as soon as it will if I give you medicine."

"When you gonna see what that Mercedes will do against a good car?"

"When I want to see you planted in Bluffwood Cemetery."

Sally Anderson, the postmistress, waited for her blood pressure to be checked. She had mild hypertension which responded well to medicine, but she had also developed a massive blood-pressure phobia. During each visit she asked for reassurance five or more times. When she was again reassured, she offered her assistance to Ned.

"I don't know what I can do, Ned, but I'll do it. I'm not above a little peeking in the mailbag, you know. Lord knows, it never hurts to cheat the cheaters."

Ann hadn't returned.

He saw an old farmer with a cold. Ned wrote a prescription.

"Don't I get no shot?" the man growled.

"Don't need one."

"How in the hell will I get better?"

"This pill is twice as powerful as a shot. Something new."

"I always used to get a shot."

"If you want a shot, you go to T. B. Travis. If you want to get better, take this."

Another fifteen minutes passed. Nothing had happened.

He hurried through a one-year checkup on Milly Graem and removed a flat mole from a college student. Sheryl brought back an itinerant highway worker who had asphalt burns on his hands and arms. "Soak them in cold water for a while. He might be a little sore, but they don't look bad."

He heard Ann's voice. She led the leather-faced sheriff to Ned's office.

"Carlisle, my kids phoned from Gatlinburg, Tennessee. Can you call down there and have them arrest Johnny?"

"Not for kidnapping like Amos said."

"What for, then?" Ned asked.

"I don't know, Doc. It's a screwball situation to me."

"The hell it is. You don't know your ass from a hole in the ground. You call the sheriff down there and have him arrest Johnny. They can hold him until I get there."

Ann stood by the door, observing.

"I can't have a man arrested for just anything. That's illegal arrest. Against the law."

"How about car theft? If you won't say he's a kidnapper, you can say he stole a car."

"He's got his own car, doesn't he?"

"All I want is you to call and have them stopped."

"I don't see how I can do it."

"You know what's going to happen if you don't?"

"What?"

"See that woman there. I'm swearing to her and to you that if you don't get your ass in gear and get me some action you'll never win another election in this county. Ever! You call down there. Give them his license number and have him stopped. If you don't, I'll spend all day and all night until I've talked to every Democrat in this county about what kind of a sheriff you are."

The man paled. "OK, Doc."

"And don't worry about Johnny and any false arrests. He'll chicken out of anything.

"OK, Ann. Let's get these patients seen. When you get a moment, call Gail Tamlin. She's either at the college or you can get her number from her record. Tell her to bring me some lunch. I don't want to leave the office this noon."

The last patient walked out of the office at eleven-thirty. Gail was waiting with sandwiches. They sat in his back office, waiting.

"What are you going to do if they catch them?" Gail asked.

"Fly down there. Here. Look at the map. Tell me where's the closest place to fly. I'll call the airlines."

When he had reached the United reservation desk, Gail told him that Chattanooga was the closest city.

He waited as the man checked schedules. Ned could fly out of Des Moines at 2:17 and arrive at Chattanooga 7:35, Eastern Daylight Time. Ned made reservations.

"I hope they find them. God, Ned, how did you feel when you heard the kids' voices?"

"I almost passed out! It was great! They both miss me. They think they're on a vacation. Win told them I couldn't go because I had to work."

"She hadn't told them they're not coming back?"

"I don't think so."

"I hope they catch them."

"If they don't, the sheriff can kiss his job goodbye."

"Would you really make him lose the election?"

"You're damn right."

Gail clapped her hands. "Fantastic! That's the most spirit I've seen in you since San Francisco."

"Wait until you see what I do to Johnny."

"Not murder, I hope."

"One swift kick in the balls."

"How are you going to handle the kids?"

"Easy. Announce that the trip is over and bring them home."

"What if your wife won't cooperate?"

"She will. Don't worry."

"Why don't you continue the trip, Ned? They might like that."

"What do you mean?"

"Take them someplace neat. I bet they'd love Disney World."

"Good. I never thought of that."

At one, Ned called the sheriff's office. Carlisle answered.

"Did you call them?" Ned asked.

"Gatlinburg is in Sevier County. The sheriff will check it out."

"Is he going to call you back?"

"I suppose."

"When did you call him?"

"When I left your office."

"That was over an hour ago. Call now."

"He's got a whole county to check out."

"Call now."

"Doc, I can't be calling down there every few minutes."

"I'm holding this line. You call."

Ned waited five minutes. Telephone equipment hummed.

The sheriff returned to his line. "They checked it out. Someone thinks they saw a car of that description, but it was going toward the park."

"Did they look in the park?"

"It's a national park. Out of their jurisdiction."

"Carlisle, call the park, talk to the rangers."

"I don't know how to do that."

"You ask the operator for the number and you dial it."

He held for another ten minutes.

"They need a federal warrant, Doc. But they said if they saw a car of that description, they'll call back. They'll check camping areas and the lodges. If they locate him, they'll call me. In the meantime, get Amos to figure out a warrant."

Ned bypassed Amos and called Emily Hart. She thought it over and said there was nothing they could do.

"If it's a national park, we have to have a valid reason. Other than adultery, I can't think of a law they've violated and it's almost impossible to pin someone down on adultery without photographs or the like."

"Should I fly down there and take a chance?"

"I wouldn't. They can drive through the park in an hour and be in Atlanta by the time you get there. If the rangers report back that they're staying in the park, then you can go. Your kids will phone again. We'll locate them. At least you have good information. They're in the South. The children miss you. Most of all, they're all right. They haven't been injured or abused."

Ned called the ranger office at Smoky Mountains National Park. He said he was a deputy sheriff. They had no information for him.

He canceled his flight reservations at two.

Gail returned about four with a book. She asked Ann if she could read in his office. When Ned found her, she said, "Thought you might like a familiar face around for a while."

Ned finished the afternoon with a series of emotional impulses. He wanted to move, to act, to hurry and strike out, but these urges were undercut by the awareness that he might go out on a wild-goose chase.

Gail waited in the Mercedes as he finished hospital rounds. They ate hot dogs, then bought beer and drove to the pond.

There was an hour of sunlight. They opened a can of

beer and lay back against the hill. The pond had become full of algae and other plants.

"For five dollars I'll dive for your radio."

"You're on."

"Later," she said.

They acceded to the quietness of their surroundings and were quiet themselves. Each looked at the pond, the trees behind, the pasture land, the idle, benign clouds in the sky. A breeze tousled the leaves of a seedling poplar tree. Ned said it was the first sign of autumn when the poplar leaves dried and crackled with the wind.

"Where were your kids born?"

"Lizzy was born in Toledo. Ellie was born here."

"Did you deliver them?"

"I would have dropped them, I was so excited."

"Were they cute?"

"Have you ever seen a baby after it's born? They're covered with cheesy white stuff and their heads look funny. Lizzy looked awful. Win had a long labor and Lizzy's head was like a football. Ellie was fat as a pig. Squealed like one, too."

"Did you name them?"

"Mom did. She named them after relatives in Wales."

"Was the minister right that night? When he said you never spent time with your kids?"

"What do you think?" Ned threw an empty can onto the sandy beach. "I talk to them every day. I took them to the hospital on Sundays. We ate breakfast and then wandered around; the nurses all made a big fuss over them. We watched TV. About every other week we came out here. They gave me a boat for the pond on my birthday. We usually brought wieners to roast. The preacher was full of shit. Maybe Win made that stuff up. I don't know. Hell, I never did half as much with my mom and dad. But they were around, like me. I haven't taken the kids on big trips, but you don't need to with a pond like this. The ocean just has more water in it."

"Were you mean to them?"

"My kids?"

"That was a dumb question."

"Sure as hell was."

"Did you ever wish they were boys?"

"I'm glad they aren't."

The moon was overhead, appearing and disappearing as a low cloud-layer moved in patches toward the east. There was too much light to see the algae; the mystery of the pond had been replaced by a feeling of comfort and security. The water's surface mirrored the sky, refining it with a patina the texture of a fine silk screen.

"I'm sorry, Ned. The preacher's accusations affected me. He made you sound terrible. He seemed to be certain."

"I kicked one of Lizzy's friends out of the house once. The kid hit Ellie and I blew up. Screamed and hollered like hell. I didn't bother to learn that Ellie kicked the kid first."

Ned spoke so reasonably and calmly Gail could only respond in kind. He, like the pond and its surroundings, was different from the night they had made love after he had lost his radio to the watery depths. He was a bit like the surface of the pond, reacting to available light and moods, seemingly aloof; but she knew of, and had touched, the warmth beneath. "The preacher was wrong, wasn't he?"

"You heard what I said to him."

"You were good. Now I want to see your campaign to dump the sheriff."

"What can I do to him?"

"I thought you were going to ruin him."

"That's too much work. He isn't worth it."

"If he's a bad person, maybe it's your obligation to get rid of him."

"Only Carlisle would have the job. If people wanted a good sheriff, they'd pay for one. I should do something, though. Piss on his lawn, maybe."

"It's hard to get back at stupidity."

"Maybe I'll call him up and swear. There was this guy in college who could say every swear word in a row."

"I have it," Gail said. "I'll do a little number for you. I'll make an obscene phone call. I'll tell him I'm naked with my legs spread out, lying in front of a mirror. I'll breathe hard."

"You're making me breathe hard."

"I'll tell him he can lick and suck anything he wants."

"Don't."

"I'll tell him he can sniff my panties and rub his cock with them."

"Gail."

"I'll get him so excited he can't stand it when I'll give him the finger."

"Over the phone?"

" 'See this, Sheriff, screw yourself.' "

Ned gave her another beer.

"I used to think things like that during the war," Gail said. "You do that because of frustration. You can't fight idiots and stupidity, so you want to get back at them. It's the need to get revenge. I want to get revenge."

"So do I."

Friday, August 6

Ned called Gail to tell her he couldn't meet her for lunch.
"I tried to get out of it, but they gave me a hard time."

"Who gave you a hard time?"

"A bunch of guys who belong to a club."

"Is it like the Lions or Rotary?"

"I don't know what they do. I don't want to go."

"But you are. Why are they insisting you go?"

"They said they wanted to do something for me."

Gail hesitated. "They haven't asked you before." When
he said no, she said, "Maybe they're worried about you—
not worried, perhaps—concerned."

"I don't know why."

"You'd better go, Ned." Her voice was knowing and
resolute. "I have an idea they don't want to lose the town's
best doctor."

The Fat Man's Club sent three members to escort Ned.
Warren Kunkel was the spokesman. He was the old man
of the Fat Men, a successful turkey farmer and retailer.
He looked and acted like an old politician. With him were

Jerry Strabala, vice-president of Cathlin College, and Stew Penningroth, editor of the *Denby Mirror*.

"We should have had you with us a long time ago, Ned. Everyone said you were too busy to be a Fat Man." Warren wore a vest although it was nearing ninety degrees. "Somebody made a rule a while back. We couldn't take new members unless someone moved or died. They keep looking to me to do one or the other. Now the reason I came to get you is because I'm the Joker this time. Once a month a different man brings special food. The café cooks it and we eat it. We have twelve members. You'll make thirteen. I said we should eat twice in October. Nothin' much else to do in October."

They walked to an alley and entered the café from the rear. The Fat Men awaited Ned. Arlen Jenson. Ralph Loess. Gene Hoyt, insurance agent. Andres Niebuhr, car dealer. Rod Jurries, implement dealer. Tim Vanderwaal of Vanderwaal's Department Store. Brad Mahanna, president of the furniture factory. Dough Ellis, attorney. Fats Kelly, janitor, Commander of the American Legion—founder of the club.

Andy Niebuhr was the first to shake Ned's hand. The car dealer was a compulsive drinker and gambler. His only visit to Ned's office was for referral to a psychiatrist who might cure him of his curse. "The wife and I and a few people from around the state are going to Vegas in a couple weeks. I made a deal with that doctor at the university. Las Vegas twice a year and the old lady holds the checkbook. She gives me a five-hundred-dollar limit. I can stay in Vegas long as I keep winning! That's a good deal, don't you think? And I was thinking maybe you ought to get out there sometime. If you're looking for women, Doc, Vegas is a clean number."

The gavel sounded. Fats Kelly ordered them to sit. "A moment of silence for taps."

Brad Mahanna stood at the far end of the room. He put on an old top hat and played taps on a trombone.

Ned was sitting between Gene Hoyt and Warren Kunkel.

They clapped and cheered after taps. "Tell the doc the history of that, Stew," Warren said.

"Not much history to it. Four years ago we began by singing 'God Bless America.' Then Rod Jurries brought back what he called venison from a hunting trip in Montana. The meat was dressed out and he brought it back in his trunk. Truth of the matter is the stuff was rotten. Cook here didn't know the difference, since we eat a lot of different things, so she cooked it. It didn't take us long to figure it out. Smelled, honest to God, like fried skunk piss. We ended up at the Captain's Wheel eating cheeseburgers. So the next time we got together Brad brought his trombone and played taps. His playing beat our singing, so we kept it up."

"Rod didn't know the difference between dry ice and plain ice," Tim said.

"The hell I don't. It was packed wrong."

"You ruined my taste for venison. The smell was a bitch," Arlen said.

A waiter brought them elderberry wine from the Amana Colonies.

"None for me," Ned said. "Can I have a glass of milk?"

He was booed soundly.

Ned didn't laugh, and when he told them his stomach hurt, they were quiet.

"All right!" Fats gaveled the table. "Joker takes the bets!"

Warren moved around the table collecting five-dollar bills. A piece of paper was attached to each bill. When they were collected, Warren sat and looked through the bundle.

"Side bets on the whole works," he said.

"I got ten," Tim said.

"No side bets," Arlen insisted.

"Put your money away, Tim," Jerry said.

"If that's the way you want it," Warren said. "No winners today. We're having smoked turkey."

"I said turkey," Tim protested.

"This is smoked turkey."

"What's the difference?"

"Three days in the smokehouse and a lot of work."

Ned looked at the men gathered around the table. Ralph Loess was the only one not involved in conversation. He was picking a string on his raspberry jacket; unable to remove it, he smoothed it with a finger.

"Ever have smoked turkey?" Warren asked Ned.

"Don't think so."

"Just wait."

Tim Vanderwaal asked for more wine.

Jerry Strabala passed the bottle. Bald on the top, Jerry had trained hair over his left ear to cover his head. Ned stared at his hair, shiny as resin, with patches of skin beneath.

After another glass of wine, Tim made a toast to the doc.

"He did it the hard way, but he's one of us now."

Half of the glasses were raised; the others were touched but not moved, tentative. Arlen opened his mouth, then looked, as did the others, toward Warren.

The old man of the Fat Men stood. "No one bothered to tell Ned here what this organization does. We don't do charity. We quit singing songs a while back. Mainly we bet against each other. Five bucks will get you twenty-five if you guess what the Joker brings to the table. Takes a good man to do what I did just now—beat 'em all. With my own turkey, even. Another thing. We don't have rules, but we do. Because I'm the old man and because I've got more money than anyone else, I broke the rules. I said, 'Men, there's one man in this town who could use a little good cookin' and we could use a little of his money.' Ned, we'd be honored if you would join this table."

"Hear, hear."

Two waiters brought the smoked turkey. The meat was

cooked so well it fell apart with the touch of a fork. They were served bowls of sauerkraut and cranberries and spiced stuffing and mashed potatoes and creamed corn and watery gravy.

The Fat Men were alive with talk and good will. Their guest watched them, their complicated interaction—moving silverware, gesturing, daubing gravy with napkins, laughing, belching, speaking with mouths full. They talked about the stock market, real estate, their wives, cars, planned vacations, their children. A happy and uncomplicated lot of revelers. When Ned was found silent or preoccupied, they enlisted his participation. He was their guest.

They each ate two or three portions of the turkey. The walls of the room caught Ned's attention. Thin white paint covered old wallpaper, like whitewash. The pattern of the wallpaper was veiled but distinct: gray squares ordered, confined by wide vertical stripes; each square protected a colorless flower.

"Finish up. Finish up." Fats gouged the table with his gavel. "Andy, you can't eat the whole turkey."

"What's the hurry?"

"Something special."

"I thought we didn't do anything special."

"We do today. Warren and Stew thought this up."

"Today is awards day," Warren said. "Stew, get up and give the awards."

There was general surprise at the innovation.

Gathering a portfolio of papers, Stew Penningroth began, "We are a proud and venerable group—"

They laughed.

"It was brought to my attention the need for recognition of our most deserving members. People whose blundering and tomfoolery make them stand out." The editor searched through his papers. "First. The Art Karp Barnburner Award."

They clapped.

"August twenty-five, nineteen fifty-two. Spring Falls receives its newest and most up-to-date fire engine. Fire Chief Art Karp drives it through the town with sirens blaring. The community is at ease knowing it's well protected. Not satisfied, the master fire chief went about preparing the people for Fire Protection Day. He wrote a letter to the newspaper. He made leaflets. He talked to the children in our school. Fire Protection Day was designed to display the new truck and was to be highlighted by a demonstration. Art found a deserted shed, and at three o'clock in the afternoon children and adults gathered to watch the new truck and the volunteers extinguish the fire. All was ready. Art made certain the kids were away from the building. He took kerosene and covered a wall of the shed. He lit the fire. Firemen pulled out the hoses. The shed was old. Flames shot upward. A wall fell in. Then it was apparent: There was a tractor inside. It caught fire; the gas tank exploded. Flaming boards landed near the children. Art had forgotten to look inside the shed before he lit the fire."

They laughed and cheered.

"The Art Karp Barnburner Award goes to Gene Hoyt for selling three insurance policies to terminally ill people."

"That's not true!"

He was given a scroll.

"Sir Charles Denby," Stew continued, "not only founded our college and this county, he was the biggest mouth west of the Alleghenies. He sold education like snake oil peddlers sold patent medicine. The award goes this year, as it should every year, to Andy Niebuhr!"

The man clapped loudest for himself.

"Next, we have the Midwest Corncob User's Trophy. This goes to Warren Kunkel for successfully breeding a turkey with a canary."

"You got that wrong. I bred a turkey with a buffalo, and it flew over Arlen Jenson's house."

"You should get the BS award," Andy yelled at him.

"Last but not least, we have the doc here." Stew nodded to Ned. "He gets the Roadrunner Award. I have official testimony from the head of the Iowa Highway Patrol that Ned has been clocked faster than any other human being. They quit bothering him 'cause they know they'd never catch him. So, for being the best doctor in Spring Falls and the fastest man in the state, I award this scrap of paper to Ned."

They clapped loudly.

With that, they looked at their watches. The meeting was over. Warren shook Ned's hand and told him to call when it came time to bring the food. Warren had a lot of ideas about unusual food. "And don't forget, these guys cheat. They'll come over to your house the day before or call your wife to find out what's to be served. But you'll catch on. Really isn't hard to fool this bunch of guys."

A little past three, Ned's stomach began hurting. The pain was at the top of his stomach, constant, and he felt a twinge of pain in his back, near the shoulder blade. He gulped some Maalox, then drank a small carton of milk. Returning to his private office, he shut the door, took cigarettes from a desk drawer and had a cigarette with coffee. The cigarette relaxed him, but caused a sharp pull in his stomach. He stared at the wall for ten minutes before he called for Ann.

"Ann. My stomach hurts. Can I sneak out of the office now?"

"Are you sick, Doctor?"

"No. Sick of work, maybe. My stomach is just a little upset. A ride in my car will fix it."

"Do you want me to call someone? Dr. Markham?"

"Byron would tell me to drink some milk. I did."

"And smoke a cigarette with coffee?"

"Don't know! Maybe he would."

"I don't know who's out there, but why don't you go?"

He left and drove to Gail's house. She wasn't there, so he drove through the campus. He found her walking home.

"Hey there, woman! Wanna ride?"

"What are you doing at this time of day?"

"Going for a ride. Come on."

"Why aren't you working?"

"I need to get out of the office."

"I'm not going with you."

"Why not?"

"Last time I did that we came back to chaos."

"I'm going to visit my folks. I haven't seen them for a while."

"Where do they live?"

"Colfax. We'll be back by eight."

Ned drove past the old mineral springs, through Main Street and around the residential area. They stopped for a few minutes by the shack where Win was raised. It was empty. Windows were broken and the back yard was a collection of rusted tin drums and refuse. His house was four blocks away, halfway up one of the hills. It was small and tidy. Shutters were painted and the yard was mowed. Ned parked the car and showed Gail a peach tree he and his dad planted when he was a child.

"Hey, son." A tall man, slightly bent, approached. His voice was high-pitched and rough at the same time. He was like a bear, almost waddling. His reddish hair was thin, revealing freckles on his scalp.

"Who's that?" he enquired of Gail.

"This is Gail. She works at the college."

"You wanna see something nice?" he asked her. A child-like smile erupted. "Come on, then." He turned and they followed his short footsteps to a side door to a small basement. "Watch out, now," he warned.

A gray-and-white kitten jumped from a rag-filled basket. Ernest bent slowly and caught the kitten with one hand.

"See what it does? Look at this. It won't show its claws."

"I like its face," Gail said.

"Take it. It won't hurt anybody." He gave it to her. His hands were huge, worn.

"Does Mom know you have this?" Ned asked.

"She said I could keep it in the basement."

"She doesn't like cats."

"That's fine," Ernest said. "The cat and I get along good. Nice one, isn't it?"

"How's Mom?"

"We'll see her when we're done here." He put a finger in the kitten's mouth. "See there? See that? Won't even bite. Neighbor gave it to me. The Jones boy. He comes up every morning after his paper route."

A door opened upstairs and a woman's voice boomed, "Are you down there with your dad and that fool kitten? If you are, come up. Did Win and the kids come along?"

"You put the cat away," Ernest told Gail. "We can come back again and see it. You should meet Ned's mom."

Ruth was five feet one inch tall. She was heavy and moved quickly. Her face was delicate: small mouth and clear eyes. She spoke with a slight accent. "Your dad's more like a kid every day. He won't go to church and save himself but he'll play with that fool cat, Ned, from morning till night. I hate to say it, but you'll be the same way."

Ned introduced Gail and apologized for Win. He said she was busy.

Ruth looked puzzled. "Everyone come in the kitchen and I'll warm some coffee while I cook."

"Oh, God, I forgot."

"Don't cuss like that," Ruth said.

"I did it again. Mom. Don't cook. I'll take you out to the place on the highway."

"It's almost ready."

"If I come anywhere near eating time, she cooks a whole meal."

"The good Lord says you got to eat. And don't be so

ungrateful. For two guys who never go to church you're lucky to have food. And, Ned, I swear, your dad gets worse every day. He was going to fix the back stairs but he hasn't. But he has time for that animal."

Ernest winked at Gail. "She don't like cats."

"With the Lord as my witness, the old man talks to the cat like it was a child."

"You have to, so's it knows what you think."

"Then it knows more what you think than I do."

Every burner of the old gas stove was cooking something. The squat woman moved quickly, catching the potatoes as boiling water spilled over the pan, frying sausages and leftover roast beef. Ernest left the room, his feet almost shuffling.

When he was out of the room, Ruth quietly asked Ned, "He looks good, don't you think? I worry about him. He forgets, you know. But he does good. We're lucky he's that good, Ned."

"You don't look so bad yourself."

"I'm an old goat." She laughed.

Ernest returned with a tattered, overflowing scrapbook. "See?" There was a lisp in his voice. "Here's Ned and his medical school class. We went to the graduation. That was something."

"I don't mind saying it, but I spent a lot of money for a dress. Pride is a sin, but I didn't care that day." Ruth's voice was strong. "Not many kids from Colfax ever get to medical school. When Ned went, it raised a few eyebrows. Now they're all used to it. They come up to me in the store and ask me, 'How's the doctor?'"

"Here, woman." Ernest poked Gail. "See this. That was an old car I had when I worked for Maytag. Ned drove it on the creek once."

"How'd you know that?"

"The Morgan boy told his dad a couple years ago. Said you almost didn't get the car back over the bank because of the snow."

The scrapbook held clippings and pictures of relatives. Ernest's thick fingers sorted and tucked in the faded memoirs.

Gail found a picture of Ned when he was seven. "This looks like a Walker Evans photograph. Patched pants. Anemic-looking face—"

"Nothing anemic about that child." Ruth laughed. "For a long time I swore I was visited by a plague. But the Lord was merciful. Ned got all the devilment out of his blood. He's made up for it a hundredfold. He couldn't be better to us. Visits us more than once a month. The TV he gave Ernest was a blessing. He takes care of us."

"I love your house and this town," Gail said. "It reminds me of pictures of the thirties. Take away the cars and the TV antennas and it looks like America looked then."

"Might look like it, but it doesn't act like it," Ruth said.

"We have good trees," Ernest said. "Ned put 'em in with me. Two cherry trees and a peach tree. Grows real peaches. Kinda small, but they have lots of sugar in 'em."

They ate supper in the dining nook. The plates didn't match and there was no tablecloth. Ernest ate his beef with ketchup. Ruth made them eat rhubarb pie.

After eating, Ned apologized and said he had to leave. The four toured the lawn and the fruit trees. Roofs of small frame houses were spread about below them. Ernest left to visit the kitten and Ruth walked Ned and Gail to the Mercedes.

"Silly car," his mother said.

"Gotta go fast when you're a doctor," Ned said.

"Men have to have foolishness. Cars or kittens or alcohol. Lord save us."

"Ma really likes the car. I saw her sneak out and drive it one day."

"Ha! I've never been in the thing and I never will. Bring the kids next time. They're growing faster than you did." She kissed him and waved goodbye.

Gail wanted to see the town again. "I bet it hasn't

changed in twenty years. It would make a great set for a thirties movie."

He didn't agree but drove her through the streets. He showed her a place that had been a hobby shop; the old hotel where people came by train for mineral water treatments; his mother's Baptist church.

"I should spend more time here, Ned. Will you bring me back so I can walk around and talk to people?"

"Why?"

"To get to know you. It's my own method. I made up a phrase for it: psychictopographic investigation. I think you can get to know someone by walking their paths. I used it in my research."

"I can tell you more than you can learn by walking around here."

"That's what everyone thinks." She pointed at a street. "Drive over there. That's a pleasant-looking street."

"That's where the schoolteachers live."

"You can drive by and give them the finger."

"I'll give you five bucks if you give the finger to the whole street while I drive."

"I know you. You'd stop and leave me holding the finger."

"I'll drive as fast as I can."

"I like your town. I would have been one of your friends. I almost took you up on your bet. This town does something to you. Gives you reckless abandon."

"Look up there."

"Oh, God. Your mother."

"I should have made it ten bucks."

"I think she still worries about you."

"She's wondering what I'm doing with you."

"Let's hope she never finds out."

Ned drove around a corner, his face changing. He drove slowly, then stopped. He began to cry. "How can I ever come back without the kids?"

"They wouldn't understand, would they?"

He cleared his nose and drove out of town.

"Slow down so we can talk," Gail insisted. "Ned, I don't know what to do. I can't leave you, but I can't stay. It's a terrible position. If I go, I'll hate myself, and if I stay I'm only waiting for the day your kids come back; then I'm excess baggage. God, I hate your wife. Whimpering little cunt! Do me a favor. I never want to see her. I'd choke her. She's a spoiler, a bitch and a spoiler."

"When is your school over?"

"A week. I should be out east in three weeks. I can push it to four."

"You have to go. I'm OK."

"I don't believe that. You don't look good. You don't laugh. I'm staying. I'm stupid, but I'm staying."

"Don't."

"It's my life, buddy. I'm your only friend right now. And—you're my good friend. I'm staying, but you have to pay the price."

"A hundred bucks?"

"Not so cheap! You don't know who I am. It's time I told you. The price of my staying is a lecture."

"Can I give you the bird if it's a bad lecture?"

"You do and I'll jump out of the car. I want to tell you who I am and what I do. Somehow we haven't gotten around to that. If you don't care to know, auf Wiedersehen."

"Let's go to my house."

"Nope. Let's go to a bar. Call the hospital and turn off your radio. I hate houses. I was a cocktail waitress, informed mistress and a mobile sculpture programmed to smile at request. My husband's colleagues propositioned me. I had to entertain their wives. One of them propositioned me. I was taking her sailing. She wanted to play fingers on the boat, so I jibed and damn near knocked her out of the boat when the boom came around. Have you ever sailed?"

"No."

"You wouldn't understand. Where can we stop for a drink, so we can talk?"

They stopped at the Holiday Inn near Newton. The bar was nearly empty.

"Are you up for this? I've got to talk. We've been waiting, waiting, waiting and nothing happens. I'm going to stay so I've got to talk. I want you to understand. That's important. A good screw just won't take care of everything anymore. I'm lonely like you and I've got to talk."

Ned ordered drinks and told the waitress to keep their glasses filled.

"Do you know why I took up with you? The truth? I was horny. I was on the make. I liked your laugh and your looks. I knew you were married and that made it safe. No entanglements, nothing to keep me here, and I could leave with a memory of a good summer. A story for my fantasy life. We all do that, don't we? Some nights when we're alone and horny and playing with ourselves we desperately think back to a time of nice sensuality. We let our minds run away with the fantasy. Know what my favorite is? When I was in high school, I went out with this guy. I courted him and we finally got together in the back seat of a car. God, it took an hour to get anywhere. I had to take the lead. He was frightened. I did everything I could to let him know it was OK. I slouched. I spread my legs and wiggled. Finally he pulled up my skirt. I helped him pull down my pants. Then I attacked! The zipper. The damn zipper! It took me forever. He was touching me. Seems to me he was in the wrong place. I worked my hand through the opening in his underpants and found his cock. I think I scratched him. Any rate, he couldn't take it and came, on my hand and on his shirt. He was so embarrassed! I love that episode because I can carry it to all kinds of extremes. I thought about fantasies when we were in San Francisco. We didn't need them then. But someday you and San Francisco will save me in an hour of need. If your damn wife hadn't left, I could have gone out east with an absolutely pure and true fantasy."

"How can you talk about things like that?"

"Are you embarrassed?"

"I'm not used to it."

"Christ. How old were you when you put your hand in a girl's pants?"

"I don't know."

"Sixteen."

"Maybe."

"You won't admit it. Stop and think. Think of the girl. You can remember. She's your age now. You don't think she doesn't remember it, too? You men think you do all the diddling and women forget it, like dime store dummies. I bet if you asked that woman right now, she'd remember. Men don't realize that. Women think about it, too. Ah, hell, that's neither here nor there. I feel like I've taken speed. It's all your wife's fault. She got you but she got me, too."

Their glasses were filled again.

"Did you know I went to high school in Paterson? New Jersey? William Carlos Williams lived there and I used to walk by his house for inspiration. I knew he was good, but a lot of people there didn't. Once I walked by the mental hospital he wrote about. My dad knew him, sort of. Dad taught physics and geometry. That's probably why I teach. A noble profession. Sometimes. My ninth-grade teacher almost changed my mind. She was an old bitch named Mrs. Smythe. She caught me reading Kerouac. 'Impropriety and rudeness never survive as literature,' she said. I went to high school in Manhattan, near Washington Square. That was where Dad's last job was before he retired to cooking and writing. I think I got married because of my father. I liked being around him, so it was natural to marry a professor. Jesus. When the marriage was no good, I blamed Mom. Actually I pitied her. I didn't write her, I was embarrassed to talk to her on the phone.

I was wrong, as usual. She was better than I thought. We get along great now. We have a common love—cathedrals. It began in New York. Since we've been all over the coast looking at cathedrals. Even to Montreal. Someday we're going to Notre Dame in Paris. When I'm stoned, I mix my mother's religion with my father's physics. I daydream about the massive spaces in cathedrals and imagine God as ionized particles dispersed throughout the air; everywhere you go, bits of God touch you. There aren't any bathrooms in cathedrals in Europe. They were built before plumbing. Imagine going to church and watching peasants relieve themselves as you enter. It was so bad in the time of Louis the Fourteenth that women took special crocks to church and peed in them during services. That's true. They lifted their skirts and let go. Rabelais liked to write about people farting in church. He didn't believe in an ionized God."

Ned laughed. "I hate churches," he said. "Always did. Vietnam clinched it. God never made sense after that."

"You should become a member of the Sun Dance. Indian religion. Maybe you are. Oh, I forgot. You're Welsh. The druids! That fits. Druids and bonnie rats. The dark and forbidden rites. Human sacrifice and blood. Too bad the druids didn't teach macramé. All their secrets could be tied into thousands of knots and historians could spend lifetimes unraveling them. Of course they'd end up with a piece of twine. Nihilism. That's finally what you and I believe. Once we're dead, we're dead. Vietnam did that to me. Willy P-3 did the same to me. You and I believe we'd better get it now because we sure as hell can't take it with us. That's nihilistic. Maybe that's why we ravished each other in San Francisco. We knew damn well there may never be another San Francisco. Something inside told us."

Suddenly she stopped talking and drummed her fingers against the table. Two men were staring at them.

She looked Ned in the eye. "I know why I'm talking

like this. You don't respect me. I'm not an equal. And I have to be. You don't understand me or my job. I won't stay unless you do. You're dumb sometimes. But you have a good mind. You'll change. I don't think you know the discipline I needed to get where I am. Probably as much as for medical school. Then there's the matter of our tryst. The pond, San Francisco. You never had anything like that. It makes me a whore and a hero all at once. I'm a good woman! You're a good man. When the likes of us get together, it's good. Nothing bad at all. You'll learn. Do you know what I do when we're not in bed or looking for your wife? I work. My Ph.D. thesis was titled 'Psychologic Determinants of the Depression, 1929–1939.' I took twelve people and analyzed their lives and beliefs and proved—hell, I'm less certain of what I proved the more I read. I proved I needed a scapegoat, a simple explanation to prove what happened."

She was sitting against the wall of the lounge, impervious to a sloppy waitress and the noise of the bartender's blender. It was semi-dark and her face appeared heavier, losing its freckles and fine wrinkles. Ned responded to her conversation with a laugh or a smile, attentive. She was a drink behind. Ned pushed a drink toward her and she took a sip, politely.

"I had the good person–bad person theory," she went on. "Hoover was a bad person. FDR was good. My theory fell apart one day when I read a speech Hoover gave immediately after the depression to rich businessmen at the White House. It was an impressive occasion. W. C. Teagle of Standard Oil was there, so was Alfred P. Sloan of GM and Owen D. Young of GE and Gifford and Klein and Lamont and Mellon and Henry Ford and E. C. Grace of Bethlehem Steel—the power brokers of America. Know what happened? Remember this was in November of 1929. Hoover outlined the New Deal! He told them the work week needed to be shortened and that make-work jobs had to be created. Hoover knew what had to be done.

But he believed business would do these things as a favor! Of course they didn't. FDR took the same ideas and turned them into laws with teeth. Ruined my theory. I always thought Hoover was stupid. Not so."

Gail relaxed for a moment. The waitress had been standing by the table, hands on her hips, churlish, anxious to clear empty glasses and the ashtray. Seven women in softball uniforms claimed the back table, demanding immediate service.

"Ned, I wish you could sit up with me some night and we could look at my books and I could tell you so much— so much. History is a dream world. Visiting your hometown did something to me."

The noise level of the bar increased as customers arrived for the Double-Bubble hour. The softball team was joined by two cross-country truck drivers. Gail paid no attention save to raise her voice in unconscious defense. She had talked to Ned as if he were a class of students and now she spoke as though she was addressing a political rally, hands alive, voice strong, commanding—a believer.

"What a glorious and pathetic past we've had. Want a useless fact? In nineteen thirty-one Winston Churchill was hit by a car on Fifth Avenue in New York. Want another? In nineteen thirty, one hundred million movie tickets were sold a week. Do you know what John J. Raskob, vice-chairman of GM, said in 1929? 'Everybody ought to be rich.' That was right before Black Thursday, the start of the depression. In 1933, Hart Crane, a poet I love because he loved words and he reminded me of my dad, jumped off the stern of the *Orizaba* and solved his problems. He was a homosexual. Then there's another man who never dated a woman in his life and collected blown glass and antiques—J. Edgar Hoover."

Ned was smiling, his face on the verge of laughter— not in derision or mockery but in delight. She was so different from the others in the bar, especially the other women. Gail's oratory and the street language of the back table formed a counterpoint: beauty versus the beasts.

"Ned, this stuff is off the top of my head, like you think of penicillin and pelvic exams. It's my fantasy world that was true—or sort of true, because the more I read the more I wonder. Do you ever see an infection and know it's caused by bacteria and wonder why bacteria? Why not something else?"

The bar was filled and nearing Double-Bubble chaos. Patrons knocked against Ned's chair; a drunk businessman spilled a drink on the floor, part of it splashing on Ned's ankle. The waitress, per Ned's order, was keeping their glasses filled. Gail was far behind—three drinks waited for her—but she continued talking as if she'd been drinking heavily all afternoon.

"I learned a lot about you today. I do the same thing in my research. I went to the country home of Mantis and Oris Van Sweringen outside of Cleveland. They were men who began as office clerks and ended up owning, by manipulating stocks and loans, the Chesapeake and Ohio, Erie, Pere Marquette, Missouri-Pacific and Nickel Plate railroads. They bombed out after the depression and J. P. Morgan had to remind them quietly one day that they were insolvent. I went to the place where they lived. My God, what an experience. First of all, the two of them slept in the same room until Mantis got married at the age of fifty-five. The place reeked of loneliness and sparseness. No big parties, no garish statues. Two sniveling, conniving bachelors. I never wrote about my trip. How can you verify emotions? How did Mantis explain to Oris that he'd found a woman? A woman—at fifty-five! How did Oris sleep the first night he was alone in that bare room? The depression ruined them; their empire folded, only silently, because the real big money couldn't allow the truth to be known. The Van Sweringens were broke! Morgan and Rockefeller shielded them from public disgrace."

Ned went to the bathroom. Upon his return, she apologized for talking so much. He said he liked it.

"Do you want me to stay?"

"Sure. If you want to."

"I'll leave when the time comes. You have to make me a promise. OK?"

"What?"

"I'm staying because of what happened to your world, but I'm bringing my own world into it. OK? I don't like Iowa. You'll have to come to my place, look at my books and talk about my world, too. I can chase the ghost of Wildman Brookhart only so far, then I get scared—and lonely."

"I like going to your house."

"Ned—" She put her drink aside and cleared the space between them. "What if your wife hadn't run off, but simply asked for a divorce? What would you have done?"

"Stopped her. Bothered her the same way I got her to marry me. I wouldn't let her do it."

"I'm glad you admitted that. My divorce still bothers me. It was terrible to tell Willy P-3 I didn't love him. He couldn't understand. Everything was perfect. We had this modern house on Lake Skeaneatelas, a sailboat, good friends. He cried and cried when I told him. He promised to do everything. It got so hard, I ran off for two weeks and stayed with my parents. Finally I got the nerve to go back and face him. Poor man! He wears tweed suits and smokes Borkum Riff in his briar pipe. But there was no magic, no love. I could have ripped him off for some money. His family had money though he was very thrifty. He'd never spend sixty bucks for a bottle of wine. He'd never throw his radio into a pond."

"How do you feel now?"

"I felt great until your wife ran away."

"You don't have to stay."

"Will you come and read books and talk to me, Ned?"

"Sure."

"We can always screw, you know."

Tuesday, August 10

He was sick from the alcohol he drank the night before. At seven in the morning he walked to the bathroom, urinated, drank a large amount of antacid and took thirty milligrams of codeine. He slept until nine, called the office and told Ann he would be late. The sky was overcast. He considered raising the top of his Mercedes, but it was too much of an effort.

His first patient was Elmer Groote. Ned mumbled a greeting and told the man to slip down his overalls. Ned put on a glove and smeared his index finger with KY jelly. Massaging the man's prostate was painful to his finger and arm, but in an act of self-punishment he continued the massage past reason. When he was casting away the dirty glove, Elmer said, "Say, Doc, that was real good today." Ned walked out of the room.

He went to his back office and drank a cup of coffee quickly, then another, smoking five cigarettes. A sip of coffee, a puff of smoke. There was a tremor in his hands when he finished. Holding them in front of him, as though doing a neurologic exam on himself, he saw them shake visibly.

His hand continued to shake when he held his stethoscope to Natalie Cooper's breast. She needed an athletic physical for track. Aware of his tremor, Ned quickly finished the exam, signed the forms and smiled; when smiling, he felt the skin about his eyes; the sides of his eyes were tight and puffy.

Rather than see his next patient, he returned to his back office. He drank more Maalox and practiced deep-breathing exercises to restore his nerves. It helped the nausea but did nothing for the fine and uncontrolled palsy in his hands.

Ann walked into the room and asked him how much coumadin he wanted to order for Mr. Feldstein. "The nurse said she missed you at the hospital this morning."

"Five milligrams."

He inspected a burn on Ralph Coggin's arm. The man had accidentally leaned against the exhaust of a tractor. "It's doing fine." He instructed Sheryl, "Put some more Sulfamylon on it and redress it with fluffs and Kling."

Walking to another room, he was overcome with so much nausea he was forced to stop. He concentrated on breathing deeply. When Ann walked by, he chose to stare ahead, breathing, fighting the nausea.

Grace Worth sat bare-chested on the end of an examining table. Emaciated, dying of breast cancer, she came once a week to have the fluid from her chest removed. Her skin was scaly brown from radiation treatments. Needle scars lined the lower ribs like track marks on a junkie's arm. In half-breaths, she told him most of the fluid was on the right side this week. He tapped the back of her chest like a vintner checking a cask of amontillado; there was resonance where there was air and only dullness where fluid lay. He told her it would be a while and covered her with her blouse.

He found another cup of coffee. Against his better

judgment he lit a cigarette. Three puffs and he was aware of his hands and the nausea. His headache seemed related to his powers of concentration; when he relaxed, the pain increased. For a moment there was a memory, obfuscated, of pouring Scotch after the beer was gone. Two Scotches, it was, before he kicked his shoes and, standing, holding on to the bed, pushed himself out of his pants, turning them inside out in the procedure.

If he could endure the morning, he might be able to rest with more codeine over the noon hour.

"We're ready with Adam Roberts," Sheryl said.

"What?"

"The Roberts kid. You told Jane to bring him back today to remove the sebaceous cyst from over his eye."

His flesh was jellied, uncertain—a state midway in the transubstantiation from strength to atony.

"If we do it now, we can get going with Grace."

He followed Sheryl into the surgical room. Adam Roberts lay on the new Ritter table. Sheryl had scrubbed the area above his eye with Zephiran and draped three sterile towels in a triangular fashion over the cyst.

"Hi, Ned." Jane Roberts stood in the corner. She was wearing a matching tennis outfit; trim body and walnut hair.

An opened surgical pack lay on a Mayo stand. It contained a stack of 4 x 4 sponges, straight hemostat, needle holder, suture scissors, pickups, self-retaining skin retractor, roll of 6-0 nylon, knife handle and a No. 15 Bard-Parker blade.

Ned looked at Jane quickly, then pulled a stool next to the Ritter table. Without speaking, he found the surgical gloves and put them on. Leaning over, he picked up the small, sharp knife blade with a hemostat and began fitting the blade onto the knife handle. His hands shook, but he was able to snug the blade onto the tip of the handle.

He felt the cyst on Adam's forehead. It was half the size of the tip of a little finger, immediately above the eyebrow.

"Xylocaine," he said.

Sheryl handed him a syringe with a small needle.

"Might hurt," he said quickly.

He began to inject the anesthetic through the eyebrow, upward, away from the eye. Skin welled and blanched as he saturated the tissues around the cyst. His thumb was uncertain as he put pressure on the barrel of the syringe.

Looking up, he saw Sheryl and Jane standing directly over him. He reached for the knife, touched it, then grabbed a sponge and rubbed it slowly over the cyst. He looked at the floor, breathing deeply, inhaling and concentrating. His hand was shaking worse and he couldn't stop it. When there was nothing else to do, he again reached for the knife. Carefully, resting his elbow against the table, he began the incision over the cyst. When he was halfway finished, the boy opened his eye, looking at him. The blade was poised but an inch or two away from the top white of the eye. His hand shaking visibly, Ned lifted the knife into the air and placed it on the table. He sponged the partial incision. Sheryl and Jane hadn't moved.

"Sheryl, go tell Ann to double-check that hospital order. I can do without you for a while." She left. "And, Jane. You can sit if you like."

"That's OK. I don't mind." The chairman of the Democratic central committee didn't move.

Ned took the scalpel and after a deep breath completed the incision, removing the knife to the Mayo stand as quickly as he could.

He dissected fat around the cyst with scissors. He was only able to expose the very top of the cyst. With care, he took the pickups in his left hand, piercing the outer layer of the cyst and pulling upward. His hand was shaking, so he rested an elbow on the boy's chest. Taking the knife, he began slow, chopping movements to cut the cyst from the threads of tissue which held it. Sheryl returned. With full audience and both hands trembling, Ned chopped quick and brief strokes, his breath held in and his heart racing. Suddenly his left hand jerked upward: The cyst was freed. Surprised, he dropped it on the floor.

He managed a laugh and, while doing so, said something to the boy, something that would make him respond, open his eye and look. When the boy opened his eye and Ned saw it was normal, he exhaled in relief. His hands didn't stop trembling when he placed sutures to close the wound, but he did so hurriedly, happy for his reprieve and angry at the night before.

He told Sheryl to cover the wound with a dressing and told Jane to bring the boy back in a week for suture removal. He didn't stop to talk politics.

He'd drained a liter or more from Grace's chest when she said there was pain and he'd better stop. She could feel the needle against her lung.

Without telling Ann, he walked through the laboratory entrance and took a walk. It had begun to rain and he pulled the top up on his Mercedes, matching the auger points of the top to the holes above the windshield and twisting the two levers. After closing the windows, he sat inside and put the seat backward. He closed his eyes and tried to imagine a void, quietness. With each breath, he felt a pulsation of strength return to his arms. He lay in his car for over ten minutes. The rain was soft and the quiet rested his body. He could hear the faintest of shuffling noises as the rain landed on the roof. He remembered the relief of the codeine earlier in the morning and smiled.

"Doctor! Doctor! God, hurry. I'm glad I found you." Ann opened the car door. "Hurry, please, hurry."

He'd been asleep, or close to sleep. There was a fine beading of raindrops about Ann's hair.

Ned moved slightly and his head hurt.

"You have to come. Doctor!"

He sat and began to get out of the car. His heart beat rapidly.

He began to ask.

"It's urgent. Urgent. The lady from Des Moines is calling. She said it's urgent."

He ran up the side steps, down the hallway and answered the phone in the reception area.

"This is Emily Hart. Dr. Owen?"

"Yes."

"I found your wife."

"The kids?"

"They're fine. With her. Can you write this down? They're in a small town named Clinchfield, Georgia. South of Macon."

"Are they staying there?"

"Looks like it. My guess on the Gambles store was right. The main office called me with the information. I'd told them I wanted to buy the store in your city. They've located a job for him in Clinchfield as assistant manager with an option to buy in a year."

"I'm going down there."

"I thought so. I don't have a house address. I think the place is really small. You can inquire where they're living when you get there."

"Is he living with her?"

"I told you all I know. If you can prove he's living with her, it'll help in a custody fight."

"There won't be any custody fight."

"How's that?"

"I'll drag her ass back here."

"Let me talk to you a minute about that. You can't abduct her—kidnap her. If you hurt her, you're in trouble."

"How about the kids?"

"If they want to return with you, take them."

"I don't think she'll give me problems. I'll scare her back."

"Can I ask you a question?" she asked.

"Sure."

"Do you have a gun?"

"No. Do I need one?"

"For heaven's sake, no. Please—"

"I'll just talk to her. She'll give in."

"Maybe you know her better than I. I'd caution you: People who leave like her don't do it just to act out. They're usually very—I repeat—very serious. It's their only way out. I wouldn't count on her. If it wasn't for his store and his job, we might never have found them. She didn't leave a single clue. Every possible check was used and she left clean, Dr. Owen, no traces at all. I think she's pretty intent on hiding."

"She didn't do a good job."

"We were lucky. When are you leaving?"

"Now."

"Will you call me when you return?"

"Sure. And thanks. Thanks a lot."

Ann stood by his side. When he hung up, he didn't move. There was a scrap of paper with the name of a town in Georgia written on it.

"What do you want me to do?" Ann asked.

"Call Gail."

"Who?"

"I'll call her. I need money. Call the airlines. That's right. Get me a ticket to Macon, Georgia. I want a car when I get off the plane. Do that, Ann. Call the airlines."

"Do you want to use your phone in the back?"

"Ya. Get some money, too, get me the checkbook."

"Now?"

"Now."

Ann opened the bottom drawer of her desk and gave him the checkbook. He asked for a pen. His hand still tremulous, he wrote a check to cash for a thousand dollars. "Run this over to the bank."

"Before I call the airlines?"

"I'll call. You run to the bank."

He went to the back. Sheryl told him all the rooms were filled with patients.

"I can't see them. I'm leaving."

"Can you just see Mavis Voight? She has a temp of a hundred four and a terrible sore throat."

Ned walked into the room, asked Mavis to open her mouth, looked and felt her lymph glands. Without talking to the patient, he told Sheryl to give her an injection of penicillin.

"Do you want her on oral medication?"

"Ten days of Pen V-K. Two hundred fifty milligrams. QID."

He dialed United Airlines. A recording told him to wait. He lit a cigarette, thinking.

"Sorry for the delay. May I help you?"

"I want to fly to Macon, Georgia."

"And when will that be?"

"As soon as I can."

"Today?"

"Yes. Now."

"And where are you leaving from?"

"Des Moines."

"I'll see what I can do."

Ned waited another minute.

"I have a flight leaving Des Moines at twelve thirty-two. Arrives St. Louis one forty. You have an hour and a half layover. You can fly Delta from St. Louis to Atlanta at three-fifteen. Arrives Atlanta six-twenty, Eastern Time. Leave Atlanta six-fifty. Arrive at Macon seven-twelve."

"Good. I want to rent a car."

"I'll see if I can confirm your flight first, sir. What kind of car do you want?"

"A big one."

His flight was confirmed and he was told there'd be a car waiting.

He couldn't get Gail at her house. He called the college. A secretary in the English department told him she was teaching.

"Find out where and get her for me. No. Have her be

in front of the library. This is Dr. Owen. It is an emergency."

Ann returned with the money. "Are fifties all right?"

"Anything."

"How long will you be gone?"

"Be back tomorrow."

"You sure it won't take longer?"

"Nope. I'll call and tell you when I'm back. Oh, Ann. Do me a favor." He gave her one of the fifties. "Go out and buy something for Lizzy and Ellie. A present. Something stuffed for Lizzy. Big. Clothes or something for Ellie."

Sheryl joined them. "Doctor. Oh, I hope things go right. You could use that."

"They will."

He stuffed the money into his billfold and ran to his car. Gail was waiting in front of the college library.

"Found the kids," he told her. "In Georgia. I'm leaving now."

"Great, Ned. You must feel fantastic."

She hugged him.

Then she asked, "What are you going to do?"

"Go down and get them. The lawyer says I might have to kidnap the kids back, but I don't think so. She'll come, too."

"What if she doesn't want to come back?"

"She will. If she gives me a hard time, I'll hit her. She's caused enough trouble. Damn woman. What the hell does she want?"

"Maybe she wants the other guy."

"He's a pussy. If I see him, I'll mess him up so bad he won't walk for a month. The dumb prick."

"Don't hurt anyone, Ned."

"I might."

"You're a lot better off if you do it cleanly. Talk to her, and if she won't come, take the kids."

"That sounds good."

"Oh, this is great! I really don't think you would have

survived much more of this. You are really beginning to look worn—to be polite. I don't blame you. You have a terribly strong sense of family. I was impressed, really impressed, when I saw you with your parents. I'm sure you feel the same way about your kids. You know, Ned, part of your problem is you don't talk about things that mean a lot to you. Strangely—oh, not really—I mean a lot to you. I can tell by the way you act. But you never tell me that. I'm smart enough to know, so I'm not hurt. I think you love deeply and feel deeply, but you cover it up with laughing or whatever. That's fine. A lot better than not caring and acting like it. Are you excited?"

"Yes."

"I feel a bit of ambivalence, I have to admit. We're in a screwy situation and now I'm odd person out. We'll go our different ways. Hell, I shouldn't bitch, that's what we were going to do all along. But I have a great affection for you, doctor friend. You're a good man and you know what they say about that. Just think! We can get on with our lives! You'll have your kids; I'll go out to Brown and be the local expert on the depression—and cornfields. It is a relief, isn't it? It's almost over! What a terrible time it's been for both of us. How many nights have we stayed up and drunk ourselves silly?"

"Last night was the worst. I really was bad this morning."

"I don't see how you do it. You're strong."

"I'm beginning to wonder."

"Do you want me to do anything now? Drive you to the airport?"

"No. I'll drive and leave the car. I'll be back tomorrow."

"I hope so. I really want to meet your kids."

"I'll bring them over right away. You can be Aunt Gail."

"When do you leave?"

"Now. I'll get there just in time."

"Good luck. I mean that. Won't it be great seeing your kids?"

"It will."

"Do me a favor. Don't hurt anyone, huh?"

She kissed him and he drove away.

It was raining heavily when his plane took off from Des Moines. He sat alone in the first-class cabin, smoking and looking at beads of rain outside the window. He tried to read the airline magazine, but couldn't focus his attention. When he tried to visualize his kids and the town in Georgia, his mind failed.

At St. Louis, he ate in the airport cafeteria and walked through the concession stands. He thought of buying the kids a present, but trusted Ann to take care of that.

He flew to Atlanta in a DC 10. The stewardess offered him wine, but he preferred coffee. The skies had cleared and when he stepped out of the plane at Atlanta, he felt a burst of heat and humidity. It was hotter in Macon. He ran to the Hertz desk and told the woman he was in a hurry. She asked for a credit card. "Here, use this." He gave her a hundred-dollar deposit. "Oh, and I need a map."

"There's one in the car. Where are you going?"

"Clinchfield."

"Never heard of it."

Clinchfield was closer to Macon than Emily Hart had estimated. He drove ninety down Interstate 75 and turned onto State Highway 341. He arrived at seven-thirty. The town was small and different country from Iowa: stands of scrub trees, oddly shaped fields, poverty. The main street was short, bordered by frame buildings with porches. Ned stopped at a gas station and asked the attendant about any new people in town.

"Heard of 'em but don't know where you can find 'em. Why don't you stop your car and come in. Have yourself a Pepsi. I'll call Wayne Ramsey, he'll know."

Ned followed the man into the messy station. He was given a Pepsi and the attendant called. It was a brief conversation.

"The woman and the kids live out on Baron Road. It's

out about a mile. Easy to get to. The guy with the store lives in a room above the store."

"How do I get to Baron Road?"

"Easy. Go up to the funeral parlor and turn right. Go across the railroad tracks and take the first road to your left. It's gravel. Don't let the name fool you, it's not like a city street. Got its name because of the Baron plantation. Used to be out past that way."

"How much do I owe you for the Pepsi?"

"Nothin'. Glad to help. You from Atlanta? That's a nice car."

Ned gave him ten dollars.

Baron Road was narrow. Weeds grew up to the roadside. Every few hundred feet there was an old house, small and unpainted. Ned drove slowly, looking at each house and the signs on the mailboxes.

He came to an empty lot which contained half a dozen rusting old cars. There was also an old railroad caboose. The next house sat back. The lawn was unmowed and the house was very small and, like the others in the neighborhood, unpainted. Ned looked for a mailbox, but there was none.

He saw a child near the house. She wore a faded dress and was throwing something. When he stopped the car, he knew it was Lizzy. He ran to the yard gate, threw it open and yelled, "Lizzy, Lizzy!"

She'd been feeding a goose. She turned, dropped the grain in her hand and ran to him.

"Daddy! Daddy! I knew you'd come. I knew you'd come."

She hugged him so hard, it hurt his ribs.

He kissed her, and when he looked up, Ellie was running toward him.

"Dad! You came! Thank you!"

She hugged him from the side and lay her head on his chest.

The three stood that way for a while, the girls changing

holds and reinforcing their grasp. A band of animals began to gather about them: two mongrel dogs, a goat,
several geese, a large cat looking on from a fence post.

"Why didn't you come before? You can't be that busy?"
Ellie asked.

He didn't know how to respond.

"You didn't call me back," he said.

"We tried one night and you weren't there. Then we
came here. We don't have a phone," Lizzy said.

"You kids look good," he said.

"We're so glad you came. We missed you, Dad," Ellie
said.

A figure stood at the rear of the house. She was dressed
in an old, plain dress. Her hair hadn't been combed and
she looked thinner than he remembered. Ned stared at
Win. Her arms were folded and she didn't move.

"Hello," he said.

She touched a hand to her black hair. The late sun cast
shadows on the hollows of her face. There was no smile
or perceptible emotion.

Ned walked with the children toward her. She was barefoot and there were scratch marks about her ankles.

"So you came, Ned Owen," she said with the familiar
musical cadence.

"Yes."

He stared at her and her face didn't change. She was
a beautiful woman: delicate mouth and regal forehead;
black hair and blue eyes and light skin.

There was a loud squawking sound as a goose chased
a dog.

"We have animals," Lizzy said.

"Lots." Ellie pointed.

"Are you going to stay?" Lizzy asked.

Ellie asked the same question.

"I thought you all wanted to come home," Ned said.

"Goody, goody," the girls screamed.

"Your dad and I should talk," Win said.

"We're going home! We're going home!"

"Can we take the animals?"

"Your dad and I will talk," Win pronounced.

"We'll listen," Ellie said.

"You play outside. We have to talk alone," Win said.

"We want Daddy," Lizzy said.

"You can see him. He won't wither up and blow away."

Win turned and walked into the house. Ned and the children followed. When he reached the back porch, Ned told the kids to wait, that he'd be out soon.

The house was dirty and poorly furnished. Dirty dishes sat on shelves and a wooden dining room table. Ned looked and saw a small living room with tattered furniture.

"So you came?"

"What the hell is wrong with your mind, woman?"

"I did what the books say to do."

"This? What kind of stupid book told you that?"

"There is a time, the book says, to start life anew. The Good Book told me that." She spoke with placid confidence—quietly, as if granted absolute and eternal immunity through her invocation of Holy Writ.

"Did it tell you to kidnap the kids?"

"Should I have left them with a father who goes for days without talking to them?"

"Bullshit. That's bullshit."

"Don't swear. I don't allow it in this house." She was standing by a greasy stove of thirties vintage. Looking away from him, she pushed a filthy frying pan to a rear burner.

"Win, get off your goddamn high horse and tell me what the hell you're doing."

"I'm living here. This is my house."

"You picked a good one. It's a fire trap. It's a pig pen. Why did you do it?"

"We're different people, Ned Owen. You love money and big things. You think different."

"I sure as hell do. You had everything you wanted at home and you come down here."

"You never asked me what I wanted."

"Bullshit! Every damn thing in our house was bought with your approval. You had all the time in the world and you could do anything. You didn't need to pull that crap and hide out down here. You must have known I'd find you sooner or later."

"I would have told you."

Ned pushed a chair aside, harshly, so that it fell to the floor. After composing himself with a deep breath, he spoke quietly. "Why didn't you say something before you did all this?"

"I tried, but you never listen, Ned Owen. You move like a freight train, going the same direction."

"When did you try to talk to me?"

The children were peering through the window. Ned waved them away.

"Many times. Your ears aren't for my words."

"You've gone crazy. That's what. I like to hear you talk and I never didn't listen. I always listen to you."

"Not about some things."

"Maybe you didn't try to tell me."

"You're not an easy man to talk to."

"Well, I'm here. Talk. Tell me all about it; then we can get out of here and go home."

"I live here now, Ned Owen." She could have been talking to a friendly neighbor. There wasn't the slightest edge of contempt or fear or anger in her voice, and her face was so vacant, so bereft of emotion, he experienced a moment of hollowness and dread beneath his skin.

After a look around the room, he recovered. "You can't stay. I have a car and we can leave tomorrow. Hell, I wouldn't even bother with this house. I can put a match to it and we won't have to worry."

"The children love it here. They're happy. There's no worries here. They have the animals."

"We live in a state that's full of animals. We have a farm with animals, for Christ's sake."

"I don't like your swearing."

"What am I supposed to do?"

"Why did you come?" she asked.

"To take you home, that's why."

"I'm not going home."

"That's what you think. You can't stay here. It's crazy. And how about Johnny? What's he up to?"

"He has a job at the store."

"Does he come out here to screw?"

"That language isn't for this house."

Ned stepped closer to her, abruptly, forcing her to step backward toward a window held open by an empty flower pot. "Was it his idea?"

"That's none of your worry. I did what was right."

"The hell you did! You broke up a family. What does the Book say about that?"

"It's not right to live with a man when things aren't good." She slipped past him as she spoke, easily, moving from a position of jeopardy to one of greater security near the rear door.

"Hell, we're married."

"That was your doing. You didn't give me a chance to say no."

"What's wrong with you? You turn everything backwards. You wanted to get married as much as I did."

"You chased me until there was no strength left in my body." She raised her voice and showed emotion for the first time. "I found the strength, thanks to the Lord."

"And Johnny?"

"He doesn't swear."

"He doesn't need to. He plays with himself all the time."

"There's nothing hurtful in him."

Ned grabbed the kitchen table, a hand on each side. Gripping tightly, he lifted it, holding an end inches from

the floor. He didn't let it down until the feelings of rage
subsided and he knew he could continue the conversation
without violence. The room was filling with the yellow
light of a day's end. As he let go of the table, he heard
the *caw-caw-caw* of a crow, distant but singular. "And
how about you? Coming down here isn't hurtful to me
and the kids? You'd better grow up and look at things.
I'm the kids' father. You can't take that from them. That's
worse than any sin they talk about in your fucking
church."

"The law says you can see them."

"Once a year? You think that's right? You're out of your
mind."

"You have money. You can travel."

"Sure. It's just a hop, skip and a jump. It took me all
day and three hundred bucks just to get here."

"I talked to a lawyer. You can have them a month in
the summer."

There was a pile of dirty clothes in a back corner of
the kitchen. Mixed among the bundle were the kids'
swimming suits. Ellie's was red and Lizzy's yellow. On
days when they were at the pond, when he was loafing on
the beach and the children were swimming or exploring
the woods, he could always tell them apart by their colors,
after telling them not to swim too far or to watch for a
hidden barbed-wire fence. "In the meantime they're down
here. They have snakes here, you know. Rattlesnakes and
copperheads. You want me to sit up there and worry about
them all the time? What if they get sick? Is there a doctor
in this crappy town? Probably some old quack. Win, you
can't do it. You can't break up the family. I'm not going
to let you get by with it. If you and Johnny want to be
friends at home, you can be friends. I don't care. But you
can't take my kids. I won't let you do it."

"I can't move back. There's no place there for me now.
It's your place; the people like you and need you. There's
no needing for me."

"Everybody will be glad to see you back. Everybody."

"No, they won't. There's too much talk in a small town. If I didn't hear it, I would see it on their faces and feel it with my skin."

"It's all in your head. There's no problem about your coming back."

"I can't live with a man when it's not right." Again, her voice reverted to a tone of serene unconcern—repetitive and trancelike, as though she had memorized a speech and recorded it on tape for a phone message.

"What's not right? We're married. That's simple."

"Not in my heart, Ned Owen. Not in my heart. You can't fool the Lord with your heart."

"So you run away with the kids to make it right? I'll tell you what I think of your Lord!"

"You don't have religion. That's not right for the children."

He stomped a foot and his voice boomed, "I have religion. It says you don't hurt people. That's religion." His jaw was rigid as he stared at her in contempt and hate.

"There are greater notions and greater service."

"That religion of yours is something. Lets you do anything. Win, we're wasting time talking. Are you coming with me?"

"No."

Ned walked directly to her. A step away, he shouted, "Say that again!"

"No."

"For two cents I'll bust your face to pieces." He tightened his fist, holding it aligned in front of her face, looking at her face and his fist. He compared them: Her face was thin, yet soft, and his fist was reddened and gnarled. He backed away.

"I always knew you would hurt me. That's the first thing I thought when I saw you tonight. That's a part of you, violence and trouble. I still dream about it."

"Have I ever touched you?"

"It's in your heart."

"That's the worst thing I ever heard. You don't know! Why do you think I chased you? You were the nicest person I knew. I never wanted any other woman. And you think I want to hurt you."

"You've never been gentle."

"That's a lie. A lie! I am gentle." He yelled so loudly he didn't hear the knob of the rear door being rattled in vain.

"You always forced yourself on me."

"Just because I get horny I'm not gentle?"

"You don't understand a woman."

"You don't understand a man."

"I have my own understandings."

"Win. Come home with me. We can talk all the time. It's no good with you down here. I'll do anything. You can tell me to do anything and I'll do it. I'm not hurtful and I'll never hurt you. You tell me what you want and I'll do it. Anything. Please come home."

"I can't."

Her face hadn't changed. It was lifeless. Ned looked about the dingy kitchen. It smelled of grease and cat litter. He looked at her for a long time. He could hear the children and animals outside. When he knew he couldn't change her face, he said, "I'm taking the kids back with me. I won't let them live here. It's unsafe. They're coming home with me."

"This is a healthy place for kids. They have freedom and they have love."

"They don't have a damn thing. The least you could do is buy them a new dress. Lizzy looks like a little tramp. So do you. You can't bring them up like this."

"I was raised like that."

"Your old man was a soak."

"He was a kind man, Ned Owen, kinder than you'll ever know."

"He was a drunk."

Ned looked at her again. He swore and left the house. Lizzy and Ellie were waiting at the back door, surrounded by their menagerie.

"Did you yell at Mom?" Ellie asked.

"No," he said. "We laughed a lot. Hey, kids. Show me your pets. Do they have names?"

"Not the goat," Lizzy told him. "He's called the goat. We don't have names for the gooses either. That one over there is mean. He tries to bite, but all you have to do is hiss at it and it stops. I'll show you." She ran over to the goose and hissed at it. The goose walked away.

Behind the yard was a stand of trees. The sun had begun to descend past them.

"Have you seen any snakes?" he asked.

"Yes, yes!" Ellie screamed. "Back by the fence. A huge black snake. I screamed and the dogs chased it. It went away."

"I saw one, too," Lizzy said.

"She's lying. She didn't see a snake."

"How do you know?" Lizzy made a face.

"Hey, Dad. Did you get a new car?" Ellie asked.

"No. I rented it at the airport."

"We don't have a car, so we have to walk to town. We walk in for mail and groceries. Lizzy dropped a milk bottle one day. She says it was an accident. I think she got tired."

"It was an accident. Dad, you should walk with us. There's an old man who lives in a house and he scares me."

"Mom says he's just old."

"He's scary."

"Did he try to hurt you?" Ned asked.

"No. He just looks scary."

"She's a sissy."

"Do you want a ride in my car?" Ned asked.

They said yes.

He drove them into Clinchfield and they showed him the Gambles store. They drove until it was almost dark.

Baron Road was unfriendly and desolate. He parked in front of the house.

"Do you kids want to come back home with me?"

"Yes, yes. I want to go home," Lizzy said.

"So do I. This is OK, but we miss you and we miss the house," Ellie said. "Can we go to the pond?"

"Sure. Maybe we can go camping out there."

"Camping?"

"Goody!"

"Why don't you run in and get your clothes?" Ned suggested.

"Can we wait till tomorrow?" Lizzy asked.

"Why?"

"I have a friend named Sue Lynn. I want to say bye to her."

"You can call her from home."

"I'll help you write a note," Ellie said. "She doesn't have a phone."

"Run and get your clothes. If you forget something, we can buy more," Ned said.

It was dark when he opened the car door for them.

"Is Mom coming?" Ellie asked.

"Sure," Lizzy said.

"I don't think so," Ned said. "She likes it here."

"You mean Mom isn't coming?" Ellie said.

"We can't go without Mom," Lizzy screamed.

"She might come later."

"Why don't you stay here?" Ellie asked.

"I have to work."

"That's what Mom says."

"But you can come home to Iowa with me, kids. Hurry, now. We have to leave."

"We can't leave without Mom."

"How about Johnny?" Lizzy asked.

"They can come later."

"Why doesn't Mom come?" Ellie asked.

"She doesn't want to."

"Then why can't you stay here and work?"

"I can't."

"That's not fair. You and Mom aren't fair. Aren't you going to live together anymore? Are you getting a divorce?" Ellie asked, looking at him directly.

"I don't know."

Ellie began crying and Lizzy also cried. Between sobs they looked up at him. There was a single yellow light shining in the house. The night was noisy with crickets and the foraging sounds of the pets. The girls cried for a long time. At one point Ellie looked at him and said, "You're not fair. We don't want you to get a divorce. You're not fair," and then started crying again.

Ned looked at the house. There was no sign of Win.

"I love you," Ned said to his children.

They continued to cry.

"I wanna go home," Lizzy said.

"We can't without Mom."

An old car sped by, leaving a cloud of dust which hung in the air. Ned touched his children, patting them on the back, gently hugging them. The night was very warm and he felt their interrupted breathing against his body.

"I'll walk you to the house," he said.

He escorted them around the house to the back door. Of all the animals only a dog bothered to greet them.

"I have to go now," Ned said.

"Can't you stay?" Ellie asked.

"No," he told her. "Not if your mom doesn't want me. I'll come back again. Remember, I love you. You write me and you can call me. I'll come back again, lots."

Ned kissed the wet faces of his children, then left them. He drove back to town, turning by the railroad tracks, and found Main Street. As he drove by the Gambles store, he thought of throwing a rock through the window. By the time he reached Macon, he wished he had.

Sunday, August 15

Ned made hospital rounds late, beginning at ten-thirty. His stomach had been hurting all morning. Each time he returned a chart to the nursing station he visited the medicine cabinet and borrowed Maalox or Gelusil or Amphogel. By the time he signed out of the hospital, the cracks at the sides of his mouth were white from antacids.

He took a codeine tablet and opened a beer when he got home. Finding nothing of interest on television, he played a Doc Watson recording of "Bonaparte's Retreat" several times, listening to the guitar picking and Vassar Clements' fiddling. He drank another beer. He took a third can of beer to his deck and stared across fields of mature corn toward the trees surrounding the French River.

Midway through a fourth beer he called Gail.

"Why don't you come over?" he asked.

"I'm not in shape for anything," she said. "I'm in agony. It's the first day of my period and that damn IUD is sending gremlins all over my pelvis. I took a Librium and I'm smoking a joint. It's the only cure. I told you that, didn't I?"

"Come over here. I have some codeine."

"You know how I feel about men's houses."

"That's stupid. Sundays are good days in this house. You can sit on the deck. If I turn the hi-fi way up, we can listen to music there."

"How are you feeling, Ned?"

"A little more relaxed today, I think."

"Ouch. Excuse me. A little gremlin just squeezed something down by my whatever. Damn. There. It went away. Ned, if I weren't so groggy, I'd give you a sermon I've been preparing for you."

"Come over here and give it."

"I wouldn't dare say it to your face."

"Say it now."

"I can't. My mind isn't on top of anything. This is my day of debt to biology. The price I pay for being female. You caught me at the wrong time. After a couple of Librium and a few joints, the pain becomes pleasure. It's still pain now."

"What was your sermon?"

"It sounded good when I thought it a few nights ago. Now it sounds maudlin. Wait a minute." There was a long pause. "OK. Almost burned a hole in my rug. Do men ever have genital anguish?"

"Not like cramps."

"I wish you'd get a cramp sometime."

"Come on over."

"I bet having a baby isn't as bad as what I endure every month."

"I told you to come over. Codeine is the best thing."

"On top of Librium and Colombian grass?"

"If you don't take too much."

"I have to give you the sermon first."

"Go ahead."

"I told you, my mind isn't up to it."

"Maybe it'll be better this way."

"OK. The sermon. Expurgated. Very expurgated. Ned" —she paused and laughed—"this is ludicrous. OK. October twenty-four, nineteen twenty-nine, was the day of the big crash, the start of the depression. It was a result of technology. Factories could produce more than people could buy. Factories overproduced because there was the belief that the good times could only get better. People were told to buy stock. It was easy. All they needed was ten percent down. They didn't know the market was manipulated by men of wealth and cunning. It fell apart on Black Thursday—October twenty-four. Can you hold on? I think if I put my beanbag chair under the phone, it will help the cramps." He waited for her to change position. "There. Much better. This all relates to you. The depression. See what I mean? My sermon may not hold up in academic circles. Everyone thought Black Thursday was the low point. 'Recovery is just around the corner' was the official word. Morgan and Hoover and Mellon said it. They believed it, so they didn't do anything. They believed the Keynesian theory that a free market would correct itself. They were dead wrong.

"Black Thursday was a picnic! The depression got worse and worse. People were laid off work and couldn't buy things, which caused more businesses to fail and get rid of more workers. It got worse every month. Then the depression really set in. Depression is the only word to describe it. There was no fun, no hope, no good feelings. That's why people went to the movies. It was their only escape. What I'm trying to say is that the whole thing started in twenty-nine and didn't reach bottom until thirty-two."

"That doesn't have a damn thing to do with me."

"Yes, it does. The same thing is happening to you. Your wife left, and that seemed the worst thing. It wasn't. It's what's happening to you now. You're going down and down. I can see it. Last night you stared at the wall for half an hour. You drink and stare at the wall. This has gotten to you."

"I don't feel so bad today."

"So you have one good day in five."

"You didn't finish your sermon."

"That was it."

"You didn't tell me what to do."

"You're smarter than I thought. I wish I knew what to tell you."

"How'd they fix the depression?"

"A radical change. Congress gave immense power to FDR. The National Recovery Administration regulated wages and working hours and prices. There was the Civilian Conservation Corps, the Public Works Administration and the Works Progress Administration. The federal government stepped in and took over."

"You want a small-town boy's reply to that?"

"Sure."

"Those things won't do a damn thing for me."

"You're right. But I have a feeling that things won't get better for you until something radical happens. I don't know what, but you're tearing yourself apart. I don't know how you're surviving. Maybe you should go away somewhere on a long vacation to sort things out. That would be a radical break."

"I'd drink beer and stare at the walls there, too."

"Then I don't know what to do. I wish I did."

"Come over here. That'll help."

"All right. I will. It's against my good judgment. But if you give me a codeine, I'll give you a joint. We can get stoned together."

Gail rode her Gitane bicycle to Ned's house. She parked it behind his Mercedes. The weather was refreshing: seventy-eight degrees, clear with a light wind. Ned met her on the porch and escorted her through the living room, up the open stairs to his deck. Once she was seated, he ran and got a codeine pill for her.

Gail commented on the house; especially, she cited the Scotch bottles and empty beer cans, on the floors, night stand and deck.

"You've been having a big party."

"Drinking makes staring at the walls more productive."

"We'd better find a radical cure. The booze isn't an answer."

Ned opened another can of beer. When he put his feet on the railing, two empties fell to the lawn below.

"I keep saying I'll quit drinking each morning I get up. God, I've had some hangovers. My stomach hurts a lot. I probably have an ulcer. But," he said, hoisting his can of Schlitz, "it still tastes good."

"Can't you do something, Ned? Have you talked to your attorney?"

"She's an honest person. I have two choices. I can go down and bring the kids here. That means finding a housekeeper and all that. Or I could stay home and quit medicine. It probably wouldn't make any difference after the divorce because Win will get custody."

"Can't you fight for custody?"

"I can. Emily says I'd spend a lot of money and probably lose. Win will testify that I'm . . . what the hell did she call it, negligent—there's some word that goes with it, —because I'm away from the house. It's a rotten deal— because I work and make the money, I'm not around the kids enough. So legally, I have to give Win my money because she doesn't work and needs the money so she can spend her time with the kids. But if I stop working, I wouldn't have any money to pay alimony and I'd be sued for nonpayment. Win gets off scot-free because she doesn't have a job and isn't trained for one. It turns out that because I went to medical school and because I'm a man, I'm not qualified for custody. How's that?"

"You're screwed."

"Nice, isn't it? Win tries to make it sound like I don't like my kids. Jesus. I'd give my left arm right now to have them. Win doesn't understand that I don't need to be doing things with them all the time. Just being around, having them come up to me for a minute—that's good. They see a lot of me. Emily and I spent a long time talking about this. Win would get people to testify how busy I am; she'd get that cocksucker preacher to say I'm not religious even though when the war was on, the preacher never said a word against it and I was out in the streets. But I'm the one who doesn't have religion! Emily said the courts are old-fashioned. I'd look like a shit."

Ned stopped talking for a while. Tears wet his eyes.

"But I'd never do what she did! I don't break things. I told her she could come back and play with Johnny's pecker all day long, just so the kids could be here. I don't care about her anymore. She can do anything. She's the bad person, the wrecker. But not in the eyes of the law! She'd prove I'm violent. Because I like to screw. That makes me violent!"

"You poor thing."

"It never bothered me. Sex didn't bother me. I had enough to do."

"What can you do? Is there anything radical you can do?"

"Murder."

"That's pretty radical."

"When it's all said and done, Win calls the shots. Emily tried to convince me I should accept the settlement, giving her a minimum of money and using my money to fly down there every other weekend. I would get the kids for most of the summer. I keep thinking it over and over. Over and over. Why should Win get the kids? I hate that place she lives in. There's snakes down there! That doesn't bother her. Do you know what she told me once? She was a little girl and watched a snake crawl through an open basement window into a neighbor's house. It made her happy! The snake found itself a nice place! So she gets the kids. I can't accept it. Why can't we flip a coin? Heads she gets them, tails I do. No. She's a woman. The kids are hers. Automatic. If we flipped a coin, I'd have a fifty-fifty chance. The only solution is murder. I spend hours thinking how I can do it and get by with it. If I could kill her and not get caught, I'd have my kids. She's never coming back."

"The scene you described down there is incredible. She really went back to her childhood, didn't she?"

"The whole works."

Gail opened her purse and removed a joint. "You want some?"

"Sure."

They shared the marijuana in silence. It relaxed them and they sat back in the sunshine. From time to time they looked at each other and smiled.

Gail began to laugh, almost inappropriately.

"What's the matter?"

"I'm going to do something. I'll find out what makes her tick. Maybe that will help." She laughed again, heavily.

"What are you going to do?"

"This is her house. Right?" She looked at him intently. "I told you I can learn about people by looking at where they live. I'm going to do something unique. I'm going to pretend I'm your wife. I'll walk around the house and be your wife! I'll learn her secrets."

"What good will that do?"

"Then we'll know! We'll know why she's such a bitch."

"That won't help anything. It won't bring her back."

"If you know her, you can deal with her."

"I already know what I can do. Nothing."

"Maybe there is something. Find her Achilles' heel and attack that."

"You'll waste your time. It's a nice day. Let's sit here."

"I feel good. That codeine was nice! I feel like I can walk through this house and learn things from the vibrations. Let's go." She stood.

"Go ahead. The place is a mess."

"You have to come. You're my husband."

"Bullshit. You're being stupid."

"No, I'm not. You are. We have to learn about her so we can act. We have to get her. I can help you."

"How much stuff have you taken today? Pills and grass?"

"Enough to make me feel good. I'm not out of it. Come on." She led him through the French doors.

"I'll be an archaeologist. I'll study her remains and define her."

She walked to the end of the second-floor hallway. She looked in Ellie's room, all tidy with red-and-white bedspread and matching curtains. There was a shelf with glass animals and a collection of children's books. She looked into the empty room with the TV and broken toys. Lizzy's room was a mess. Animal pictures were taped haphazardly to the wall. Gail found nothing in Ned's study.

There were two volumes of *Reader's Digest* books in the bathroom. Gail carefully searched through them. Nothing had been underlined or earmarked. The bathroom towels were plain. White toilet paper.

She tugged at sheets in the master bedroom and found two more *Reader's Digest* books under the bed. The wedding portrait hung over a chest. Gail stared at it.

"She's beautiful. I never saw her, you know. Are her eyes really blue? Delicate skin. Damn, I wish the picture would talk to me! Speak, woman! Tell me who you are!"

She tripped on a beer can.

"You're a slob. That much I've learned," she said. "Was the deck on the house when you bought it?"

"No. I had it done."

"Was it her idea?"

"No. Mine. So I can watch storms."

Gail toured the kitchen.

"Why aren't there any pictures on the walls?"

"I don't know," he said.

She found the teddy bear in the silver bowl and old Christmas cards in the china closet.

She loved the stained glass over the living room door. She looked at the mismatched furniture and the shag rug.

"How old is the house?"

"Over a hundred years."

"Who picked out the painting? The ship?"

"She got it on sale at the furniture store where she worked."

"It's dumb."

The library shelves in the living room held more *Reader's Digest* books and an assortment of book club selections. Most were untouched. Tucked away behind a dictionary was a worn leather Bible.

"Found something, Ned. Look at this." Gail opened the Bible and a picture fell to the floor. She picked it up and asked, "Is this her?"

"That's her and her dad."

"He looks sober here." She leafed through the book but found nothing else.

There was nothing in the basement but dirty clothing and laundry equipment.

"There's something wrong with this house, Ned. I don't know what it is, but there's something wrong. Those are the vibrations I get."

"I like the house. When I saw it, I knew it was what I wanted."

"You picked it out?"

"It came up for sale after I came here. I bought it on sight."

"She didn't choose it?"

"She said she liked it."

They returned to the deck and shared another joint.

"I know the answer," Gail said slowly.

"What?"

She spoke slowly, searching for words. "I'm the smart one, right? I went to school. I study people's lives. I told you about my sixth sense—a musician friend said it was a seventh sense. You learn things by checking places out. Your hometown, for instance. I liked you a lot more after being there. You made more sense."

From their vantage there was nothing between them

and the horizon to move and distract them. Gail's face was drawn, intent to an extreme.

"I was angry with you. I wanted you to face up to things, not to be deceived. It's frustrating watching you. I wanted you to admit your marriage was a mess and take the consequences. I'm the schoolteacher, the smart one. But she's no dummy! I wasted half an hour looking for her Achilles' heel, but she doesn't have one. But she knows you have a jugular and she dove right for it!"

Gail stood and pointed a finger at Ned. "Do you know what I learned? There isn't anything of a woman in this house. Nothing! I went looking for remnants, for shards. She didn't leave a thing. She hasn't put anything into this house. It's yours. The deck, the furniture, everything. This never was her house. That's how she got to you! You can't fight back because she didn't give you anything to fight back at. She left nothing here"—Gail laughed cynically, bitterly—"nothing but the bonnie rats in the attic."

Ned threw a beer can into the air. Giving her the codeine was a mistake. All he wanted was a quiet afternoon of sipping beer and small talk. She was far past anything as simple as that.

"Now I know why you kill yourself drinking and looking at emptiness. That's her gift! I don't believe in spooky shit, but this comes close to it. Maybe there is something about Celtic people and paganism! Blood of blood of blood of the supernatural. Descendants of dark rites."

Ned tried to look away from her and concentrate, however absurdly, on the scenery about him. The weather was perfect and the fields were docile, growing orderly. Shadows from the oak trees darkened spots of grass to a deeper green and branches moved easily with the breeze. But Ned couldn't avoid her gaze; drug-altered and haughty, she stared at him from a rigid posture, rancorous and accusing, not to be changed by anything he could say.

"I don't know who she is, Ned," she said finally. "I know what she's done."

She hesitated long enough for him to speak. "She's a kid," he said, shrugging his shoulders.

"Want to try that again? A kid, huh?" The drugs had also penetrated her voice, accentuating its harshness. If her visit had the purpose of bringing him cheer, the mission was failing rapidly. "Look at you! So observant. So wonderfully analytical." She slurred the last word. "You stand in the middle of a road and get run over by a truck and you say it wasn't a truck at all—it was a kid!"

Her head was unsteady, weaving slightly in circular movements to her left.

"What's in there?" She pointed to the bedroom.

He answered the obvious.

"That wasn't that bad, either?" Her lips were curled into a grin.

Ned responded angrily. "Maybe I'm not so dumb either. You really want to know why I didn't get out of a bad marriage? What's a bad marriage? So I didn't have all the sex in the world and she got nutty with the church. I made up for it. She didn't hurt me, not until she left. What if I didn't talk much to her? I talk to people all day."

Gail tried to interrupt him, but he continued, "I was getting along fine. We made it to San Francisco, didn't we?"

"That's how you planned to spend the rest of your life? Running away on little weekends while everything around you was decaying?"

He laughed at her. "You went along."

"Don't drag me into your pit. She's your kid. Good Christian wife. I say she's the most castrating bitch I've ever heard of." Gail leaned forward to an extreme. Her body unsteady, she continued her line of reasoning. "Look what she's done. You let her do it to you. She's turned you into a weak sot. And me! She's getting me just like she got you." A film of wetness covered her eyes, stopping short of becoming tears. "I thought you were this wild, daring, crazy doctor who had the world at his fingers. Maybe you were."

"I said I wasn't so dumb," he said, again in anger. "Because I knew if I left the marriage the same thing would happen, only I'd be sitting somewhere else. I'm not stupid."

"Why are you turning into a cripple? You don't do a damn thing to change things. You didn't even bring your own children back when you had the chance. You get drunk and cower like a wounded dog. I'm beginning to wonder if you'll ever recover. I'm beginning to think you'll spend your life in the goddamn fucking house and when you die, they'll carry you out in a laundry basket. Why don't you fight? Why don't you take what's yours?"

"I can't."

"Then I don't think I can help you," she said, muttering and sanctimonious. "I don't even think I like you anymore."

Ned looked away from her at a blurred horizon. His lower lip was all sadness and defeat, drawn, flat above the chin, pushing his upper lip. He blinked his eyes to focus them, but his vision remained fuzzy. It was bright outside; colors were strong and elemental, the tinted sky and growing things were as sparkling and incandescent as in an Impressionist masterpiece. The muscles on the sides of his face, beginning near his eyes, and those of his jaw gradually weakened until his face was limp.

"You'd better leave, then," he said.

Something within her attempted to respond in palliation, but the Librium and joints and codeine prevented her from reacting. He left, walking into the house, through the bedroom, down the stairs.

"Ned." She got up and fought her unsteadiness. Hurrying as best she could, she moved through his bedroom, swearing at a bed sheet that almost tripped her. The drugs were exacting their toll: Her mind was in a foggy panic; nauseated, she tasted acid from her stomach and her arms and legs were weak. She struggled to maintain her coordination and to keep from retching.

He had put her bicycle in his trunk and sat waiting in the car.

"Ned. Please." She tried to smile in conciliation, but failed.

"I don't think you should ride your bike. You might hurt yourself," he said.

"I didn't mean—"

"Sit over there. I'll drive you home."

"I'm sorry. God, I'm messed up. Can't you understand?"

He looked at her with an absolutely vacant face. She got into the car. She tried to touch his arm, but he started the motor and drove away.

"I didn't mean what I said," she insisted. "I'm stoned and getting sick. I like you. I like you a lot. Believe me!"

He drove through a stop sign. The trunk lid bounced repeatedly against the bicycle.

"I said all that because of the drugs. And your house. I shouldn't have come. I can never go back there. It does things to me. Don't you understand?"

"I heard what you said." He turned up a hill toward the college. "I know what you mean. I don't like myself, either."

Tuesday, August 17

The pain had awakened him twice during the night. The first time he swigged Maalox from his nightstand and went back to sleep. It was more intense upon his second awakening, cramping the entire upper part of his stomach, penetrating to his back. He arose, again swallowed the antacid and walked around the empty house. It began to ease after fifteen minutes, so he sat on his deck in the dark until he knew he could sleep again.

He was better during morning hospital rounds; the walking helped. If not cheerful to patients and staff, he was attentive. He spent ten minutes in the record room, completing charts that needed dictation or a signature.

While he was driving to his office, the pain returned. His first request to Ann was that she run down the street to the supermarket and buy milk. Between every patient he either drank milk or took antacid.

Mail came at ten-thirty and he received a letter from Lizzy and Ellie. It was a mutual effort, immediately obvious because half of the letter was tidy and the other half was legible only with careful deciphering. They said they missed him. Not only they; all the animals, including the cat, a friendly stray, and their mother missed him. Ellie inquired as to the possibility of his practicing in Clinchfield. Lizzy circled the query; from her circle there was a meandering line to "YES," written on the bottom of the page.

Gail had called in the morning and apologized. He had accepted the apology but couldn't talk long. Too many patients, he'd told her.

At noon he toyed with the idea of having lunch with her, but went home instead, napping as best he could for an hour.

When he drove back to the office for the afternoon session the temperature had risen and the humidity was tropical. The pain never completely went away. All afternoon he kept away from coffee and cigarettes, drinking his milk, whitening the sides of his mouth with antacids.

He looked forward to the evening, when he could take codeine and perhaps risk a beer or two. He trusted the codeine to solve things. A hospital admission and two minor emergencies delayed his arrival at home until after eight. The component of pain in his back was worse, though he didn't feel the tightness of his upper abdomen. Milk and codeine took away the sharpness for a while.

He was looking at a medical journal in his study when he heard the sound of thunder. Invigorated, he looked outside and saw that the sundown would be premature because of a thick cloud front advancing from the west. The pain hadn't gone, but the excitement of the coming storm led him to the refrigerator and he opened a can of beer. Thinking ahead, he tucked two more cans under his arms and walked to his deck.

The frontal plane of the storm came from the southwest. Above the wall were hues of the receding sun. Great bands of lightning danced randomly within the approaching dark interior of the storm.

It excited him and he responded by calling to it, encouraging it. He was like a spectator in a box seat in Yankee Stadium, clapping, cheering, coaching. He drank the first beer quickly and though it heightened the pain, he paid no attention, opening another and drinking it rapidly. He quickly calculated the amount of beer left against the speed of the storm. Not wanting to miss anything, he ran wildly downstairs, grabbed a six-pack and ran back again to the deck. Little had changed. He'd calculated right.

A cigarette was appropriate. He had two with the third beer and lit another with the fourth can. Details of the storm were apparent. There was more turbulence to the north; the clouds were higher with more lightning. All things considered, it was a remarkably solid front. Ned felt the first rush of cooler wind across his face. Updrafts and swirls of clouds did combat. With the storm much closer, each bolt of lightning illuminated the inner formations. He loved it. The wind was heavier and darkness had surrounded him, but the frequent streaks of lightning let him participate. The rhythms of lightning and thunder increased in tempo as the wall encroached on the fields near him.

Ned raised a fist in excitement, to cheer the storm on.

As his fist reached its high point, he bent over in severe pain. He lost his breath. None of the pains he had suffered were anything like the intensity of this pain. He had the urge to vomit; the urge itself was a part of the pain. He sat bent over as the first large drops of rain walked across his back. He didn't notice them. When he began to breathe, the pain eased slightly. He waited for it to improve more. Attempting to sit, he felt a pain so severe he thought the muscles of his stomach wall were being pulled apart. Unable to stand, he rolled forward to his hands and knees. Fighting, he took two deep breaths and crawled through the French doors. He moved toward the phone, thinking he would call Gail, when he remembered, somewhere in his mind beyond the pain, that she had asked not to visit his house again.

Mustering all his energies, swearing beneath his breath and biting his teeth, he stood and began to walk out of his room. He could do this if he stayed half bent and didn't move too fast. He fought for strength with his breathing. Walking stooped and almost sideways, he made his way outside into the rain. The pain was worse than ever, but he continued to move, to wince, to breathe, to swear, to moan, for he knew if he didn't he would die.

He started his car engine. Leaning against the door, he drove out of the lane onto the street, the rain pounding heavily. His body weaved forward and backward like a drunkard's. He tasted blood in his mouth and he tried to spit, but it only trickled onto his lower lip. Raindrops immediately diffused the blood into a thin wash which tinted his chin.

He drove haltingly, giving wide passage to oncoming cars. Each street corner marked an achievement, distance gone. A first wave of dizziness came and he countered with rapid, forced breathing. Another street corner, another success. He turned down a private lane and smiled.

Gail heard a sound in the storm, persistent. Looking outside, she saw car lights, and with the lights she recognized the sound of a car horn, stuck.

She found Ned crumpled, halfway out of the car. The door was open; his left leg touched the ground, but his right arm was caught in the horn ring of his Mercedes. He was unconscious.

She smelled the beer on his breath and the smell of blood. When she eased his arm from the horn ring, the weight of his body folded against her. She tugged at him, pulling him out of the car. He was too heavy to carry. She left him on the grass. It was raining heavily and she didn't have anything to use as a cover.

She scanned emergency numbers above the phone and dialed the hospital.

"I need an ambulance. For Dr. Owen. He's unconscious."

"Where are you, ma'am?"

"Oh, God, I'm sorry. The Raffensberger house. Second house in College Row. And, and please call that doctor that's his friend. Byron something."

"Markham. I'll send an ambulance immediately."

She ran outside and crouched over him, shielding his face with her body. He was very cold. Touching his chest, she felt it moving rapidly, breathing like a sick baby.

She couldn't speak to him, though wanting to. She wiped rain from his face and waited, numbed.

She heard the siren as lights of the ambulance appeared over the hill. The attendants rushed out and she told them she didn't know what had happened. They lifted him onto a cart and she watched the cart's legs fold as Ned was put into the ambulance. She helped push the cart and climbed in alongside him.

They reached the hospital and moved him inside. Under the lights of the emergency room she could see that his skin was blanched and without blood. His lips were blue, his chin colored from the blood.

A nurse took his blood pressure. "Get someone! He's forty over zero. Get someone!" She ran and found an IV set. A tourniquet was placed on his upper arm and she inserted a needle into a vein. "Call the lab and get some blood down here."

Byron Markham was wearing riding pants with black boots. Upon seeing him, the nurse pulled him to Ned's side. Gail stood across from them.

"He's complained of his stomach for the past week or two."

Byron pulled Ned's shirt open. Ned's stomach was stretched and tight. Wherever Byron put his hand, there was resistance from the abdominal wall. Putting the bell of a stethoscope to the abdomen, Byron heard nothing.

He turned to the nurse, demanding, "How much blood do we have in this hospital?"

"I'll call."

"I'll do it." He phoned the lab and was told there were nine units of blood. "How many O negative?" They had three.

The ambulance drivers leaned against the wall. Byron returned to Ned's side and reexamined the abdomen.

"Has he complained a lot about his stomach?" he asked Gail.

"Not a lot but every day." She studied Byron's brow.

"Get me another IV set," he yelled to the nurse. She took a set from the shelf. "Give me five liters of Ringer's and run to the lab. They have three units of O negative. I want them now."

Byron turned to the ambulance drivers.

"How fast can you drive?" He continued without waiting for an answer, "Do you have a radio?"

They looked at each other for an answer.

"How far is it to Iowa City?"

"Hundred miles."

"Can you drive a hundred?"

"We can try."

"Get on your radio and tell the highway patrol. We'll leave as soon as I hook up a couple units of blood. Come here. Take these bottles of Ringer's and put them in the ambulance."

They did as they were told.

Byron spoke to Gail. "I have a choice. He's in shock. High possibility of a perforated ulcer. He's bleeding inside. A lot. I can operate here, but we don't have enough blood to back me up. I could lose him. The other choice is to get to University Hospital, and if I can talk to them over the radio, they can be ready with surgeons and enough blood. I think we should risk moving him. He's bled down to nothing. I have barely enough to keep him going, but if I open him up here and don't get the bleeding stopped immediately, he'll die. We're going to be lucky if he makes it either way."

"I'm coming along," she said.

"Stay out of my way, then."

He connected a unit of blood to each of the IV's, placing a pressure cuff around each to speed the delivery of blood.

"Let's go!" Byron pulled the cart as the nurses held on to the IV's. "Move!" he screamed. They ran with the cart out the door into the rain. As soon as the rear door was closed, Byron told the ambulance drivers to get going.

They bounced around a corner and drove on Main Street to the Interstate, swerving once to avoid a car.

A dim overhead light allowed Gail to watch Byron's hands. He pumped on the bulbs connected to the cuffs which squeezed the blood. Byron's eyes looked up at the blood bags.

"Did you get the highway patrol?" he asked.

"They're picking us up in a mile. I'll holler when I see their lights."

"How fast are you going?"

"Ninety."

"Go faster."

The first unit of blood was finished. He took the final bag of blood and connected it, tucking the cuff about it.

Gail held Ned's hand. It was wet and cold. His pulse was but a murmur against her palm.

She looked out the window at the storm in progress. They passed a car as if the car was motionless. The siren sounded far away but was insistent, never leaving.

"We have two patrol cars ahead."

"Can you talk to them?"

"We can talk to them, but not to University Hospital. Maybe they can."

"Tell them we have a doctor aboard. Have them relay

this. I'll say it slowly." He waited until they had made voice contact with the patrol.

"He is a thirty-five-year-old male. Previously good health. Presumed perforated, that's perforated, peptic ulcer." Byron waited for them to repeat the message.

"Tell them there is a surgeon aboard. It is a severe emergency. I want a staff physician. That's a staff physician, waiting. The patient needs immediate surgery. Tell them we need blood. O negative. No time to cross and type."

They gave part of the message and asked Byron to repeat the last.

The second unit was empty and Byron attached a bottle of Ringer's lactate to the IV. He repeated the message as he worked.

"Tell them to really lay it on. The people at the university sometimes have a mind of their own. Lay it on thick."

The attendant spoke to the patrolmen, translating Byron's words into his own. When he finished, he asked Byron, "How's the doc doing?"

"All I can tell is that he's alive."

Gail looked between the attendants at the lights of the highway patrol cars. They were in close tandem, clearing a path in the left lane of the Interstate. The speedometer on the ambulance read a hundred and ten. Every now and then lightning illuminated the back of the ambulance and Gail saw the fixed jaw of Byron and Ned's silent face.

"Do you know Ned very well?" Byron asked her.

"Pretty well."

"That's better than most. I didn't know he was in trouble. He never asked. I feel bad."

"He'd be ashamed to ask another doctor," she said.

"Probably so. He's too private. That's what got him in trouble. He should have talked to his wife more. Maybe she wouldn't have left him."

The ambulance radio came on with a burst of static.

"University confirms message. Surgeon and blood waiting. Which approach to the hospital do you recommend?"

"Hold a minute." The attendant asked Byron.

"I don't know."

"Your choice," the attendant told the patrol. "We don't have a preference. Your choice."

Gail's knees were wet from kneeling next to Ned. Her instincts were to hug him and shield him from all harm. She was afraid to talk to Byron. The surgeon's voice was harsh and absolute.

The radio buzzed. "Be prepared to take the shoulder. There's truck traffic ahead and if that one clown doesn't see us, we'll have to go around. Be prepared."

The ambulance driver sat forward. He saw the truck lights the moment the patrol cars moved to the far left, keeping as close to the truck as possible. The ambulance swayed and tilted. They made it around the truck and continued.

Byron added another bottle.

"How far is it?" Gail yelled.

"Fifteen minutes maybe."

"How is he?" she asked.

"Alive. Barely. How did you find him?"

"He was in my driveway. His arm was caught in the steering wheel. I didn't know he was sick— Oh, God," she moaned.

"What's the matter?"

"I know why he didn't call me."

"Why didn't he?" Byron asked.

"I can't tell you," she said. She looked at Ned and swore to herself, bitterly.

Suddenly she saw city lights through the window. They approached quickly; white lights of houses and the red of highway businesses surrounded them.

"Dr. Markham. We're turning off onto the Coralville exit. Looks like they've got more patrol ahead. Yes. I can see more patrol up there."

They slowed, but not so much that they didn't swerve turning from the Interstate.

Lights were all about. Predominant were the emergency lights of patrol and police cars ahead. They rushed past gas stations and motels and turned onto another road. The intersection had been cleared by police cars. In another minute they turned again and after slowing were at the Emergency entrance of University Hospital.

Orderlies waited in the rain and jerked the rear doors open the moment the ambulance stopped. They rushed Ned's cart into the building. Byron and Gail followed.

Three gowned men waited. Byron ran up to the oldest.

"He's perforated an ulcer. I didn't have enough blood. Mind if I scrub in?"

"Take him up to the OR," the surgeon said. "We'll get going and you can join us. How much blood did you give him?"

"Three units and about three and a half liters of Ringer's."

"Good."

Orderlies ran with Ned's cart; the wheels wobbled violently as they ran. The three in green scrub suits hurried behind. Gail followed them and ran so she could ride the elevator with them.

Ned's face was almost yellow. She couldn't see a sign of life. The surgeons felt his pulse, checked the IV's and felt his stomach. They talked about blood and site of incision and the possibility of brain damage from the shock.

The elevator door opened and they took Ned into an area closed to visitors. Gail found herself alone in an empty hall.

She sat on an old wooden chair. The walls had recently been painted green. The smell persisted. There were no windows and she couldn't hear the storm outside. Her stomach began to hurt mildly. She didn't know how long they would be. She had no idea what they were doing, what technology they were applying. She tried to imagine blood and his stomach and none of it made sense.

A janitor with a huge sweeping machine entered the hall. Having made it halfway to where she sat, he stopped and lit a cigarette after stopping the machine.

Gail had never been in a place like it. Green walls, emptiness, the silent janitor. Nothing offered comfort. She waited a long time. None of her thoughts were productive. Very little made sense, including her remembrance of Ned unconscious, his elbow hooked in the stainless steel ring of the steering wheel. To ask why was ludicrous.

A long time after she had arrived, the older surgeon emerged from the forbidden area. His belly was covered with blood.

"Are you Dr. Owen's friend?"

"Yes."

"I think we're OK. Dr. Markham was correct. He perforated a duodenal ulcer. In a rather difficult place, posteriorly. Dr. Markham exercised good judgment risking the ambulance ride. At the latest count, we're gone through nine units of blood and I think we're a bit behind. We've been able to give him matched blood for the last five units."

For no reason, Gail asked Ned's blood type.

"He's A negative."

"He'll be all right?"

"He should be. He was in profound shock, but he's putting out urine. That usually means he had enough circulation to keep things going."

"His brain? Is that all right?"

"We'll keep our fingers crossed. He's just waking from anesthesia. During surgery he had good reflexes and his pupils reacted well. Those are gross signs, but all of them are good."

"Thank you," she said.

"I'll be getting back. We have to watch him closely for six to eight hours. You're his friend, right?"

"Yes. I am."

"Good. Do me a favor and notify his family. You can tell them what I told you. I think we're lucky."

He returned to his patient.

The only visitors his first postoperative day were Gail and his parents. Gail rented a car and brought Ernest and Ruth to the hospital. Ruth asked Gail if Win was at the hospital. Gail explained with all the delicacy she could muster the events of the past month.

"That girl never was right, you know," Ruth said with little emotion. "Ned gave her too much. He spoiled her. You can't make a canary out of a blackbird." Ruth displayed little concern that Ned's access to the children was severely restricted. "The Lord put love in those little girls. When the time comes, he'll be repaid in full. I know his girls."

Ned lay in bed with his head slightly elevated. A nasogastric tube ran from his nose to a suction pump. One IV remained, and his other arm was immobilized with a catheter which led to a glass tube. His urinary catheter would be removed later that day.

If there had been any damage to his brain, no one, including Gail, could detect it. His speech was hampered by the nasogastric tube and the Demerol, but he showed great emotion upon seeing his parents. Ernest didn't know what to say, but Ruth made up for his reticence. She hugged Ned without regard to his external plumbing.

"I worried about you and that girl from the day you met. You're lucky you had her as long as you did. You were too crazy as a kid to understand the Welsh. And this one! Her father never let her grow up. Ah, what a liar he was. Not even his wife listened to him, but the girl believed it. God dealt the old man a terrible blow, it's true. He hated America. He dreamt of Wales and playing soccer. That was his life. Soccer and singfests. Heaven only knows what he told her. They say he killed a man in the mines over a pint of whiskey." She laughed. "Ah! You're better than all that. No one would believe it, but you are. And those kids of yours will be like a dog in a strange kennel. Wait and see. They'll break out. Worry about yourself, Ned, not those kids. And you don't think that your pa and ma won't fuss over them like they were the king's own? I know a trick or two for an old fat lady. Might even get another kitten for the house." She turned to Ernest. "We'll leave now. He doesn't need our talk all day."

Ann and Sheryl visited the next day. They brought flowers, candy, an Exotic Hideaways travel brochure, get-well cards from twenty patients and news of interest from the office. "You won't believe this, but yesterday afternoon Byron Markham walked into the office and said he'd be in every afternoon at two to handle patients. Doctor, please don't laugh now, but that office has never been so crazy. It's a comedy act. He spends about half an hour with each patient and after they leave he asks us what you would have done. He hates kids. He says he's afraid they'll vomit on him. Then he told Mrs. Washburn she was neurotic. When she left, she told me she wouldn't ever pay her bill. Anyway, we'd better get back because he insists he'll come every day. I think we'll make a movie of it for you. When he left yesterday, he told me he doesn't know how you do it."

He ran a fever the third and fourth postoperative days. It was diagnosed as a focal pneumonia and treated with a combination of antibiotics. He asked that visitors be limited to Gail and his parents.

Bowel sounds returned to his stomach when his temperature returned to normal. His nasogastric tube was intermittently clamped to prove that he was hooked up and functioning properly inside. The tube was removed. After a day of clear liquids, they removed his IV and central venous catheter, the tube in his other arm. He began walking and needed little Demerol for pain. It was on the sixth day that Gail made an embarrassing request. "I'm broke. Sorry. But I wondered if you could loan me some money—like five hundred dollars."

"When do you need it?"

"Now. I have to pay a bill by tomorrow or the bill will go to collection."

He phoned his bank and had funds transferred to an Iowa City bank.

"It'll take some time to straighten out my business," she said. "You'll have to survive without me for a day or so."

Ann and Sheryl alternated visits. Every other day they brought Ernest and Ruth. Ernest became more verbal with Ned's improvement.

Gail was gone more than a day. She returned to find him walking rather comfortably down the hall of the surgical ward. It was eight days after his operation.

"Where have you been?" he asked.

"If I told you, you'd be upset. I'm not very good with money. I got into a real mess. Anyway, your loan helped me, but I wonder if you'd cosign another loan. I have to buy a car and I don't have collateral. Will you do it?"

"What do you need a car for?"

"To drive."

"Where?"

"Hopefully on streets and highway."

"What kind of car are you buying?"

"Ned. The guy is down there with the paper. Will you come down and sign it so he can leave? He went out of his way to come here."

Dressed in his striped gray-and-white robe, he rode the elevator with Gail to the main hospital lobby. When the elevator door opened, Lizzy and Ellie yelled at him.

Each had a rose for him.

He knelt to hug them, but they held their distance. "This is to make you better. Gail told us not to hug you too hard because it might hurt you. But we can kiss you," Ellie said.

He bought them French fries and a Coke at the cafeteria.

"This is funny, Dad. Gail came to our house and asked Mom if we could come visit you. Mom thought Gail was going to hurt us, so she made Johnny call your office to make sure. Then she said we could go. Ellie got sick on the airplane, but I liked it. We got chocolate cake with our TV dinner. Gail bought us presents at O'Hare. That's the Chicago airport."

When Ned returned to his floor late that afternoon, the charge nurse lectured him severely for his absence. Gail returned for a short visit in the evening.

"That's the nicest thing anyone has ever done," he told her.

"It was a ball! Give me five hundred bucks and I'll do it all the time."

"Did you have trouble with Win?"

"No. But what a scene. She's back to the basics! She made certain that I wasn't a kidnapper before she would let me take them, but she didn't object once she knew the situation. She definitely has an accent! Very different. But she isn't as pretty as I thought she would be. I thought she looked haggard."

"How long can the kids stay?"

"You ask that! How long do you want them?"

"You're smart, for an old schoolmarm."

"How soon can you get out of here?"

"Three days if I'm lucky."

"Great. We're staying at the Holiday Inn. I think between the swimming pool, TV and the city park in Iowa City I can keep them entertained. Then I have a suggestion. How about all of us going somewhere? Disneyland or someplace like that?"

"I'll have to check and see what's going on with my practice."

"No way. You need the vacation. I'll kill you if you don't take us somewhere."

Ned's release was delayed because of a persistent low-grade fever. He felt well, but they insisted he stay. Each day he wandered about the hospital, where he had trained as a medical student. Most of it had been refurbished or completely changed.

The day before his release he took Gail by the hand and asked that she follow. He led her down three flights of service stairs, very similar to the stairs they used for an escape from the Mark Hopkins. They walked a long corridor, turned a corner and stopped by a huge window. On display were row upon row of newborn babies. He asked her to look at them.

Mothers of babies came to the window dressed in bathrobes, talking to one another and pointing at the bassinets.

"Aren't they nice-looking?" he asked.

"Sure are. And you can't hear their crying from out here."

"Just look," he said.

"My God, Ned. You look like your dad the day he showed us the kitten. I feel like crying, it's so good."

"There's one over there that has a whole head of hair."

"Wait a minute! Ned. I hope you're not telling me something."

"Maybe." Ned laughed for a moment, an instant. His face then became somber and sad, more than sad, defeated and without life.

Gail looked at him, confused and worried. Her voice

was soft, yet retained an analytical tone. "Do you want—because of what happened to your kids—for us to have a baby?"

"We've got enough trouble," he said, planting four fingers against his receding hairline.

"Why did you bring me here?"

"To show you the babies."

When he was unconscious and in shock, the doctors had voiced concern about the blood supply to his brain: It was a moment she'd never forget. Gail stepped away from him, wary, looking for other signs of mental aberration.

"I came down here yesterday and remembered how much fun it was delivering babies."

"You said you didn't deliver in your practice."

"Not for eight years. It was too complicated in solo practice—leaving a full office to go for a delivery. But I liked it. It was fun. Maybe that's what I'll do."

"Do you have to take a refresher course?"

"For three years. I'd have to finish a residency." Ned's enthusiasm dwindled. He kicked the wall before the sad mask tightened his face and tears wet his eyes. "Shit, damn, fuck, balls, bastard, whore," he muttered. "It's a son of a bitch."

"Let's go to your room." Gail took his arm.

She closed the door and he rested on the bed. The shadow of depression hung about him.

"You're not going back to your practice—to Spring Falls?"

"I can't go back. Not by myself. It's all done." He threw a pillow aimlessly into the air.

"So you think you should deliver babies?"

"I have to do something."

"What do you want to do?"

"What I was doing. That's what I want." He stared at the wall.

"Are you certain you can't go back?"

"Not now. Everything was just the way I wanted it. Even if Win wasn't such a good wife. I had everything. The house. The kids. My practice." Again he became tearful. "How can I tell Sheryl and Ann? I don't know how."

"You must like them a lot."

"They're like my own kids. I was lucky to have them. It was really special. They made fun in the office. What will they do?"

"You'll have to tell them."

"Maybe I'll send them a letter with a lot of money in it."

"Sounds like a divorce."

"Worse."

"Do you really want to deliver babies?"

"It's good. Some nights you stay up late, just the nurses and you and the woman in labor. The best thing is show-ing the baby to the mother. Like giving her a present. She thinks you did it all. When I was an intern, I delivered this fourteen-year-old. She was so hysterical, she rolled all over the table. After the baby came, I showed it to her and she began to cry, she was so happy."

"You love women, don't you?"

"Sure."

"You poor son of a bitch."

"That isn't the problem," he said. "I don't want to waste three years. In a residency you have to walk in a line down the halls like a bunch of penguins. Baby-sit with medical students. Listen to boring lectures on experiments. Take a bunch of shit from the staff. I'm too old for that."

"Why not set up a practice somewhere else?"

"Where?"

"I have the perfect place! Providence, Rhode Island. I have my job there. And since it's in the East you'll be closer to your kids."

"You're going back?" he asked.

Gail jumped on his bed, lay next to him and snuck a playful finger through the opening of his hospital pa-jamas.

"Ned. Let's talk. You've learned one thing. You can't go back. And I've learned something. I can't leave you. Not now. If I leave you, you'll go back to drinking beer and staring at the walls. I'm staying with you." She bent over him and smoothed the tape of his bandage. "From now on you'll wake up with my legs curled around you and we'll listen to records and we'll get some things sorted out. Mostly with your kids." Gail sat up, confident and bright. "How'd you like the way I got your kids? Had you fooled all the way. I felt like a trophy hunter invading that African safari your wife runs down there. Bring 'em back alive, Tamlin."

She didn't change his face. He insisted on asking questions. "Where are we going to live?"

"My God, you're a flawed individual. We can probably trace it to your zodiac or your Celtic blood. You ask 'Where are we going to live?' " Gail laughed as cynically as kindness would allow. "We've been kicked out. We're displaced persons. We don't have a home."

"What are we going to do?" His face was so encumbered with doubt that she kissed it and touched it with her hands.

"Survive! How's that for starters?" She rubbed his nose in circles. "I think I read too many paragraphs on your face. Am I right? You want to know answers. Where are we going to settle? Are we going to get married? What will we do on Christmas Eve when your wife has the kids in Georgia. Does Santa Claus know where Georgia is?"

He laughed for the first time since they had come back to his room.

"You wanna go home," Gail said. "Buddy, even if we had the tickets, the train don't run that way."

"I like the idea of waking up with you in the morning."

"It requires our going to bed together at night."

"I figured that out."

"How much money do you have?" she asked seriously.

"I can make a guess. Six years ago I bought a farm and the value has doubled. With what I've got in stocks and the farm and the pond, I should have over four hundred thousand dollars."

"That'll pay my bill at the Holiday Inn."

Ned stood and pointed a finger at her. "What do you want to do?"

"Visit Disneyland."

"I mean for real."

"That's as real as anything right now."

Ned wasn't satisfied. "Look. You have a job. You have to think of that. And . . . " his voice trailed off as he struggled for words, "I think I should be honest. Remember when we met? I told you I didn't like schoolteachers. What I meant was I'm not an academic person. I have to be doing things. I am smart, though. I used to make difficult diagnoses, then sent the patient to the specialist with the diagnosis. But I have to be going all the time. You're be embarrassed with me. I'm a small-town kid. I don't read intellectual books. I'm not like you. If you had a party, I'd probably sit in a corner like a dummy."

"God, I feel sorry for you." Gail sat at the foot of his bed and broke into laughter. "Have I ever asked you to quote Proust? Poor little country boy. Get off it! Join a book club and you'll know as much as anybody I associate with. Ned. This is a lovely comic scene and I hate to turn it into something serious. You're breaking me up. You're worried because you're not like my first husband!" At that she bent over in laughter, which turned to tears when she looked up at him. "Christ! He was perfect. He was a Yale graduate. He spoke three languages. He was an expert in international law and he smoked Borkum Riff in his meerschaum. He was perfect—a perfect ass!" Ned smiled at her exposition. "You, you clod. You've got real class. I know that about you. You'll do just fine—anywhere. If the Ivy League types knew your secrets, they'd give up their clothes and cars and simply grin."

Gail snuck a drink from his water pitcher. "I thought about us. Who we are. I even thought about those things that bother you." She sat very close to him; her hands were on her lap. "Then I think of the night you came here.

The ride in that rainstorm. Your freaky friend acting like Dracula—even though he saved your life. I remember sitting in the hallway so stunned that to be able to cry would have been a godsend. When they came and told me you were alive, I was the happiest person in the world. You'll never know. And when I saw you awake in the morning. Beautiful. Now I want to see you laugh again, like you laughed the day we met." She continued to speak, with her hands in her lap. "So? What's going to happen to us? Who knows? Maybe someday we'll get married and have babies. You're not even out of the hospital. We're in no hurry."

She halted. She walked to the window and played with wilting blue carnations, plucking dead petals. "We know what we can't do." She gave him a rose to smell. "There's a hell of a lot of things we can do. You can do your baby thing. I can teach. You can work in Providence. Or I can get a strange illness, with your signature, and delay my work there. For Christ's sake, we can put on robes and study Zen in Nepal. We have money. We have time. That's more freedom than most people ever had. The way I see it we have only one choice right now, packing up the kids and going to Disneyland."

She had lifted the mask from his face.

"We'll make serious decisions when you get your laugh back. You know, I look at you and realize something. We live in the electronic age; we're wired into so damn many circuits it's no wonder fuses blow now and then." Her voice changed. "There's one thing I want." She thought and stared at him. "No, I demand it," she said. "You have to do right by your kids. They're your blood. I'll make you do it. The reason I say this is because for a long time my mother and I were at odds. For dumb reasons. Then something happened and we found a common love for cathedrals." She took the rose and waved it in front of his face. "I want you to show your kids the cathedrals in the world, in your own way. Will you promise me that?"

The next day Gail rented a car and drove to her house, where she picked up Ned's Mercedes. He'd asked a favor and she'd agreed. She drove to his house. She parked by the station wagon, which was draped with dust. Grass around the house hadn't been cut for a month. She hadn't realized how apart the house was from the rest of the town. It sat alone, pressed against the edges of mute and inanimate farm fields. The paperboy had continued his rounds; newspapers, yellowed the color of urine from the rain, were stuck between rails of the porch and wind-pressed into shrubbery like folded linen.

She went to his bedroom and emptied his closet, putting his clothes into large plastic bags and stuffing them into the trunk. Each trip up and down the stairs frightened her. She thought she heard noises. When his clothing was packed, she went to his study and gathered all his records, fitting them behind the seats of the car. She left his mass of journals, taking only his medical texts. With some difficulty and an increasing sense of urgency, she unwired the components of his hi-fidelity system and arranged them on the seat and floor of the car. Having done that, she made a last inspection of the house, peeking quickly into each room. Her feeling of unease grew intensely. He'd requested she find something, but she couldn't remember what it was.

Looking around at the debris of the empty house, she couldn't think. A shadow from the late afternoon sun darkened the living room. Gail ran as fast as she could down the stairs, across the living room and out the front door. She didn't care what it was she'd forgotten. Without looking at the house, she drove wildly out of the driveway, through the city streets. Checking the contents of the car, she was slightly more at ease. Looking ahead, she studied the arrows to the highway.

She was doing eighty when she hit the Interstate.